FRANC

# THE VATICAN'S LAST SECRET

# *THE VATICAN's LAST SECRET*

*by*

FRANCIS JOSEPH SMITH

A JAMES DIETER NOVEL

# THE VATICAN's LAST SECRET

Copyright by Francis Smith

All rights reserved. No part of this book may be reproduced, stored in a retrieval system, or transmitted in any form by any means without the prior written permission of the publisher, except by a reviewer who may quote brief passages in a review to be printed in a newspaper, magazine, journal, or on-line.

First Printing

This is a work of fiction. Names, characters, places, and incidents either are the product of the author's imagination or are used fictitiously, and any resemblance to actual persons, living or dead, businesses, companies, events, or locales is entirely coincidental.

PUBLISHED BY FJS Enterprises

Printed in the United States of America

**Titles by Francis Joseph Smith:**

The Vatican's Deadly Secret
(James Dieter Book 2)

The Vatican's Final Secret
(James Dieter Book 3)

Long Buried Secrets
(James Dieter Book 4)

Secrets from a Father's Grave
(James Dieter Book 5)

The Devils Suitcase

THE VATICAN's LAST SECRET

*For my Father.*
*He never saw the Final Draft,*
*but I knew he was looking over my shoulder the entire time.*

## FACTs:

*IN the early spring of 1945, a German train comprised of 46 rail cars packed with five tons of gold, 700 pounds of diamonds, 1,200 paintings, 5,000 Persian rugs, and 1,000 cases of silverware, left Eastern Europe and the advancing Russian army, hoping to reach the relative safety of Germany within a few days. In early May 1945, after two weeks of dodging Allied Forces, it was finally captured by the US Third Army. But on final accounting it was missing 17 of its original 46 rail cars, and most of its cargo of gold and silver.*

*ON October 21, 1946, a Top Secret report from a US Treasury Agent declassified in 1997, quoted a "reliable source in Italy" who alerted his superiors about confiscated monies sent to the Vatican Bank "for safekeeping." A sum largely in the form of gold and silver.*

*IN a 1998 report issued by the US State Department, Nazi Treasures were identified as having been illicitly transferred to the Vatican Bank after the end of WWII. The Vatican has repeatedly denied any involvement in crimes or the disappearance of any Nazi treasure.*

*SINCE 1945, the Vatican has refused to open its wartime records to substantiate its innocence...*

# THE VATICAN's LAST SECRET

# CHAPTER 1

**TODAY, 10:50 a.m., VATICAN CITY**

Saint Peters Square on a sunny May morning contained the usual tourists as Father Jonathon Lester turned down a narrow service alley, a block off the main square. He was a few days shy of forty-five, lean and fit, standing a hair under six feet, attired in an elegantly tailored black jacket with matching pants. A stiff white clerical collar graced his neck.

At the alleys end a solitary door welcomed him, a brass plate attached to it read in English and Italian: "*Staff Entrance Only.*" As he reached for the doors buzzer, the door suddenly swung open with a loud, metallic click. Father Lester laughed to himself as he realized dozens of security cameras had followed his progress down the alley. After he had entered, Father Lester watched as the door slowly closed behind him, its titanium bolts sliding effortlessly back into place within the buildings two-foot-thick concrete walls.

# THE VATICAN's LAST SECRET

He nodded to the uniformed guard who now blocked his entry. "Good morning, Heinrich," he said with some familiarity.

The burly middle-aged guard stepped aside in acknowledgement, well aware of Father Lester's identity. "Welcome back, Father. It's been a couple of weeks since your last visit," he replied in perfect English. "No need for a walk-through for senior staff." He motioned Father Lester around the metal detector.

Father Lester smiled in return. "Thank you, Heinrich. You know how I try to avoid this building as much as possible."

Heinrich grinned, fully aware of Father Lester's aversion to the Vatican Vaults. "Yes, I understand. Shall I notify the boss of your arrival?"

"No, let me surprise him this one time," Father Lester replied over his shoulder as he walked the remaining 10 meters to where an empty elevator awaited him. He stepped inside and waved back to Heinrich, sliding the old-fashioned cage doors closed. Once alone, he withdrew a 9mm Beretta from a leather shoulder holster, holding the weapon in his palm as if weighing it. Satisfied, he withdrew a bulbous silencer from his jacket pocket and expertly screwed it into place.

It was almost eleven o'clock. He would have to hurry.

*Take a deep breath,* he thought to himself as the elevator neared the bottom.

A soft shudder signaled he had reached his destination: The Vatican Vaults. Considered one of the most formidable facilities in the world, with its hand-carved tunnels dug deep into solid Italian bedrock ten stories below St. Peter's Square. For over 300 years the vaults had proved a formidable deterrent which no enemy had ever penetrated.

Father Lester slid the cage doors open. "Jesus forgive me," he said aloud, stepping into the brightly lit concrete hallway that offered itself. A black windbreaker draped over one arm concealed his weapon. He felt a rising excitement inside him.

No more than ten meters away at the end of the hallway, a member of the Vatican's elite Noble Guard snapped to attention, an Uzi machine gun slung low across his chest.

*"Personal bodyguards to the Pope,"* thought Father Lester. *"His Excellency must be close."*

A Dell laptop in front of the young Noble Guard employed the new *Scan works Facial Recognition Software.* A camera mounted atop his desk continually scanned Father Lester's features as he approached. Within seconds, an exact match appeared on the computer screen in front of him displaying both his picture and profile.

The young soldier touched the tip of his blue beret in acknowledgement. "Good morning, sir," the soldier barked mechanically. Behind him, a thick steel door slid open in response.

Father Lester nodded as he walked past. Suddenly he stopped, whirled around, flung his raincoat to the ground, and pointed his Beretta at the soldiers head.

The young soldier's eyes went wide before he could react.

"Bang, you're dead, Johann," said Father Lester, his free hand slicing through the air in a sign of the cross at the young guard. "You owe me twenty euros this time. Next time it is fifty. How many times have I told you to search *everyone* coming through these doors, including me?"

The young soldier shook his head at the Vatican's Chief of Special Action Teams. "Bastard," he mumbled under his breath.

Father Lester allowed a slight grin to escape upon entering the bunker.


**FRANTIC ACTIVITY ALLOWED** Father Lester to gain entrance without much fanfare. He eased through the initial ring of standard government office cubicles, low fabric walls, and gunmetal gray desks before reaching his objective: the offices of the Vatican Special Action Team. Its members were frequently compared to those of the American Navy SEALS or British SAS but on a much smaller scale, with the Special Action Team lucky to number in the low teens. *However, they all handled their respective government's silent, dirty work.*

Father Lester eyed his superior, Monsignor Sims, as he sat on top of his desk speaking into his cell phone, one leg draped over its side, the other firmly placed on the concrete floor.

Monsignor Sims nodded to Father Lester as he handed him a Cuban Romeo y Julieta cigar. "Sit down, I'll just be just a minute," he silently mouthed. After a few seconds he absently rubbed his shaven head with his free hand, his black shirt sleeves rolled up to reveal arms betraying his younger days as a Boston College offensive lineman. As he sat there, he looked nothing like a man who possessed the full authority to speak and deal on behalf of the leader of the Catholic Church.

Father Lester overheard bits and pieces of the conversation before he realized the discussion was in Hebrew—one of six languages Monsignor Sims spoke fluently.

"I no longer have it, *we* no longer have it," Monsignor Sims replied angrily before slamming his cell phone on the table. "That arrogant bastard," he said aloud before he realized Father Lester was staring at him. He smiled as he paused to compose himself. "I know how you detest visiting our little hole in the ground, but I wanted to inform you personally of the ghastly news. We have a potentially humiliating situation whose existence, if it were leaked to the general public, would utterly disgrace the Holy See."

A puzzled look graced Father Lester's face.

Monsignor Sims handed Father Lester a red folder before he continued. "Our contact in the United States sent that message to us over thirty minutes ago. It seems that after some seventy years in hiding our enemies have returned home for a little scavenger hunt. You know what that means don't you?"

Father Lester casually scanned the message, having written his doctorate on the papers original theory in his former life of clandestine service for the British Government. "Yes, I understand," he replied assuredly, "retrieve our product and protect the church at all costs."

Monsignor Sims nodded at Father Lester as he repeated his last three words back to him:

*"At all costs."*

**AT A FAST PACE**, Monsignor Sims hurried through the lush grounds of the Vatican Gardens before he stopped at the Lourdes Grotto to eye the Pope deep in silent prayer. He waited patiently until the Pope looked up and signaled for Sims to join him as he sat on wooden, patio-style chairs admiring the grotto.

Monsignor Sims sat beside the leader of the Catholic Church, his head bowed in reverence.

The Pope nodded in greeting. "It must be of some importance for you to intrude upon my prayer, Monsignor."

"You must forgive me, Your Holiness. It is of the worst possible kind. I have just authorized the elimination of some of our enemies—*all in your name."*

The Pope reached for Sims' hand as he nodded in understanding. "Don't feel any guilt, my son. You can only turn the cheek so many times before you must strike back. In our situation we can't always afford to play by the rules."

His message delivered, Monsignor Sims rose to leave. "Thank-you, Your Holiness."

The Pope smiled at Sims. "Remember one thing," he said slowly, emphasizing each word. "Death comes to every man at one time or another."

# THE VATICAN's LAST SECRET

# CHAPTER 2

**MARCH 1945**
**145km NORTH of BELGRADE, YUGOSLAVIA**

A dry wind sliced its way through the sprawling old growth forest, the sun having set an hour before. Captain Hans Dieter knew his enemy lurked before him, waiting, watching, just as a jungle cat readied itself before it struck its helpless prey.

He was a man of medium height, light brown hair, and piercing blue eyes. A dirty and disheveled army uniform clung to his unwashed body; on his head rested a leather officers cap tilted jauntily to one side.

Dieter strained his eyes in the night's darkness as he absently pulled at a weeks' worth of stubble that graced his chin.

Suddenly a flare burst upon the nights sky followed by a burst of automatic fire no more than 500 meters forward of his position.

## THE VATICAN's LAST SECRET

"Here they come," Dieter shouted to the fourteen weary souls that constituted the remains of his command.

Cigarettes were quickly extinguished as the men took up defensive positions to his left and right.

From the enemies position came the high-pitched roar of a single, diesel engine.

Within minutes Dieter and his troops viewed two round beams of light that seemingly weaved in between hundred-year-old birch trees as the vehicle sped towards their position.

Dieter had no desire to see the inside of a Russian prison camp. "Open fire," he commanded.

Fourteen weapons heeded his call. The soft thud of lead bullets impacting sheet metal and shattered glass signaled their limited success as the vehicle still pushed forward, only now weaving in and out of control before crashing into a cluster of trees only meters from the Germans' position.

Dieter scrambled to the front of the truck as it lay on its right side, its two left side wheels still spinning. His men soon followed and expertly took up positions to encircle the truck. One of his men motioned toward the drivers cab. Dieter nodded. From a crouched position Dieter pushed his weapon up and over the trucks hood and fired on full automatic as he sprayed the front cab from side-to-side. He ejected the empty cartridge in one smooth motion and reloaded. He then crept silently along the trucks undercarriage using it as cover until he reached its rear.

Using hand signals, Dieter motioned for two of his men to take up positions on either side of the truck. He counted to three before he cast aside the trucks heavy canvas flap. Streaks of moonlight aided him as he examined its inside. Dozens of small wooden crates lay scattered about the bodies of seven bullet-riddled corpses.

Dieter closed the flap in disgust. "We killed some of our own soldiers," he said aloud before opening the flap once more. This time he used his flashlight to better view the carnage, focusing its narrow beam on the bodies nearest to him.

Three of the dead soldiers lay clad in heavy gray woolen uniforms, white piping lined the edges of their uniform, the notorious white Deaths Head emblazoned boldly upon their shirt collars. Not German soldiers in Dieters mind *but the dreaded SS.* Political soldiers. *Fanatics.*

He aimed the flashlight's beam to the middle of the trucks cargo bed as he eyed the uniforms of the other soldiers. Upon closer inspection he noticed they appeared more ceremonial than fit for a combat soldier. Dressed in fanciful black baggy silk pantaloons that gave way to yellow stockings and soft black leather shoes, a red woolen shirt covered the chest area topped with a golden breastplate that bore the crest of a lion emblazoned on its face.

*Each belonged on a parade ground, not a battlefield,* Dieter thought as his flashlights beam moved from body to body.

Dieter nodded to Private Selig who now stood over him. A puzzled look graced his face. "Captain," he said matter of factly, using the tip of his machine pistol to point to one of the smartly attired soldiers. "The ones with the fancy uniforms all have their hands behind their backs."

Dieter wondered why he had not noticed something so obvious. "Here, help me," he said to the private. They managed to flip the closest body over.

Metal handcuffs bound the dead soldier's wrists. "Handcuffs? Why are they in handcuffs?" Dieter said aloud. "Help me flip the rest of them over."

As Dieter grabbed the second body, he heard a soft cry in response.

"This one's alive," he said. "Let's move him outside into the night air."

Once outside, Dieter gently laid the soldier on the ground.

# THE VATICAN's LAST SECRET

One of Dieters men thoughtfully wet a piece of cloth with water from his canteen before he applied it to the soldier's lips.

The soldier managed a slight smile in thanks.

Dieter leaned over the soldier as he took care to wipe blood from the soldier's mouth. "Who are you my friend?"

The soldier coughed several times. Dieter quickly positioned the soldier on his side so he would not choke on his own blood. Pools of crimson now spotted the ground beside the soldier's head.

Dieter leaned down beside the soldier once more. "Your time is near my friend," he said softly. "What were you doing in this God forsaken place? Why did you come from the Russian lines?"

The soldier struggled to speak. "I am…," he replied in German with a heavy Swiss accent, "an emissary for my Pope." The blood flowed more freely now. "I must deliver…, I must. I have many secrets in the truck." His eyes rolled back in his head before he could finish.

Dieter shook his head in disgust before he mumbled a short prayer in response.

With time in short supply, Dieter turned his attention to the bodies that remained. He now searched for wallets, identity tags, or photographs of loved ones. Anything that could assist them in identifying the men. After several fruitless minutes, nothing was found.

Dieter ordered his men to strip the uniforms from the dead hoping their true identity lay beneath their garments. After several minutes, the naked bodies lay side-by-side. Only a crude tattoo of a black orthodox cross was visible over each soldier's right breast—the Latin words *Filiolus Humilis Servo* scrawled beneath each.

*Gods' humble servant,* Dieter mumbled to himself, his Catholic upbringing betraying him. Speed was of the essence. No doubt the Russians were just as curious about the trucks fate. Flashlight in hand, he probed about the trucks cargo one last time.

On each wooden crate, a hastily painted German Eagle stood side by side with a royal crest—the crest matched the crest on the breastplates of the dead soldiers.

Amid the darkened interior Dieter spied one crate whose contents lay partially spilled about.

Curiosity edged him on. Dieter knelt closer to the box for inspection before removing its remaining wood slats.

*His eyes grew wide when he viewed its contents.*

# THE VATICAN's LAST SECRET

# CHAPTER 3

**PRESENT DAY - CHEATEK, NEW YORK**

Brilliant sunshine flooded through the bedrooms floor-to-ceiling windows. Hans Dieter indulged in the view his fifty-two-acre property afforded him: lush rolling green hills, interspersed with patches of majestic oak and maple, and numerous marble statues of Greek Gods and Goddesses placed discreetly about the property. *My little Versailles on the Hudson,* he would frequently say to his friends.

Hans turned to the reflection in the window before him, the figure required no acknowledgement. His once thick, silver mane was now almost entirely gone. Nothing but empty eyes stared back at him. He turned away in disgust. The doctor's prognosis said it was only a matter of days or possibly weeks until he would receive a visitor he had avoided for some ninety plus years.

The soft metallic click of a spade hitting rock reminded him that he was not alone. Hans looked down to where one of the estates gardeners worked diligently in the prized Lincoln and Grant rose beds, pruning the same roses his long-departed wife had originally planted so many years ago.

Memories suddenly flowed over him. He recalled standing in the same spot spying on his wife as she labored in the midday sun. Surely her beauty outshone the roses she had planted. He reminisced how her silky, long brown hair clung to her skin as she turned to see him standing in the window. He remembered her radiant smile as she pushed back the battered straw hat she constantly wore. She waved to him.

Suddenly the pleasant memory faded and another slid cruelly into its place. One that took place some 40 years before when she died in an apparent robbery attempt, at least was how the New York City Detectives recorded it. *Another robbery gone astray*. However, all Hans could remember was his life-long love dying in his arms, taken from him in a filthy Chinatown alley.

The bastards were after him, of this he was sure. The message of her death was clearly addressed to him.

"Damn you!," he cried aloud as his rage increased. He thought they had a deal. It was an unspoken deal. *But still a deal!*

He grabbed the windows wood frame to steady himself. "I would give anything to see her beautiful face again," he murmured. "Anything."

A slight smile now graced his face at the thought of his wife looking down upon him from the heavens above to say that it wasn't his fault.

"Everything I own for just one more minute of her as she sung off key, or the spontaneous slow dance that would break out in our living room," he said silently—the bedroom about him still empty. "Just one more minute with her as she breathed softly on my chest in a restful sleep after we made love."

Gold had killed his wife, millions of dollars' worth of gold. He used to think the gold was cursed. After his wife's murder, he was sure of it. The memory of her as she lay helpless in his arms as she gasped for her last breath, her eyes searching his own as if he could make the pain go away as the blood continued to ebb from the corner of her mouth.

*Her beloved Hans would save her. He always knew what to do.*

The frustration of not being able to help her haunted him to this day. He never meant to place her in jeopardy, *not her.*

He closed her eyes after she had silently slipped away. He then pulled her lifeless body tight to his chest and held her for what seemed like hours, until the paramedics delicately separated them.

From that day forward, he vowed to seek revenge. *He swore it.* He knew who they were. For years they had tormented him, *hounded him.*

His day for revenge was close — *very close.* They had stolen something very dear to him and he was about to do the same to them.

However, his revenge would rock the very foundation of their empire.

**AFTERNOON THUNDERSTORMS** rumbled in from the west. Dark clouds soon followed. Raindrops began to pelt the open window where Hans stood. A clap of thunder snapped him out of a drug–induced haze in time to view two cars slowly approach from the estates main drive.

This had been the first time in over a week Hans felt the genuine will to rise from the safety of his bed as he sought one last glimpse of his estate before his death. Eyeing his Rolex, he was shocked to see that thirty minutes had elapsed.

**FATHER DAN FLAHERTY** quietly entered the bedroom where Hans stood, brushing water droplets from his coat. He had expected to see his friend bedridden. A look of surprise spread across his face when he saw Hans holding onto the windows frame. "Hans sit your ass in bed before you collapse where you stand," he said in a sarcastic, heavy Irish brogue. "Don't rush your death. We all know the Lord can't wait to meet you."

Hans smiled at seeing his old friend and confidant.

Father Dan was tall and slim, his face aged from years of hard drinking and smoking. Also being the principal of the local high school, plying the dead language of ancient Greek to the children of well-heeled parents, had obviously taken its toll.

"All right you Irish Mick," Hans replied. "Keep your tongue and save your words for my eulogy. For a so-called man of the cloth you're the best damn liar I know."

Father Dan laughed heartily in reply.

Hans swallowed his pride as he allowed Father Dan to take his arm and ease him back to his bed. "All right, all right, don't make me laugh. I have enough morphine flowing through my veins to keep me laughing for days."

Hans leaned back against the beds metal headboard. "Dan, I'm obliged that you could show up here today on such short notice and listen to a story of my youth," his voice trailing off.

Father Dan simply nodded to his friend, well aware that the doctor's prognosis was a week, tops. "It's not one of your nasty Nazi war stories where you are once again the big war hero is it?" he replied in jest. "Because if it is, I would rather go listen to old Mrs. Perkins speak about the ghosts' that reside in her bedroom."

Hans leaned over to open a drawer on his nightstand only to produce a twenty-four-year-old bottle of Irish whiskey. He held it up for Father Dan to admire. "The old witch couldn't supply you with this, could she now?"

Father Dan eyed the bottle appreciatively. "You old codger. You are the devil in disguise. Where did you get the bottle? Or is that considered some type of miracle drug the doctor has discovered?"

"The cleaning lady brings it to me, the lovely charmer that she is."

Hans picked up the phone beside his bed and dialed a two-digit number to reach his duty nurse stationed just outside his door, a recently converted anteroom. "Sissy, I know he is out there. Could you please send him in?"

Hans beamed with pride upon seeing his only child enter the room. "Jim, my boy, I'm glad to see you again. Please come in and greet Father Dan, for the two of you are about to become partners in a little venture of mine."

At 6'2', 210 pounds, Jim proudly maintained his physique from his Naval Academy days. This combined with his rugged features were enough to keep many a night occupied. He had recently chosen to take his retirement from the Navy due to the unfortunate circumstances surrounding his father's ill health. Still single, he recently ended his third engagement in as many years. Unfortunately for Hans, grandchildren would not to be in the picture before his death.

Jim grabbed his father's extended hand in greeting before he decided a hug would be best. "What's this all about, Dad? You and Father Dan haven't been drinking already have you?" Jim chided.

"No, I haven't been drinking and no, I'm not delusional," Hans spat out in reply as he waited for yet another sarcastic response to follow. Satisfied they were indeed finished, he elected to continue. "I just want you gentlemen to sit back and listen to a little story I have. Humor an old man whose time has come." Looking to Jim, he pointed to a chair that occupied the corner of his room. "It's a story about a time some seventy plus years ago, so I would recommend you get comfortable, son."

Hans gestured to the bottle that occupied a space next to his medications. "Would you both join me?" The crystal glasses chinked as Jim passed them one by one to Hans, him pouring generous glasses of the Irish.

Hans raised its amber contents, waiting until Jim and Dan followed suit. "*Prost,*" he said before he consumed the whiskey in one long swig.

"Good. On to more important matters," he began with an air of seriousness about him. "This is going to be a short but lucrative tale for you both. I must swear you both to an oath of secrecy. Only Jim's mother, *God rest her soul,* and myself know the full story. So this must never be spoken of again."

Both nodded to Hans's simple request.

"Good. Now it begins," he said. "And remember, only when my story ends, will your real adventure begin." Hans leaned back once more.

*"It was April 1945, Berlin. The war was in its final hours…"*

# CHAPTER 4

**APRIL 1945 - BERLIN, GERMANY**

The sun rose on yet another Berlin day, its rays battling columns of dark smoke slowly drifting across the ruins of a once vibrant city.

*At least what was left of it.*

For as far as the eye could see, acre upon acre, lay gutted; windowless, roofless buildings open to the elements. Entire neighborhoods had simply ceased to exist. Grand boulevards and elegant shops that Berlin was known for now contained nothing more than rubble pushed to the sides, narrow trails snaking through the rubble for people to traverse and go about their daily business.

The bells of Feuerschutzpolizei, or Fire Protection Police, could be heard as they raced from fire-to-fire, still battling the previous nights consequences of a British bombing raid.

The bells of the Fire Protection Police where soon overtaken by the whine of air raid sirens, no doubt warning of the American bombers who chose to bomb the city by day. The drone of hundreds of airplane engines could be heard overhead as they approached the city.

In the center of the city stood what remained of Berlin's largest park, the Tiergarten. At one time royalty and their courts consorted about its 630 acres of exquisitely manicured grounds as they strolled through its famous Dutch tulip beds or chose to take in its world famous Equestrian Rink.

Now it lay in utter ruin.

Allied bomb blasts had cruelly upended centuries-old oak trees and had tossed them about as if they were mere matchsticks. The parks pristine lakes once used by lovers in rowboats and children for sailboat races now lay drained of its precious water, the water used to fight Berlin's numerous fires. Even the equestrian stables found new use as makeshift soldiers' barracks.

The oddity of the landscape seemed even more bizarre due to dozens of Luftwaffe 88-mm anti-aircraft guns positioned about the area, their telephone-pole sized barrels now busily firing at American B-24 bombers that passed 8,000 meters overhead.

A close look at the soldiers who operated the guns revealed they were mere boys, teenagers at best, in uniforms much too large for their young bodies.

*The madness was truly in its last days.*


**"SERGEANT, I AM** going to say this but once. Drop your weapon," Captain Hans Dieter yelled above the deafening blasts of the Tiergartens' anti-aircraft guns—his machine pistol pointed directly at the sergeant. He had just witnessed the sergeant shooting one of his young charges at point blank range.

# THE VATICAN's LAST SECRET

The sergeant was quite drunk as he turned to face his new adversary, gun raised. "Screw yourself, Captain," he spat out, his words slurred. "I don't have to take your orders. Shoot me if you have the guts. These little children were my gun crew before you came." His free hand swept across the park where the youngsters operated the anti-aircraft guns. "I trained them. They answer to me. Go back to your nice clean hospital bed with your pretty little nurses, and wait for the Russians to come so you can raise your hands in surrender."

A lopsided grin creased the sergeant's face as he squeezed his weapons angled trigger. *Nothing happened.* He squeezed it once more. *Again, nothing happened.* The grin suddenly disappeared. He realized the predicament he was in as he continued to keep his weapon pointed at Dieter in an effort to maintain the ruse.

Dieter watched as the sergeant frantically reached for additional bullets from an ammo pouch on his waist, his ferret-like eyes never left the captains.

Dieter allowed the sergeant to load the first bullet before he tired of the charade, firing his weapon on full automatic.

The sergeant was dead by the time the third and fourth bullets pierced his skull.

Dieter walked over to where the now headless torso lay to kick the pistol from the sergeant's lifeless hand. "I do believe you were being insubordinate, sergeant, and I found you guilty. Hence my summary execution," he said aloud to no one in particular.

Suddenly, one by one, the anti-aircraft guns in the Tiergarten fell silent. The boys crewing the guns chose to leave their posts and gather by the dead bodies of their young comrade and the loathed sergeant.

Captain Dieter turned to those who had witnessed the carnage. He now held his weapon above his head for all to see before he chose to lay it on the ground. He wanted them to see he was no threat to them.

"Boys," he began, his steady gaze taking in each of them, "this sergeant did not deserve to wear the uniform of the Wehrmacht." He noticed the taller boys nodding in his direction, a good sign for him. He continued: "And for his summary offense of murdering the boy and his open disregard for my direct order, was himself executed. Anyone who disagrees with my version can take it up with the commanding officer. I will not stand in your way if you wish to press charges."

The boys eyed one another until one of them, a shade over thirteen who wore a black woolen uniform of an anti-aircraft gunner three sizes too large, spoke up.

"Sir," Axel Schmitz began, his teenage voice cracking as he spoke. "We witnessed the entire incident and you were right to execute him. The man was a worthless pig who needed butchering. He treated us horribly since our first day we reported here over two months ago. I guess I speak for everyone when I say *thank you*."

In the eyes of the young boys, the captain was right in his distribution of battlefield justice. *At least he would not be facing a firing squad anytime soon.*

Dieter surveyed his young charges as he walked up and down the ragged line they now formed, none taller than 5'5" or older than thirteen years of age. Suddenly he felt sick to his stomach. Pure exhaustion stared back at him. He saw mere boys who should be in school playing sporting games and learning history, *not making it.*

Dieter had been wounded fighting on the eastern front and sent to Berlin for surgery and recuperation. With manpower at an acute shortage in Berlin, the hospital discharged him two weeks early and assigned him to command one of the Tiergarten 88mm anti-aircraft batteries. The posting marked a brief respite from the constant hit-and-run skirmishes he had experienced first in France, then Russia, Poland, and now in Germany itself.

# THE VATICAN's LAST SECRET

After five long years of war, he was physically and emotionally spent. He had finally reached his breaking point. The child's senseless death being the final straw.

Dieter pointed over to the sergeant's lifeless body. "You were a witness to the type of people left in this city." He looked at the youngest boy then up the line to the oldest. "It might be best to escape back to your homes and families. You must see that your obligation to Germany is, from this point on, over. If there were ever a good time to abandon something, it is here and now. Please get out of Berlin. Save yourselves."

*In effect, Dieter dismissed them from any further service.*

The youngest of the group, not knowing what to say or do, looked from side-to-side in obvious fright. The rest of the boys had a look of confusion upon their faces. What was left of their small world had been thoroughly turned upside down.

"Captain," Private Schmitz began, obviously the unspoken leader of the group, "we have no one to return to. We are a special unit composed of orphans whose families were killed in the Dresden and Berlin air raids. The military thought it would be best to place us all together in one unit." He looked to his small group for support. All nodded in response. "I think I can speak for the rest of the group when I request we stay together as a unit, with you in command, sir."

Dieter felt ashamed for the way he had just spoken. "I'm... sorry," he stammered. "I wasn't aware of the unique situation involving your families."

To their left, no more than a hundred meters away, chaos was in plain view at the Brandenburg Gate. Rioters had just overturned an Army field kitchen—stealing what precious little food was available. *This is just the start. The city is in panic.* Dieter could not leave the children to fend for themselves. He had a responsibility to uphold.

Dieter straightened his cap before he proudly declared. "I accept your request to remain as your captain, and I thank you for your vote of confidence." He championed his responsibility as he patted the boy closest to him on the head and smiled. For

Captain Hans Dieter, it had been a long time since someone had afforded him the opportunity to smile.

"All right, everyone gather around for a look at our objective." He pulled a Berlin transit map out of his rucksack, one that sold before the war for five pfennigs, spreading the map on the ground for all to see. The boys eagerly looked to him for direction as they formed a circle around the map.

They had only one option in front of them: they would have to escape to the West — *or die trying.*

# CHAPTER 5

Night had settled in. Fires from the earlier American bomber raid raged out of control but provided them with an eerie glow, almost as if it were daylight, as they hiked to their destination. Since they had left the Tiergarten, it had taken them eight hours to reach a position two hundred meters south of the Zehlendoffer Damm Bridge.

*And one of the last escape routes out of Berlin.*

Dieter watched as a band of rag-tag German troops defended the century's old stone bridge from the advancing Russian Army. The bridge resembled nothing of its former self. Regal marble lions that originally stood guard for over two hundred years now lay destroyed, its pieces lay scattered along what remained of the bridges roadbed.

For Dieter and his young charges, the bridge was their last hope for escape to the West and the Allied Armies. With their hopes dashed, Dieter chose to reposition the boys in a defensive line along the sloping dirt banks of the 50-meter-wide canal, taking cover behind anything that seemed solid:

heavy wooden boxes, stonewalls, brick sections. No need for them to be caught in the open by some Russian sniper.

On an earthen bank above their position, Dieter adjusted his binoculars as he watched wave after wave of Russian troops foolishly charge across the bridge into a murderous German crossfire, this courtesy of two Tiger tanks dug in on the eastern side of the bridge.

After he viewed the debacle that was unfolding in front of him, Dieter realized the bridge was no longer an option. The situation was deteriorating at a faster pace than he expected.

"Boys," Dieter began as he looked back at the bridge, than to the boys, "if we attempt to cross that bridge with this kind of fighting going on, the odds are that most of us will be killed. I can think of only one other way to escape this nightmare. We should take our chances and float on the canal to where it intersects with another canal by the city of Potsdam. If you all agree let's get a move on because we have no time to waste. A quick show of hands will be sufficient."

Private Schmitz looked to the others then to Dieter before he spoke. "Captain, just give the order and we'll follow your lead. If it wasn't for you we would all be dead in the Tiergarten by now."

The boys all nodded in agreement.

Dieter smiled. "You have provided a boost to my ego young man. All right then, I want you to search for items like large pieces of wood or barrels. Anything that you think will float."

For safety's sake, he confined their search to a seventy-five meter area along the canals shoreline. After five minutes, Dieter and his charges were fortunate enough to come across a group of bullet-riddled collapsible canvas rafts. Each looked large enough to hold five average-sized persons. The rafts were still littered with their previous occupants; dead Russian soldiers. Evidently the remnants of an attempted canal crossing that went awry. After an additional five-minute search, three were considered serviceable.

Contending not only with the sounds of battle but also the whine of the nightly visit of British Lancaster's as they dropped their ordinance less than 200 meters away, Dieter tried his best to yell above it. "Bring the rafts over here and lash them together so we don't get separated," he screamed. He used hand signals to aid the ones who could not hear him. "Let's go people. Hurry up or be left behind."

*Dieter knew no one would be left behind, not while he was in charge.*

Satisfied they were indeed ready, they shoved off. Unfortunately they found themselves with the additional predicament of having to paddle through the start of what was a very intense air raid.

"All right, everyone count off," Dieter yelled into cupped hands. He continually scanned the opposite canal bank for any sign of enemy movement.

Schmitz tapped Dieter on the arm to provide him with a *thumbs up*.

Everyone was safely aboard.

*They were now ready to escape Berlin.*


**AS THEY SLOWLY DRIFTED DOWN THE CANAL**, the bombings destructive force ravaged apartment buildings on both sides of the river, its resulting fires casting an eerie glow on the river ahead. Ash and embers from the fires swirled about them as if fireflies in summer.

After the days horrifying events, the boys drifted off into a restful slumber—the crackle of the buildings' blazing timbers providing a form of somber background music.


**STREAKS OF LIGHT** dashed across the morning sky in greeting as the sun began to announce itself over the countryside.

Dieter roused Schmitz with a slight nudge of his foot, which in turn started a chain reaction until all were awake. As they looked about them, pastures and curious farm animals stared back.

The body of water they now floated on was a lot wider, more a river than canal.

Dieter pointed to heavy outgrowth of scrubs and trees on the western bank. "Private Schmitz, let's put in by that bank of trees and try and find out where we are."

Reaching the shoreline, the boys quickly jumped from the flimsy rafts to form a U-shaped defensive perimeter. Dieter used hand signals as they proceeded up the muddy embankment, not wanting to speak aloud until the area was indeed secure.

From atop the embankment Dieter scanned the immediate area with his binoculars, locating a whitewashed stone farmhouse no more than 100 meters directly ahead of them, curling white smoke billowed from its chimney. A long grassy track led up to the house. Freshly plowed earth occupied both sides of the track.

Dieter motioned to the solitary house. "That's going to be our objective. The only problem being we don't know who occupies it: could be either Germans or Russians."

Schmitz looked puzzled. "But why even take the house? Can't we just go around it and be on our way?"

The boys to his right and left nodded in agreement.

"Private Schmitz," Dieter replied in a Fatherly tone, "we have to find out where we are in reference to Berlin. If something went wrong during the night and we drifted down a tributary to the Russian side of the lines, we will no doubt soon find out. Somebody or something in that house will tell us where we are."

Schmitz responded by removing the safety from his weapon.

# THE VATICAN's LAST SECRET

Dieter beckoned to the boys still down by the rafts, their weapons at the ready. "I want the rest of you to be prepared to shove off should our little operation go astray. That is an order. Do not wait. If you hear any shooting get the hell out of here."

The remaining boys nodded nervously.

He turned back to their objective. Dieter assumed the lead, the rest of the boys fell in behind him as they charged over mounds of freshly plowed soil, metal canteens banging loudly against their web belts—the element of surprise clearly lost.

"Handel, break for the front door. I'll cover you."

Handel dove for the door rather awkwardly and lost his helmet in the process. He then slid up against the heavy wooden doorframe. He looked to Dieter for what to do next. Dieter made a knocking motion with his hand. Handel nodded before he cautiously extended his arm to knock on the front door, hoping for some type of response—German would be best.

After several seconds, a feeble, male, Germanic voice answered from inside the farmhouse. "What do you want?"

Handel enjoyed his newfound authority and was quick to reply. "The German army has come to requisition your property for a few hours old man. Now come out with your hands up."

The door slowly creaked open to reveal a disheveled, graying man of sixty, unshaven, medium build with crude patches affixed to his clothing on both the knees and at the elbows.

"Identify yourself to me boy and put that damn gun down," the man replied angrily. "If you don't, I'll put you over my knee and smack the be-Jesus out of you." He reached for the boys' rifle and grabbed it in one swift motion.

Dieter ran up and managed to cut off any further escalation. "I am sorry for the disturbance, sir. We just escaped from Berlin and were wondering where the hell we are."

"Ah, Berlin," the old man said as if he secretly understood their predicament. "Is that bastard Hitler still in power?"

Dieter immediately took a liking to the older man. "No sir, he committed suicide yesterday."

"Good, I never cared for that son of a bitch. Come inside and let's have a little celebratory drink and toast his journey to hell." He flung open his door. "Where are my manners? If my wife were still alive, I would have received an earful from her. How rude of me. Allow me to introduce myself," he bowed slightly at the waist. "Gentlemen, my name is Peter Goot and you are all welcome to what I have, which, due to the war and rationing, isn't much."

Dieter waved to the rest of the boys at the riverbank signaling everything was okay.

Having monitored the whole situation as it unfolded, the rest of the boys now trod over the same field Dieter and the boys had just traversed.

Goot laughed heartily. "I see your little flock is growing," he said. "Please come in boys and join the crowd. I haven't had this many people in my home since the last Christmas before the war started."

Goots' three-room farmhouse appeared to be as disheveled as its owner. Books lay scattered about— dirty clothing lay on chairs—unwashed dishes were piled high in the sink—newspapers littered the long wooden table where they performed double duty as a tablecloth.

Goot searched frantically as he moved piles of clothing looking for something clearly of value. "I have a bottle of schnapps hidden around here somewhere," he said. After several seconds he smiled as he held up his prize for Dieter to see. He then turned his attention to the boys. "Please sit down and rest from your journey while I serve up some fresh-baked bread."

Goot placed the foot-long loaf of bread on the table in front of the boys. Then he stood back as he watched the boys first sniff the warm luxury, then as they took small bites as if savoring their last meal. "Living on a farm has its benefits. Eat boys, or it will go to waste."

"And for us, Captain, *schnapps*."

Dieter could not believe their luck. First in their escape from Berlin, then in finding this easygoing man.

"I could stand a good belt after our little trip," he said. "I also need some information if I may."

Goot poured two generous glasses of the popular Berliner Apple Schnapps, some of it overflowed onto the newspaper that covered the table. "I will try to be of assistance if I can, Captain."

Dieter eyed the schnapps appreciatively before he sampled it, then emptied his glass. He smiled at Goot. "I haven't had a drink in a few weeks. Needed that." He then turned his glass upside down on the table, signaling he was done. "Can you tell us exactly where we are in relation to Berlin?"

Goot nodded at such a simple request. "That's easy, you are about twenty kilometers southwest of Berlin as the crow flies." He proudly pointed over to a makeshift radio, its antenna running out an open window for reception. "According to the latest BBC radio report, the American patrols were known to be only seventy-five kilometers away at a town called Torgau, having met up with the Russian Army just a few days ago."

Dieter realized their luck held out as they unknowingly floated off the main portion of the canal into a river tributary sometime during the night, winding up closer to the American lines than anticipated.

Goot refilled his glass. "Are you still fighting the war, captain, or will you escape to a safer environment?" He studied Dieter for his response. Goot had met some fanatical Nazis in his time, all expecting to fight to the death.

Dieter looked first to the boys then back to Goot, his expression one of melancholy.

"Hopefully I can get these boys to a safer place, a better life, anywhere but to be captured by the Russians."

Goot nodded.

Dieter continued. "I am to be a farmer when this war ends." *This was a semi-truth. Due to the unfortunate death of Dieter's parents' during an Allied bombing raid, the Dieter farm was now his to do with as he pleased.*

Goot looked on in surprise. "I would not have guessed it. A farmer you say? But you will need an experienced hand to assist you around the farm, not just these boys."

"I will require all the help I can get," Dieter was quick to reply.

Goot walked over to the mantel above his fireplace, removing a silver picture frame that held a prewar picture of his wife and sons. He softly stroked the frame at the cherished memories it held before he turned to face Dieter. "Captain, would you consider taking on an old hand such as myself? Since my wife died of cancer last year and my two sons killed at Stalingrad, I no longer have an attachment to this house."

Dieter nodded. "It would be an honor Mr. Goot." He directed his attention back to the boys, the bread now long gone. "All right, break time is over. We have many kilometers to go and little time to accomplish them. But before we do, I want you to welcome a new man to our outfit, Mr. Peter Goot," Dieter pointed over to Goot. "He is going to join us on our little journey."

A chorus of cheers greeted Goot as he was welcomed into the fold.

# THE VATICAN's LAST SECRET

# CHAPTER 6

Goot lay beside Dieter in a waist-high wheat field, their position lay just above the main road into Weimar. The boys were several meters back, their uniforms disheveled from their ten-day march through forest and backcountry hiking trails, sleeping where and when they could. All were bone tired and hungry, their rations having run out two days ago.

Jeeps cautiously approached their position.

"Are they German or American troops, Captain Dieter?" Goot said in a hushed tone as he watched as two jeeps drive slowly past the group's concealed position, four soldiers to a jeep, their 50 caliber machine guns pointed straight ahead. The smell of cigarette smoke lingered in the air as the first jeep passed.

"Looks to be an American reconnaissance patrol," Dieter replied.

"Captain," Goot exclaimed, starting to rise. "Let's surrender to them now and get this war over with."

Dieter grabbed him roughly by his shirt collar and yanked him back down to the ground. "I need to see if a friend of mine is still located in town," he said calmly, still eying the soldiers. "Then and only then can we surrender."

Goot thought Dieter had gone utterly mad. "Is the information you seek worth possibly dying for?"

He turned slowly to face Goot, a smile upon his face, nodding. "However bizarre it sounds, it most definitely is my friend — *most definitely*."

**IN HIS TEENAGED** years, Dieter would sneak into town from his parent's farm for some innocent mischief. Now he retraced the same medieval cobbled stone alleyways where 10 years earlier he had avoided the local constable when he stole a case of wine from a delivery wagon. Times had certainly changed. The town looked to be devoid of troops, neither German nor American. Behind him the motley army he had assembled followed as he weaved his way through town to the back-alley door of the Black Cat Club. Numerous cases of empty beer and wine bottles were stacked high on either side of the door.

Dieter cautiously eased the door open before entering the Black Cat Club. He stopped just inside the doorway to allow his eyes to adjust to the partial darkness. Goot and the boys followed. They kept their weapons drawn, never knowing who would be in residence, even at this early hour. In front of him, Dieter could see the immediate area was devoid of people. He breathed a sigh of relief. *He was almost free.*

As they moved forward toward the dimly lit bar area, they were fortunate enough to encounter the club manager, Lisa Chevier, as she walked down the back stairwell.

Still a head turner, Lisa was a slightly overweight, fortyish expatriate from Paris whose tight pink silk nightgown strained to conceal her ample breasts.

"We are closed for the day gentlemen. Come back in two or three hours," Lisa said politely in her most seductive French accented voice through her many years of practice.

Dieter removed his leather officer's cap to afford her a better view. "Lisa, it's me, Hans Dieter. Remember? I am Inga's friend—the officer that took up residence here during my leave many months ago. I'm the soldier with a farm just outside of town."

The boys worked their way in behind Dieter to get a better look at the sexily clad Lisa, eyes bulging.

Standing on the steps, Lisa paused to gather her thoughts for a moment before she slammed her hand down hard on the wooden railing. She then pointed at him with some recollection before she ran down the few remaining steps. Lisa embraced him for a second or two before she pushed him to arm's length, the stench of ten days on the march a bit overwhelming for her.

"Oh my goodness, why of course, Captain Dieter," she exclaimed. "I didn't recognize you in your unkempt uniform. We all thought you were dead or missing like so many unfortunate others. But what are you doing here? Weren't you fighting the Russians on the Eastern Front?"

"I was on the Eastern Front until I was wounded several weeks ago and then stationed in Berlin with these young boys until we deserted our posts. I must apologize, but we don't have much time for details. I must see Inga right away. Is she still working here?"

Lisa nodded in understanding, having personally consoled many a soldier whose last posting lay on the Eastern Front.

"Inga? Why yes, of course she still works here," she replied, slightly offended. "Why wouldn't she be here? I pay the most lucrative wages in town."

Lisa turned to Goot and the boys. "Is this what the mighty German army is comprised of these days, old men and boys? No wonder your Germany is losing the war."

Goot took offense to her choice of words, more for the boys' sake than his own. "Who do you think you are to make such a comment? The Queen of Sheba in a tight dress?"

Dieter patted him on the back in an attempt to calm him down.

Lisa was quick to respond. Never one to lose a customer, she could see she had evidently offended the gentleman. "Now, now, my dear," she purred as she grabbed his arm.

Goot pushed her away in horror.

"Break it up you two. I need to see Inga right away," Dieter said, the urgency in his voice apparent to all. "The Americans are in town and we don't have much time before they stumble upon this place."

Lisa pressed her hands together as if in prayer. "The Americans are here? Now? This is the best news I have heard all month. And business has been off for far too long."

Dieter laughed aloud at the savvy businesswomen. "You really change sides quickly don't you Lisa?"

A look of seriousness crossed her face before she responded. "The only side I am on is the side of money, Captain Dieter. No one else pays my bills. Now, you can go see Inga in room twelve while I entertain this charming older man you brought with you."

Lisa once again grabbed Goot by the arm.

Dieter glanced back in time to see Goot having his wallet expertly picked by Lisa as she escorted him to the bar area.

**FINDING INGA WAS EASY** enough, still singing the same old Bavarian tune she had sung to him four months ago. With the door that led to her room slightly ajar, Dieter quietly eased himself into the Victorian-appointed but cramped room. He maneuvered along the foot of her brass bed as she sat brushing her brown, waist-length hair in front of a dresser mirror.

Admiring her beauty for several minutes, he waited until she had finished and then he cleared his throat to attract her attention.

Immediately she turned to face the sound. When she saw Dieter she dropped her hairbrush on the floor in utter shock, her mouth agape.

"You bastard — where have you been?" she demanded angrily. "My letters to you for the past two months were returned with no forwarding address! I thought you were dead!"

Dieter smiled as he embraced Inga. She allowed his hands to roam over areas he was all too familiar. "You really did miss me, didn't you? And I thought you would have forgotten me by now."

Inga grabbed his neck using it as support as she wrapped her long tan legs around the base of his back. "Forget my long lost love? Maybe I should have."

He brushed aside her jasmine scented hair, their eyes meeting. "No games this time, okay?"

As their lips were about to touch, Lisa burst into the room. "Dieter," she said nervously. "American soldiers are downstairs. You and your little flock must hide right away."

"Can you believe this? I haven't seen this beautiful woman in over four months and now this has to happen." He continued to eye Inga appreciatively. "Damn it, just fifteen lousy minutes is all I would have asked for. It just goes to prove all good things must come to an end."

Inga released her leggy grip and slid back onto her bed.

"Inga there is one thing I must know before we part ways," he said before taking a step back to gaze lustfully upon her body's fullness. "Has anyone come looking for me in the past couple of weeks? Anyone at all?" He searched her face for any sign of betrayal, never truly knowing whom he could trust anymore.

## THE VATICAN's LAST SECRET

She moved closer to him, tilting her head to one side. "No, not that I'm aware of. Who would want to look for you here?"

"It's a long story, one that I can't explain right now due to our particular circumstances. Another day, another time, I promise."

Dieter turned to face Lisa and the boys who had now gathered in the hallway. "Lisa, please go and fetch our friend Goot before the Americans find him and decide to shoot the poor old bastard."

Dieter broke into a mischievous grin, truly realizing for the first time that he was about to become a very rich man.

# CHAPTER 7

The rush of heavy leather boots charging up wooden steps signaled the American soldiers had indeed arrived.

Dieter ordered the boys to take up a defensive position in order to repel any advance for the moment.

Goot was puzzled at Dieter's response to the Americans. "I thought you wanted to be captured by the Americans," he exclaimed.

Dieter extracted his Lugar sidearm to check its ammunition. "I do, but on my own terms and conditions." He turned to face Inga. "Is there an attic where the boys can hide?"

She pointed down the darkened hall. "Yes, of course. It's where we hide our black market alcohol from the police." Inga took Dieter by the hand, walking the short distance to where she pushed aside a large, gaudy oil painting of an alpine mountain scene that revealed a secret door.

Dieter pulled Inga out of earshot of the boys and Goot. "Is there enough room for all of the boys to hide for an hour or two while we surrender and distract the Americans from this place?"

"But of course. It runs the whole length of the club. It's at least twenty meters long."

He turned back to face the boys, marveling at their youth and determination. *They are a bright group of kids who deserve better.* He had rescued them from the perils of Berlin and the Russian Army. Now it was time for the next stage of their lives to begin.

Dieter turned to Schmitz. "Private Schmitz, I require you to take the boys into the attic."

"You heard the Captain. Move out," Schmitz ordered in turn, thinking they were maneuvering to surprise the Americans in an ambush.

"Damn it, quietly!" Dieter said. "Do you want the Americans to hear you?"


**IT WAS ALREADY TOO LATE**. The American soldiers could not help but hear the commotion on the wood floor above them.

The Sergeant in command responded by removing a grenade from his web belt. He now moved closer to the bottom of the stairwell.

"Drop your weapons and come down peaceably," he yelled up the steps in his best schoolboy German, albeit with a Texas drawl. "I'll give you one minute to reply and then we come up shooting."

Dieter required additional time. He had to stall the Americans until the boys could safely hide themselves in the attic. "American soldiers, we mean you no harm. We just want to talk before surrendering," he replied in near perfect English, a product of several years' schooling in England prior to the war.

# THE VATICAN's LAST SECRET

"No problem, buddy. You can do all of your talking down here," the Sergeant replied. "Now, I order you to drop your weapons and come down with your hands up."

Dieter realized the Americans were an impatient lot judging from the cowboy movies he had watched before the war. A minute was too long for them, more likely he would count to ten before he choose to fire.

He turned to Inga, taking her by the hand, his expression betraying his feelings. "The Americans have no idea that the boys are up here," he said, pausing to gaze into her violet eyes. "Goot and myself will sacrifice ourselves and surrender to the Americans in order to distract them from the boys. After this is over, I want you to take the boys to my parents' farm and set them up with some money. I will pay you back double as soon as possible. Can you do this for me? Please? For their sake?"

Inga was taken back by his request. "How am I supposed to settle down on a farm?" she replied abruptly. "Do you just snap your fingers, and I change into a normal house frau and take in all of these boys? Am I also supposed to turn over my life savings to you?"

Dieter realized the position he was placing her in, but due to the circumstance had no other choice. "The Americans won't hold us for long," he replied.

Inga averted his eyes.

He gently placed his hands on her shoulder. "They will set us free in several months and then you can resume your wonderful life if you like. The boys need you, Inga. Do this for all of the little boys and girls who didn't make it through the war."

Inga still chose to look away but Dieter could hear the soft sobs as tears began to run down her cheek.

Dieter took her in his arms and held her tight. "For once in your life please don't be a selfish bitch."

"Selfish? Me — *Selfish*?" she repeated, the sting of his words apparent. She pushed him away. "Am I the one who is selfish? You bastard! You have room to talk. You don't show up for months on end and expect me to drop everything for you?"

Dieter used his uniforms sleeve to dab at the black mascara that now streamed down her cheeks.

"Inga, I'm sorry. I only have about thirty seconds before this place becomes a battle zone. I am only doing this for the children's sake and their well-being. I gave them my word. Please, can you help me? It will only be for a short time."

Inga studied his face. She reached up to brush his cheek with her hand. "Only a couple of months? *You promise me*?"

"Yes, I promise," he said before turning back to check the boys' progress down the hall. "A couple of months tops, no more." Dieter placed his left hand over his heart.

"If it were anyone else but you, Hans Dieter, I would spit in their face," she said. Inga paused for a few seconds as if ready to change her mind. "Okay, I'll do it. For the children's sake only," extracting some satisfaction at his omission. "I will see that they get to the farm and I can even kick in some money to get them started. But I can promise you this, if you don't return in a few months I'll hunt you down myself," she said in jest before reaching up and engaging him in a deep passionate kiss.

Goot looked away in embarrassment.

"That's the Inga I have grown to love," Dieter said as he spun her lithe body around in a tight circle.

Inga gazed longingly into his eyes. "Please take care and come back as soon as possible."

"Now that I have somebody to come home to, you know I will," Dieter said before releasing her.

Dieter walked to where Schmitz and the boys had positioned themselves in the doorway of the attic, heads poking out, faces covered in soot and dirt. They resembled the youngsters who worked in the coalmines a hundred years ago. He nodded to each before informing them in a low voice that they were to wait out the war and go with Inga after he left. She was now in charge until he returned.

Schmitz protested. "No, sir, we go with you as soldiers. We can fight our way out of here. There is no need for you to surrender for our sake."

Each boy nodded in unison — *loyal to the end*.

"I gave you an order gentlemen and I expect you, as soldiers, to carry it out. Is that understood?" Dieter declared gently.

"Yes, sir, captain," Schmitz replied, all the boys snapping to attention in response.

Dieter admired their dedication to him. "Stay in the attic and close the door. I promise we will meet again when the war is over."

Dieter turned his attention to the pressing issue of the American soldiers' stationed one floor below. He sought encouragement from Goot and Inga, both only able to provide a meager smile in response. He straightened his uniform. "It's show time."

Dieter approached the top of the steps. "Attention, Americans," he yelled in his best English. "We would like to surrender. We mean you no harm. There are only four of us up here, two of whom are woman, so don't shoot."

Dieter turned to see tears running down Schmitz cheeks as he executed a near perfect salute from his position at the attics door.

Dieter nodded to the young man, returning the boys salute, before proceeding down the wooden steps, and into captivity.

# CHAPTER 8

**SEPT. 1945 - DIETER FARM, WEIMAR GERMANY**

Schmitz was busy in the barns hayloft when he suddenly noticed two familiar figures approaching the house from the main road.

"It can't be," he said, mopping the sweat from his brow with a well-worn handkerchief. "Look, look," Schmitz shouted to those below. "The Captain and Goot have returned." He pointed at the fast approaching figures. "Go and round up the rest of the boys and tell them the Captain and Goot have returned. Hurry!"

Schmitz jumped down from the hayloft into the hay cart positioned below. "Captain, you have come back," Schmitz yelled excitedly as he jumped into the arms of Dieter, Dieter staggered back a few steps under the boys weight, undoubtedly a product of Inga's cooking.

"Schmitz, it's good to be home," he said as he wrapped his arms around him in a bear hug. "You can't believe how much I've missed this place. It's been a long time without home-cooked food and such pleasant surroundings."

"Captain you must see what we have done with the farm," Schmitz said, yanking on Dieter's sleeve. "We have cleaned the fields and the surrounding area of the overgrowth and even planted beets and turnips in their place. We even painted the farmhouse and put on a new roof with material we stole."

"Borrowed," Inga corrected him, having walked down to where the boys now stood. A smile graced her face, one that she reserved only for Dieter.

"Yes, excuse me, *borrowed* from the American soldiers in town," he said. We even bought chickens and a milk cow with some money Inga had saved."

As he surveyed the house, Dieter took note of the new roof and the surrounding fields and nodded with approval. "You have transformed what was a rundown farm into a home," he said, knowing it was Inga's motherly spirit that had transformed the farm into a real home.

The rest of the boys soon made their way in from the fields, gathering around Dieter and Goot, all offering their congratulations on a safe return home.

"Now to more pressing matters," Dieter said. "Goot and I haven't had a decent meal in months and could quite possibly eat a bear." He rubbed Goot's stomach for effect. The boys laughed heartily in response. "So if there's enough food for Goot and myself, let us proceed to the table and eat our full share. After that, we have some additional work to be done."

*Only Goot knew what Dieter was referring to.*

# THE VATICAN's LAST SECRET

# CHAPTER 9

**PRESENT DAY - CHEATEK, NEW YORK**

Hans refilled his glass with a jigger of Irish before returning the half-empty bottle to its bedside perch. He felt like standing by the window one last time but exhaustion had settled in.

Father Dan and Jim sat on the edge of their chairs, awe struck by Hans' revelation. A defiant Father Dan helped himself to the bottle, refilling Jim's glass, then his own.

"It can't end there, Hans," Father Dan demanded. "Tell us more you old coot. You have to tell us what happened to everyone who was involved: Schmitz, Goot, Inga, the rest of the boys."

Hans shook his head at Father Dan's simple request, having unburdened himself of a story he had not entrusted to anyone but his dear departed wife. "I told you before we started that my story would shock you and by the look on your faces it has."

Hans quickly downed the remainder of his glass before he continued. "Don't worry, in due time you will be privy to the information which you seek. You will become detectives and find additional pieces of the puzzle on your own."

He wished he were ten years younger and able to go along on the journey they were about to undertake. He looked down at his pale hands holding an empty glass, purple and green veins clearly visible. He could see his body slowly withering away. *The meat was leaving the bones* his grandmother would say. After all these years, he finally understood the expressions meaning.

Father Dan and Jim sat discussing the story Hans had just imparted to them.

"Okay, gentlemen," Hans said. "I did withhold one small but very important detail of information from my tale." A mischievous smile creased his face. He toyed with the glass he held in his hand, the pause planned. He reached for another pain pill, washing it down with water, foregoing the Irish for the moment. He turned to fluff his pillow. Comfortable once more, he began. "Now after my unit ambushed the truck, we moved the gold back to my family's farm and I buried not one but two piles of gold and documents. The rationale was simple. If by chance one pile was exposed, we still had the other as a safety net. Later I recovered one pile and decided to keep the remainder of gold and documents hidden in the best possible place I could think of. It was my insurance policy against anyone who wanted to take action against my family."

"All right, Dad, you know the situation better than any of us," Jim said, "but I do have a question concerning your story?"

Hans motioned for him proceed.

"What ever happened to the older gentleman in your story, Mr. Goot? Did you ever see him again? He sounded like a real interesting character."

Hans smiled. "It was because of him the three months I spent interned in the American POW camp were a lot easier to deal with. It was during our imprisonment that I informed Goot about my little insurance policy."

Hans gazed up at the ceiling as his mind wandered back to days long past before he continued. "Unfortunately, my friend Goot was to experience none of our riches. A heart attack claimed him less than a month after we left the POW camp. We were in the process of moving the second pile of gold and documents to a safer location when it happened. At the time, I was certain no one from my old unit was still alive, but what if one of them had mentioned their share of the pot to a friend or two? Moving it eased our fears. No one could steal what he or she could not find. But getting back to the story. As we prepared the second pile of gold for movement, Goot suddenly grabbed his chest and fell to the ground in obvious pain. He motioned me to his side, whispering what would become his dying words. It was something that would comfort me all of these years. In his last breath he said, 'If it weren't for you and the boys, I would have died a lonely old man on an empty farm. You gave me hope once more. I was lucky enough in life to have had two families. Thank you, my friend.'"

Father Dan was the first to speak. "He sounded like a hell of a man."

"That he was," Hans was quick to reply. "I acquired the best possible tombstone and coffin so he could rest comfortably in his eternity. This, gentlemen, is one of the main reasons why you two must return to the land of my birth and gather the gold and documents. If it's just to honor Goot."

Jim and Father Dan concurred with a simple nod.

"Now, the gold will be easy enough to find. It is located on acreage that has been in our family for over six generations. That farm means a lot to me, more than all the money I have in my possession."

Hans reached for Jim's hand as he looked into his son's eyes. For a slight moment, he viewed a bit of his wife staring back at him. Jim obviously had his mother's eyes and smile.

"Funny, isn't it? You learn so many things about a person when they die. You get to rummage through their personal things, possessions they have guarded closely in life, things only they would find value in. You will be in a room full of junk and wonder why or what story is behind a certain picture or item. Me, I beat you to the punch. I have provided you the story, now you need to live the ending."

Hans sat back, content with his story being in the open. After several awkward minutes, he turned to face his son. "Jim, I need a minute or two in private with Father Dan. There are several issues for his ears only."

Jim nodded. "No problem Dad. I can just wait outside." Jim turned to Father Dan, silently he mouthed the words, *"You're in trouble,"* before he left the room to take a seat in the anteroom.

The bedroom door now closed, Hans slowly focused on Father Dan. He picked up the bottle of Irish and carefully refilled the contents of both glasses before he proceeded. "And now we can turn our attention to the infamous Father Dan Flaherty, or should I just call you Dan?"

Father Dan was about to speak in protest.

Hans cut him off with a wave of his hand. "Hold your tongue until I'm through. And may I remind you that this has been a long time in coming. Ever since you first set foot in my humble house some twenty plus years ago, one big lie has hung over your head."

Father Dan tried to protest but Hans once more cut him off with a wave of his hand. "Please allow me to finish."

Dan nodded silently in agreement, alarmed at Hans's sudden change in demeanor.

Hans smiled. "The main reason you came to this country was to escape the British and Ulster factions in Northern Ireland. For they don't take too kindly to a man like yourself being involved in the IRA's militant activities, do they?"

Hans mustered an ear-to-ear grin at seeing the look of surprise, nay shock, upon Father Dan's face. Hans had looked forward to this moment since he first found out about Father Dan's secret identity.

Arising from his chair, caring neither for the sudden shift in tone nor the accusation, Father Dan slammed his half-empty whiskey glass down on the nightstand. "Damn it Hans, are the drugs affecting you so badly that you would accuse your best friend of something as ridiculous as this?"

"I'm not finished yet, Dan. Sit your ass back down and listen to what I have to say." The excitement was a little too much for him as he once again reached for his oxygen line, placing it under his nose, a wave to Father Dan signaled he was okay.

Father Dan sat back down. "All right you don't have to have a heart attack before the cancer takes you away."

Both waited several uncomfortable minutes until Hans could proceed.

"Let's try this one more time." Hans sought the right words to say to his dear friend without totally offending him. "You don't have to worry about your previous life in Ireland. I haven't told a soul. Scouts honor." Hans held up his hand up as if he were swearing an oath in court. "I've kept your little secret all this time and even deflected some inquiries by our own authorities. Hell, if you remember I even sponsored your citizenship."

Father Dan smiled in agreement. The citizenship party Hans threw for him lasted for two days.

"I had plenty of time and chances to turn you in, *if I had wanted to*," he said. "But let's get back to the reason you're here. It's simple really. I want you to use some of your covert connections in the U.S. and overseas to help my son bring back the rest of the gold to the states."

"But, Hans, I…"

Again, Hans cut him off. "Enough, Dan. I've known about your secret identity since the first years you stepped foot on our humble shores. I have made it a point to have each and every one of my close friends investigated to safeguard myself from any possible threats. It's just a precaution I take due to my own checkered past. Many years have passed since I had your records verified through an old German army friend of mine who worked at INTERPOL."

Father Dan's eyes went wide with the mention of INTERPOL.

"Have no worries, your secret will remain buried deep in some obscure file placed in a storage building in Luxembourg. I also had my friend, shall we say, remove from your record any of the real damaging accusations made against you. Of course, this will leave you free to travel anywhere in Europe…*well… almost anywhere in Europe.* Obviously not England. I understand they still have a high price on your ugly mug."

"I'm truly sorry, Hans," he said. "As your trusted friend and confident, I never should have tried to keep this secret from you. I truly thank you for not betraying me. It happened a long time ago and I have tried to put it all behind me."

Hans knew a thing or two about secrets. He reached out and tapped his friend on the arm as a signal for him to stop for he had his confirmation. "It's your turn to delight me in a story, Dan," Hans said. "I mean, I can just call you Dan, right? I can drop the *Father Dan* bit because you really aren't a priest? Are you?"

Dan nodded in defeat. "Guilty," was his simple reply.

"Tell me how you settled on the priest disguise? Why not a trucker or a steelworker? You would have blended in easier." Hans reached for his bedpan in anticipation of the story to come. "This should be a real doozy."

"You really know how to make someone feel welcome, don't you? However, I must compliment you on your detective skills my friend. Well, as you have obviously known for twenty some years, I am not a real priest, but I did live as best I could to uphold a priest's convictions. I could not and will not soil the reputation of a religion that has provided me a wonderful refuge—a forced one at that. Now, let us regress to a time when I was a young naïve lad from the country with dirt behind my ears, a time when I was more than willing to blindly follow someone for the cause. That's when I became a member of the outlawed Irish Republican Army. It was my little way to strike back against the despots who ruled our land. You know the details better then I on that one."

A well-versed student of history, Hans motioned for Dan to carry on.

"As a common soldier, I was assigned to the Belfast Feinian group which happened to be the most radical of all the IRA splinter groups. After a few years of destroying police stations and maiming Ulster soldiers, my supervisors provided me with a new assignment. Unfortunately for me, this particular job would forever shape my destiny."

Dan filled his now empty glass with water, taking a sip before he continued. "My primary assignment was to destroy a certain hotel when a militant Ulster faction would occupy its upper floors for notional peace talks." Dan stopped for a moment as if in contemplation. He smiled before he carried on. "Looking back now, if I had the brains to refuse the job, who knows? I might have been a history teacher in some Shannon middle school classroom." He allowed a half-hearted smile to escape as he thought of what might have been.

He continued. "After I performed the mission without fail, my name happened to surface at the local police constabulary as a potential suspect. Someone had dropped the dime on me. One of my many enemies I suppose but who really knew? I required a quick vacation out of Ireland until the heat wore off. So I went into hiding at a local Catholic Church that was sympathetic to the IRA cause. I helped doing various duties such as cleaning, carpentry, and handyman duties. It was about this time that I met a mysterious man who called himself Father Perluci. He represented himself as a meek and humble man from the Vatican, out to help me in my unfortunate plight. Turns out he was as much a priest as I am now. No sir, he was an agent who used the disguise of a priest in order to put his prey at ease. Perluci worked in a little known Vatican office that is the equivalent to the American CIA or British MI-6, only the people do not work for money. They do it for religious conviction. Perluci was well aware of my radical background and threatened to expose me to the English unless I crossed the line and came to work for them. Within a week, they provided me with an alias that allowed me to leave Ireland on favorable terms."

"But why did the Vatican send you here?" queried Hans. "What was their purpose?"

Dan smiled at his friend. "The Vatican needed the use of someone with my obvious talents and, well, *good looks*."

Hans laughed aloud as he shook his head at his friend. "They were definitely off in the looks department."

Dan realized it was time for him to go, him now standing. "As far as helping your son, I will protect and help him in any way I can. I promise you on my mother's grave. Moreover, one more thing, don't you die on me until we get back. Did you hear me you old coot? You still owe me a night of storytelling over an excellent bottle of cognac."

"Get out of here you Irish Mick before I call the English embassy." A lone tear slid down his cheek as he wondered where all of the years had gone. "Could you please tell my son to come in here for a moment?"

Dan withdrew to the anteroom, taking a seat on a hard-metal chair opposite the day nurse, appearing lost in his thoughts.

Jim walked into the bedroom and stood beside his father's bedside. He took his father's cold, almost lifeless hand into his own. In doing so he briefly experienced a childhood memory when his father would bring him some hot chocolate or a comic book when he lay sick, temporarily taking away the sting of whatever had ailed him.

Jim smiled. "Well, did you get everything off your chest, Dad? I know you and Father Dan go back a long time."

A grin greeted him. "Yes, everything is out in the open between that mick and me," Hans said softly, pondering how to broach the next subject. "Let's be truthful, Jimmy. I don't think I'll be alive much longer. I sure as hell won't be alive when you find the gold. So, I want you to do me one last favor." He motioned for Jim to sit down in a chair by his bedside.

"Please sit where a son belongs, beside his Father, and let's just talk awhile."

# THE VATICAN's LAST SECRET

# CHAPTER 10

Venturing outside for some well-deserved fresh air, Jim bid a hasty retreat from the mansion.

The sudden rush of air seemed exhilarating. He paused at the houses entrance before he noticed Dan standing alone by the edge of the west wing garden.

Dan was smoking one of his trademark Ashton cigars, tossing small white pebbles at the koi fish that resided in the pond's murky waters, watching them rush off in a variety of directions in response.

Dan exhaled small white ringlets. He noted Jim's approach out of the corner of his eye before he turned to face him. "May I be so bold as to inquire what your old man had to say? Did it have anything to do with the expedition we are about to embark on?"

Jim was ready to respond when Dan cut him off. "No, on second thought, don't tell me anything. Your face says it all. Nevertheless, did he happen to tell you about my actions in Derry? Or any of the other distant places that I have tried to erase from my dreams each night while I sleep? Did he tell you the main reason we both drink in excess is to douse the past in which so much of our lives are intertwined—the killings, death, bombings." He took a long drag on his cigar, exhaling after several seconds before he continued. "I have something to tell you my friend. War is horrible at best. If you are fortunate enough to live through it you want to spend the rest of your life in peace. Your father and I are part of a different breed of men, one that is gradually leaving this worlds existence for another hopefully better one." He dropped the remainder of his cigar on the gravel path, extinguishing it with a well-worn black loafer.

Dan laughed aloud before he continued. "Listen to me go on, will you? Well don't worry, when the action starts, I'll be fit to hold up my part of the task."

## Saint Peter and Paul Cemetery, Lyndhurst New York

THE FLORAL DISPLAYS were piled six feet high to the rear of the regal, walnut casket. Row upon row of multi-colored roses, orchids, mums, daffodils, and other assorted flower arrangements provided a vivid backdrop for the burial of Hans Dieter. No doubt he eyed his guests from his heavenly perch only to enjoy the politicians as they tugged at their Armani shirt collars in the sweat of the midday sun, this, as they bid him farewell.

The dignitaries were out in full force, even the governor flew in from Albany to attend. Politicians never seemed to stop seeking votes, even trying to capitalize on death itself. Each provided adoring speeches of Hans' past deeds.

With the casket lowered into the freshly dug earth, Dan played his final role as Father Dan, providing his blessing. After which he walked over to where Jim stood in respectful silence. "Your father would have enjoyed it this way. No long prayers or an ungodly viewing. Just put me in the ground and get on with your life is what he would have said. A dead body starts to stink if it's left around too long."

Jim replied with a nervous laugh. "Yeah, that and make sure everyone has a toast of schnapps when the blessing is finished, and have them toss their empty glasses into the grave with me so I have something to use in the afterlife."

Dan glanced at the mourners gathered about. "Well, judging by the attendance, he had a lot of friends. You should be proud of that. Your father had wealth in three ways: family, friends, and money itself. Judging by his funeral today, all three were in attendance."

**IN THE LAST** row, hidden by the large turnout, an attractive, well-dressed, middle-aged woman removed a cell phone from her purse, dialing a prearranged number.

*"The Angel is in the ground,"* she said coolly before she hung up.

She gracefully walked past the mourners clustered in their small groups as they recalled Hans' life until she reached his open grave. She paused as if in silent prayer, blessed herself, and then tossed a white rose on top of his casket. She turned in time to catch Dan's eye, smiling at him, waving her cell phone.

The signal had been passed.

# THE VATICAN's LAST SECRET

# CHAPTER 11

**MAY 1949 - SOVIET UNION**

For the first time in over four years of dutiful negotiation, the Geneva-based International Red Cross were granted permission to visit the Soviet Union and several of its "work camps." The camps contained thousands of German prisoners of war, prisoners from a war that ended for most in 1945.

The Soviets simply stated the prisoners were needed to "rebuild" their war-torn country.

*The world press called it slave labor.*

**BEFORE THE RED CROSS** team departed from Geneva, three of its original seven members were killed in a suspicious hit-and-run accident, run down by a truck as they crossed a street to an awaiting taxi — the truck driver not even bothering to stop.

The only witness, the taxi driver, stated he thought the truck was driven by two men, both wearing friars hats. Possibly priests.

An American and a Britain were hastily arranged to replace the first two. The third, a man dressed as a priest, showed up just as the plane was boarding.

**THE CAMP COMMANDER**, Major Fedorov, strolled up to the camps newly constructed wooden reviewing platform with the Red Cross representatives in tow. A sharp Siberian wind howled in greeting.

He was in his late forties, his black hair had a hint of gray, his green-gray uniform impeccable. The prisoners often referred to him as "*the little bull*" due to his penchant of stabbing them with the dagger he kept secured about his waist.

Even his own men detested him.

When the major reached the top of the steps, he turned to his aide-de-camp in dismay upon viewing frost on the metal chairs. *Punishment could be expected for this lack of attention.* Major Fedorov elegantly withdrew a white cloth from his pocket, and playing the gracious host, wiping the frost that had accumulated on the chairs overnight before he allowed the representatives to sit down.

Satisfied that his guests were comfortable, he directed his attention to the prisoners who occupied the muddy parade ground before him, assembled row upon row, exactly as they had rehearsed for the past two weeks.

The prisoners shifted from leg to leg in the biting cold, a Siberian wind playing out across the parade ground now mixed with a light snow. The prisoners dug their hands deeper into their coat pockets.

"I will make this speech short due to the work that awaits you in our mines," Major Fedorov said, his voice resonating across the dismal camp. "As your internal rumor mill has probably informed you by now, we have honored guests from the International Red Cross. They are based in Geneva, Switzerland and claim to be a neutral organization. They have the simple job of checking the conditions at our fine establishment. These ladies and gentlemen are here to register your complaints and review our general living and working conditions. Their delegation also includes a Catholic priest for any of you who proclaim that religion as your faith. Those of you who are Catholic will be allowed to visit for five minutes with the priest to confess your sins. To speed the process, I would like all of those prisoners of the Catholic persuasion to identify themselves and step out of line. If you do not, I will personally search the records to find out who is Catholic and invite you to my office for a more personal visit. And I guarantee you will not enjoy the visit." He smiled as he patted the ceremonial sword that hung around his waist.

Of the 770 men assembled in the courtyard, ten stepped out of line as instructed. The men then walked in an orderly procession to where the priest and Major Fedorov awaited them.

"Good, good, we have volunteers," said Major Fedorov. "Follow me and this gentleman into my secretary's office." Major Fedorov then turned to face the priest. "Father, you will have five minutes with each prisoner. Use my office. After that they go back to work for Mother Russia."

The small, balding, almost gnomish priest was quick to reply. "That is most gracious of you, major. I am your humble servant." He made a slight downward tilt of the head as if the major were royalty. Of the ten prisoners who were assembled in front of them, Peter Dems was selected or "arranged" to be first, being hustled out of line by a brutish guard and harshly pushed to the front.

At one time Peter Dems had been considered a handsome man, standing 6'1," 200 pounds, with a thick head of blond hair and piercing blue eyes. Since his arrival in 1945, pneumonia, plague, and typhoid had ravaged his body. He now appeared gaunt and weak.

# THE VATICAN's LAST SECRET

"Welcome, my son. Please do sit down," said the Priest, otherwise known as Antonio Perluci of the Vatican Intelligence staff, recently assigned to the International Red Cross for this one mission.

The guard closed the door. A small window in its center allowed him to observe the proceedings from outside the room.

Perluci smiled before speaking. "Has it been long since you have spoken to a priest of your faith?"

Peter eyed the man for several seconds, not really knowing how to respond to such a ridiculous question. "I don't mean to sound rude, Padre, but what the hell do you think we do in here?" he replied sarcastically.

Perluci glanced over Peter's shoulder to see if the guard was still monitoring their conversation. Convinced he was indeed alone with the prisoner, he proceeded. "We are here to monitor the conditions of the camp and to possibly relay any messages you may have for family and friends."

Peter tried to gauge this man for trickery. He knew it would not be beneath the Soviets to create an elaborate ruse just to torture the prisoners. "Father, I really don't have anyone at home who would still care enough to want to hear from me. Most of my family were killed in bombing raids during the early years of the war. I was hoping to just talk about current events. We don't receive outside news in this god-forsaken place. Hell, for all I know, the war could still be going on."

Perluci looked to the door once more, seeing the guard had evidently tired of his post. Perluci removed a wedding photo of Peter and his wife from his jacket pocket and slipped it across to him. Perluci lowered his voice to just above a whisper. "Please, I already know who you are. You have changed much from when this photo was originally taken over six years ago. I can see Soviet food and confinement do not agree with you."

Peter stared at the photo. Tears began to well in his eyes.

The photo had the desired effect. *He was already a broken man.*

Perluci continued: "I only have a few minutes before the guard comes back, so I will be brief. First, I have a question for you. Were you assigned under the command of a Captain Hans Dieter?"

Perluci eyed the door over Peter's shoulder as he awaited a response.

Peter traced the outline of his wife's slim figure with his forefinger, not bothering to look up. "Yes, I was, but how did you come across this information?" he spat out.

Perluci smiled. "We in the Vatican also have our own intelligence unit. I will not bore you with details about our little operation because we have so little time, so just answer the questions. Did you or did you not participate in a military action against a German military truck that you latter found to contain a load of gold and other assorted objects?"

For the first time since receiving his wife's photo, Peter looked up, suddenly concerned about the direction the conversation was taking. *He had to be a KGB agent—a plant.*

"I don't know what you are talking about. You obviously have the wrong man or unit. We only attacked Soviet troops and vehicles, not the damned German military."

Peter started to rise from his seat in order to leave.

Perluci rose quickly from his chair, catching Peter with a sharp right jab to his abdomen. "Sit down and listen to what I have to say," he barked.

Doubled over in pain, a look of surprise spread across Peter's face at the small man's agility and strength. He wisely chose to sit back down as instructed, still flinching from the blow.

"Do you think I enjoy doing this?" Perluci spat out. "Now, as I said before, I have little time and patience left. Let's get to the dirty side of my work. Do you happen to remember a woman named Monica Dems? I should hope so, because she happens to be the other person in the wedding photo I supplied you. She is well," pausing for its full effect, "*and, for the moment, very much alive.*"

A look of horror spread across Peter's face. Five years had gone by since he last saw his wife. He often wondered if she ever remarried, not that he would blame her. Five years is a long time with no communication. He looked to Perluci. "You bastard, how do you know these things?"

"As I told you, I work for the Vatican Intelligence Network. We have our people located everywhere. Nothing will happen to your wife if you provide me with the information I want to know. Now, just relax and answer my questions."

Perluci was confident he had the man right where he wanted him. The picture worked to perfection, obviously conjuring up some of the old memories.

Peter sat back down in his chair, head hung low. "I didn't think a man of the cloth would resort to such blackmail," he said, eyes narrowing.

Perluci wasted no time. "After many interviews and checks and rechecks, our records indicate that your unit was the only one to have been in the area of our shipment. This leads us to believe you and your unit might have been involved in its disappearance. Now after four years of searching, I have only tracked two people from your unit who are possibly still alive. I only want to know where the gold and documents have been hidden. My request is simple, yes?" He flashed a toothy grin. "If you do this, I will see that your wife gets a new apartment and money to live on until you get out of this rat hole in a couple of years."

"What if I choose not to cooperate?" Peter probed even though he realized the consequences, but still trying to negotiate nevertheless.

Perluci handed him a recent photo of Peter's wife, clearly taken without her knowledge. "It would be a shame for such a pretty woman to suffer an untimely death," he said.

Peter fingered the photo of his wife. "All right you bastard, you have me." He withdrew a cigarette from the open pack Perluci had offered earlier. "I never wanted anything to do with that mission. It was all Captain Dieter's fault."

After five minutes, Peter Dems had provided his version of the story.

# THE VATICAN's LAST SECRET

# CHAPTER 12

**PRESENT DAY – VATICAN CITY**

"Mr. Perluci, I have excellent news for your Special Action Team," Father Lester said enthusiastically. "Only moments ago we received a message from our contact in New York. The time has finally come. They are going for our products. It seems your team is a go."

Father Lester patted the Beretta 9mm he carried in his jacket pocket as a Special Action Team member, secretly wishing to tag along. His being a priest negated that possibility, relegating him to Vatican City duties where he could only use his weapon for self-defense and protecting the pontiff.

Perluci paced about his office as if a caged animal set to strike. "Damn it, I knew that old bastard would finally crack and tell us where it was, or at the very least our agent would retrieve the info. For years I have been telling anyone who would listen. We must be patient and wait him out, that and a little prodding from our agent would eventually get him to talk. Well, our patience has finally paid off."

Father Lester stared at Perluci for a moment. It knew it was Perluci's idea to place an agent in the United States, one close to Hans Dieter. "Obviously our deep agent is an extremely patient man to have waited so long."

"Patience?" Perluci snarled. "I don't think so, Father Lester. Our agent is not one known for his patience. No, sir. We have that bastard under wraps for atrocities he performed as a member of the Irish Republican Army before he moved to New York in our employ."

Father Lester appeared confused as he stood in front of Perluci's desk. New to the position of Special Action Team operations chief, he had reported only two months earlier. Father Lester was a "pup," as Perluci would commonly refer to him.

"I don't understand," Father Lester said. "What type of atrocities would cause such a man to turn and work for us?"

Perluci pointed to a well-worn mahogany chair, motioning for Father Lester to sit.

"I take it a story is brewing?" Father Lester inquired.

Perluci nodded as he lit a cigarette. "Nasty habit," he said, dropping the match into an ashtray before he began. "As we both now know, our agent, Dan Flaherty, was bloody IRA. In my opinion not a true follower, but a decent chap just the same. Now, let's regress a few years. This is probably long before your time. I imagine you were still a student learning your catechism," taking a stab at Father Lester's youth. "It was during the early seventies that the Catholic and Protestant factions were once again fighting in Ireland. Our boy had an excellent IRA cover as a respected and well-educated teacher who, for all appearances, was a neutral. Now, this cover earned him the trust of both sides, able to lure the top two men in the Belfast Ulster Protestant Wing to a supposed truce meeting in Londonderry. The Protestants, the trusting souls they were, showed up at the meeting with their families in tow and the organizations top two lieutenants. They hoped to squeeze in a nice long holiday along with the meeting. Our man Flaherty had a different idea. He used the disguise of a bellhop to wire the place with 20 pounds of C4, waiting until the appropriate moment before blowing the place to bloody hell. He killed ten people in that blast, including three small children."

"My God," Father Lester whispered. "Our man is a ruthless one."

"Yes, ruthless when he wants to be," Perluci was quick to respond. "Add to that sixteen assassinations of various petty criminals for crimes against the IRA, and you have Dan Flaherty. He needs us, Father Lester, and we need him."

"What about the son of Hans Dieter, James Dieter? Seems to be on the straight and narrow to me," Father Lester said, thoroughly engrossed with the story. "Only now, from what our agent tells us they seem to be operating as a team."

Perluci slammed his fist on the desk in order to drive home his point. "Don't lose the main flow of the story. It's not him we are after but something his father has, or had."

Perluci's outburst caught Father Lester by surprise.

Perluci smiled at him before continuing, his voice mellowing as he spoke. "Dieter's father used to be a captain in the German Army, a pretty good one from what I understand, rising up through the enlisted ranks. Many years ago I had the pleasure to track down his units survivors, unfortunately, locating only two, our Captain Hans Dieter and a man called Peter Dems." Perluci thrusts two dog-eared photos in front of Father Lester, both courtesy of the German War archives in Hamburg before continuing. "The rest were dead, evidently killed in the final days of the war. Dems, I located in a Russian prisoner of war camp in 1949, where I understand he unfortunately met his demise. But Dieter, the lucky bastard that he is, had already escaped to America."

# THE VATICAN's LAST SECRET

A look of confusion spread across Father Lester's face. Perluci realized he had to provide the man with a little more background.

"Okay. You have seen the records and are familiar with the theft of our product, but not how the actual events transpired," Perluci said. He was restless with the story he had told many times before—the results always the same. He continued. "Captain Dieter and his troops had no way of knowing what was on the truck. I will give them that. They were under the impression the truck contained the enemy as it sped towards their position, not fellow German soldiers and Vatican guards whose cargo were crates laden with gold bars and important Vatican documents. From all reports I've read they say the fog was so thick they had no chance for a positive identification. If confronted with the same situation my own reaction would have been the same. But I'm providing too many details here." He took a long draw from another freshly lit cigarette, before exhaling. He then looked to Father Lester with a smirk upon his face. "After the ambush Dieter's troops received a seven-day pass, routinely awarded after six months of combat. Then, using Dieter's rank, they were able to commandeer a German military truck. They retraced their steps to the front lines in order to dig up what they had wisely buried only hours before. With their luck still holding, they escaped hours before a Soviet offensive that would have kept the gold and documents hidden forever. But with a pass in hand, they were able to travel unchallenged back to the town of Weimar where Dieter's parents lived on a farm, promptly burying our product somewhere under its 300 acres. Where you ask? We have no idea, but we are positive it's on the farm. This information has been verified by Dems, the man I interrogated back in 1949. He possessed no reason to lie." A sly smile broke out on his face revealing some secret pleasure. "He had too much riding on it."

Father Lester sat in silence, wondering what Perluci meant by his last comment. Looking up, he was about to inquire but Perluci cut him off.

"In the nineteen fifties, our people scoured that farm from top to bottom," Perluci continued on, his face turning beet red. "Evidently our product had been relocated years before," turning back to face Father Lester, his hands turned upward to reveal empty palms. "Nothing! We had nothing to show for our work so we finally chose to back off and await Mr. Dieter's next move. It has been seventy plus years of waiting and one hell of a chess game if you ask me. A game we will eventually win, Father Lester — *I personally guarantee it.*"

# THE VATICAN's LAST SECRET

# CHAPTER 13

**NEW YORK CITY, NY**

Emerging from Pennsylvania station, Dan and Jim were greeted by an endless sea of yellow cabs, all jostling for a prime position at its entrance. Brilliant sunshine bathed the area as the afternoon temperature approached a balmy eighty degrees.

Well-dressed office workers took advantage of the weather by fleeing their high-rise buildings in mass seeking a lunch break away from the office.

Dan steered Jim to one of five lunch carts, each proudly proclaiming to sell New York's best hot dogs, getting in line behind four well-dressed financial types.

As they stood there waiting, Dan realized the time had come to broach a subject he had kept hidden for decades. He looked nervously from side-to-side, wondering how best to proceed.

*How do you go about disclosing a sordid past you managed to have kept hidden for so long? He decided it best to just pull the Band-Aid off.*

# THE VATICAN's LAST SECRET

Dan coughed a few times in order to clear his throat before tapping Jim on the arm, gaining his attention. "Since your father obviously neglected to inform you of one important fact, I guess it's up to me. The phony priest part you are already aware of. What you are not aware of is that I'm also ex-Irish Republican Army."

A rush came over him with the truth finally disclosed.

The four yuppies halted their conversation in mid-sentence, mouths agape, turning to face Dan and Jim.

Dan stared hard at the yuppies until they thought better and moved on, food orders in hand.

Jim waited until Dan turned back to face him. "Well, chalk one up for me, Dan. My Dad did inform me. I was just wondering how long before *you* told me."

"Good," he replied, "we are starting off on a good foot. Trust is needed. Just like a marriage." Then he effortlessly switched gears. "Now on to some particulars for our mission. If we are to travel overseas, we're going to require passports. I recommend Canada, New Zealand, and U.S., with credit cards to match. It will help us to blend in just in case we are being monitored by anyone with the capability to follow electronic transactions."

Jim shook his head as he placed onions on his Coney Island dog, dropping some onto the wax paper wrapping in the process. "Electronic transactions? Passports?"

"You just heard me say I was with the bloody IRA. Well, at least up until I had to run for my damn life or the Ulster faction would have killed me. Correction, *would still kill me if they got the chance.* Besides, from what I understand, they have a rather large price on my head. To be truthful young Dieter, I know some bloody awful people if need be."

Jim nodded. "Is that what you were alluding to back at the estate when you said you had trouble sleeping and mentioned Londonderry?"

"Let's just say I had differences of opinion with certain people and leave it at that. I don't want to stir up any old memories. They should stay just that way, *old memories*."

The crowd around them kept changing as their lunches were quickly consumed.

"I don't believe it," Jim said. "Under that mild exterior lies a real ruthless bastard. All right...*done*. I won't dig into your past or bring up the issue again."

"Good. Leave it for a later date," Dan said, knowing that provided enough time the issue would once again rear its ugly head. "I have some new instructions for you since our little discussion on the train. I need you to grab a cab and head over to the Empire Hotel on 34th Street. I took the liberty of already reserving a suite in your name. You will pay only in cash. Do not use any of your old credit cards or money cards. They are to be disposed of."

Jim stood ready to object, but Dan cut him off. "I'm going to acquire us some new identities from friends I have over in Brooklyn. I will meet you in the hotel room by five o'clock. We can have an early dinner and discuss what our next steps should be. But right now we have to get some passport photos for our new passports."

# THE VATICAN's LAST SECRET

# CHAPTER 14

**VATICAN CITY, VATICAN INTELLIGENCE BUREAU**

Perluci paced back and forth trying hard to contain himself after reading the latest text message from the US. "Our information says they will be at the Dieter farm within the week. Only then can we proceed with the retrieval of what is rightfully ours." He pointed a crooked finger at his superior, Father Lester, to reinforce the point. "I knew the old sly fox still had our product hidden at the farm. That's why he didn't sell the farm after all these years."

Father Lester was well aware of Perluci's frequent talks with Pope Francis, but hell, he was a dinosaur compared to the newer more experienced agents. Even the Pope should realize he wasn't the right man to lead this mission.

"Mr. Perluci, in your opinion, do you think we will have to activate our action teams in order to secure the farm in case of a struggle?" Father Lester surveyed the man for any sign of weakness in his response.

"Absolutely not," Perluci replied sarcastically, actually sneering at the insinuation. "Hell no! I will go alone and meet our long-lost friend. Between myself and our man, we should be able to handle the American."

"Be reasonable, you are an old man," Father Lester shot back. "You are not the same young buck you were some seventy plus years ago. This could turn out to be a dangerous situation. You could be killed. Who is to say our man has not turned? You are assuming he is still an asset, but in reality, he could become an adversary."

Perluci slowly shook his head. "I have to save the Church, *The Vatican itself.* You have no idea what is about to happen if this is exposed to the world-wide press." He forcefully pointed to a chair. "Sit down, and I will tell you the rest of the story, something that only four people are aware of," holding up his fingers for emphasis, "and you are about to become the fifth."

Father Lester stared hard at Perluci for a few seconds before choosing to sit down.

Perluci nodded to him. "Do you remember your history from World War II?" he began as if addressing an errant schoolchild.

"But of course I do, *I have a Doctorate in 20$^{th}$ century warfare.*"

"Yes, of course you do," Perluci sneered. "While I was making history, you were learning it some 50 years later. Are you familiar with the Yugoslav front in World War II?"

Father Lester nodded.

"Good, now I will tell you the part the history books omitted. In 1945, with the war going badly for the Germans and their Croatian Allies, the powers-that-be needed a relatively safe place to hide all of the gold they had looted from Yugoslavian Jews now held in Concentration Camps scattered across Poland and Germany. Which between the Jewish gold and the gold from the looted Yugoslav treasury, amounted to over $500 million in today's economy."

Perluci walked over to where Father Lester sat, he leaned into the man. "Now, for the real juicy part. The nastiest Nazi bastard of all, Heinrich Himmler, bartered a secret agreement with Pope Pius XII. Our Holy Father quietly offered them the services of the Vatican Bank if the Nazis would stop killing the Jews held in the camps. In effect, bartering Jewish gold for Jewish lives. However, Himmler had another thought in mind. The war would soon be over, and he knew they would be on the losing end. He would need access to money —*lots of it.* The Vatican provided its personal assurances that if the looted gold were deposited into the Vatican Bank, it would be safe from Allied probes once the war was over."

Perluci smiled at Father Lester, he paused several seconds before he continued. "But that's not all. Once the gold was in Vatican hands, Himmler insisted the Vatican set up escape routes for high-ranking Nazis, routes that would run from Franciscan Monasteries, to Catholic churches, to eventually South America, and freedom."

"Come now, Perluci," Father Lester spat out, "do you honestly want me to believe that farce? The Ratline was only rumor then, and is still a rumor today!"

"Not only did Pope Pius know," said Perluci, ignoring Father Lester's comments, "but I was his intermediary. For two months we negotiated the deal. Can you imagine the repercussions if this were to leak out?"

Father Lester eyed Perluci for several seconds. "Okay," Father Lester said in a conciliatory tone. 'Maybe I haven't been privy to all of the information you have in your possession."

Perluci sat at his desk savoring the apology, or what could be construed as one, from his supervisor. "Thank you for finally realizing this. Now please leave me to my duties."

# THE VATICAN's LAST SECRET

## New York City, NY

THE STORM PREDICTED by each of the three local weather stations announced itself with a horrific clap of thunder, startling Jim awake as he napped on one of the suites two king-sized beds.

Jim looked to his cell phone for the time. *Six–thirty? I can't believe it. I have been asleep for three hours*, looking around for any evidence of Dan's return. *Damn it. I knew I should have gone with him as backup.*

## Brooklyn, NY

DAN ACQUIRED HIS ability to go undercover many years before from the illustrious Michael Shawnlin, the IRA's so-called *'ghost man'*. During Shawnlin's 20 years as an active, he never saw the inside of a prison cell, and Dan intended to follow, if ever so discreetly, in his footsteps.

Employing two subway trains and a taxi to shake any tail that might have followed him, he wound up in the Russian émigré section of Brooklyn, a mere two blocks from his intended destination. Dan found it convenient to exit the taxi a few blocks from his contact in order to test for a tail. Stopping to grab a paper from a street vendor, he pretended to read the headlines, searching over the newspapers top for anything out of the ordinary on the relatively quiet street. Satisfied he was indeed alone, he crossed the street and approached a rundown pawnshop. Dan took a cursory look in the shops dirty window, using the windows reflection to view the street from both directions. Satisfied, he entered.

The inside of the shop appeared just as *tired* as the outside. As he walked Dan noticed the floor missing a few of its vinyl tiles. An undersized floor fan hummed as it struggled to cool its surroundings. One of the overhead fluorescent lights continually blinked off and on. To his left, hip-level glass counters were covered in assorted piles of well-read sports magazines and horse racing forms, many almost a year old, a trace of dust on their covers.

*To Dan, the place had not changed one bit.*

"Well, well, well, look who has returned to my humble pawn shop, the infamous Father Flaherty," said the man from behind the counter, his eyes hardly leaving the racing form he held tightly in his hands. "Come to hock the church jewels or maybe something interesting that was in the collection basket? No, maybe to pay me the $100 you owe me for when the Giants beat the Rams by three points last year?"

Luther Finch smiled as he rose from his stool. All 310 pounds seemed to move effortlessly with his infectious laughter, barely standing 5'6" in platform shoes with a protruding nose and shaven head. He was known as "the man to see" for underworld business in Brooklyn, having equal dealings with the Russian, Italian, and Black Mafias. He wasn't prejudiced — with money being the great equalizer.

Dan leaned over to peer behind the glass counter at Luther's girth. "Luther, are you losing weight?"

Luther pushed him back effortlessly. "Screw you, Padre," he spat out in a heavy New York accent. "You want to make some fat jokes around here, go see the aerobics class when their 4:00 p.m. meeting lets out."

"Okay Luther, calm down. I'm just joking. If you keep up the attitude, you are going to suffer another heart attack. The last one had us all worried, especially your wife."

Luther had experienced four heart attacks in five years. His doctor ordered him to lose weight or he would be dead within the year. Eighteen months later Luther was still being Luther. Food was meant for eating and beer for drinking.

"Now here's the hundred dollars I owe you with twenty thrown in for interest," Dan said as he laid the money on a glass counter above a display of 38's and 45's, all slightly used.

"So kind of you to repay your debts," Luther said as he jokingly picked up the phone as if to call in one of his henchmen. "I guess I can rescind the contract on your ass."

Dan held up his hands. "You got me."

# THE VATICAN's LAST SECRET

"Get the hell over here and let me see you. Has it really been a year since we were last together? Damn, how time flies. You know my wife was just asking about you last month. You'll have to stop down and let her cook for you. Big pot of meatballs in gravy. No shit. You hear me?"

"I will, Luther, I will, and tell her I'll pray for her when I'm in church this Sunday. You, on the other hand, if I were to pray for you the statues would spin."

"They wouldn't be spinning, Father. I'd call it more like dancing," Luther replied, his forefinger in the air performing a circular motion.

"Dancing my ass, they'd spin so fast you'd think an oil company paid them drilling rights," Dan shot back.

After swatting a fly on the counter in front of him, Luther directed all of his attention to Dan. "All right, smart ass, you got me. Enough with the crap. You didn't come here to inquire about my health or business. So what can I do for you?"

"I have a good one for you, Luther," Dan said. "I need two separate IDs, credit cards to match the IDs, and new passports for myself and another person. The passports will be issued for Canada, the U.S., and New Zealand."

Luther didn't bat an eye at the request as he fingered through his personal Rolodex, acting as if it were an everyday occurrence. "When do you need them by?" he asked nonchalantly.

"In twelve hours' and that's the extreme limit Luther. I would prefer a one-hour special service as a frequent customer if you can find it in your big heart."

Luther focused on the well-worn Rolodex that looked as though it contained the entire criminal phone directory for Brooklyn. A few years earlier he tried to computerize the list but gave up. It was easier to write the information on a paper card. He liked the idea that he had the option to burn the card if need be, something you could not do with a computer's hard drive.

Luther shook his head. "One-hour service you say? What do you think you're dealing with a camera store with film drop-off service? Maybe some dry cleaning?" He took his time fingering through his cards before settling on one that seemed to be whiter than the rest, either a recent addition or he didn't utilize this particular persons service often enough.

"You're in luck my Irish friend," he said as he extracted a card from his index. "Geno the forger is out on bail. I happen to know the punk needs some cash from a bet he placed with me last week and hasn't paid me yet. I'll give him a call to tell him you're on your way." Luther grabbed a pencil and piece of paper from the glass counter before scribbling down the address.

Dan slipped across five, crisp, one-hundred-dollar bills as a service fee for dealing with Luther's criminal side. "Thanks Luther, I owe you."

"One minute there, Danny-boy. Church man or not, inflation is eating into my pocket. This prime location doesn't come cheap." He waved his flabby arm around the tired shop. "Another bill and we can call it even."

Dan handed over another hundred-dollar bill as he looked around the junk-laden shop. "All right, I won't stand in the way of progress, my friend," he said. "Prime location you say?"

"Tell your friends about the excellent service. Now get out of here. Geno will be waiting for you."


**Staten Island, NY**
THE STATEN ISLAND address Luther provided took the Jamaican cab driver over an hour to navigate through rush-hour traffic. A tastefully decorated block of row homes with small manicured lawns stood before them as the driver double-

parked his cab out front. Dan thought the driver made a few wrong turns to pad the meter price, but hesitated to complain due to the genuine lack of cab availability in New York after 5:00 p.m. on a weekday.

"This is 405 Grandview, Mon," the driver said matter-of-factly in a Jamaican singsong accent, his hand on the meter. "Would you like me to wait or will this be your final destination my friend?"

"No, this will be my final stop," Dan said before correcting himself. "You know what? Maybe you should wait. I'm going to be at least an hour or so. Will a hundred bucks up front keep your butt waiting here?"

Dan peeled off a crisp, new hundred-dollar bill from his bankroll as he held it up for the driver to see, then handed it to him.

The cabdriver's eyes replied before he did. "For a hundred dollar bill I'll go pick up the devil himself at Kennedy Airport and take him to Hunts Pier for some ladies." He held the bill up to the cabs overhead light, looking for its embedded security thread. "No problem, I'll be waiting for you."

Reggae music was turned up to a deafening volume as Dan exited the cab and walked up to the house.

# CHAPTER 15

Geno Scafetti specialized mainly in credit card forgery, but was also known to pick a pocket or two if times were lean. He once lifted the mayor's wallet at a local campaign appearance. He also had "the look" for someone in the criminal element: average height, weight, black hair, and brown eyes. If described to a police sketch artist, the unlucky victim could only describe him as your average white male.

The door opened as Dan approached, Geno obviously awaiting his arrival.

"Come on in, Mr. Flaherty. I've been expecting you," he said, poking his head out the door for any neighbors that may be lurking. "Luther called about an hour ago to tell me you were coming. That little heads-up provided me time to set up my equipment and get things rolling a little quicker."

Geno led him through the tiled main foyer, down the houses small, unfurnished hallway and into a dimly lit kitchen. The smell of burnt meatloaf still hung in the air.

"Some of my gear needs to heat up before it can process the hard plastic needed for the passports," he said as he lit a cigarette, discarding the match in the dish-laden sink. "Now let me get this straight. Luther tells me you need two sets of complete IDs, credit cards to match, and three passports. Is that about it?"

"That would be the extent of it, Geno," Dan replied, "and I've got five grand in large bills for your services when complete." He tapped his breast pocket to indicate he had the money on him. "A potential problem though. If possible, I need it in one hours' time."

Geno produced a grin lacking four or five teeth, probably lost in some prison fight gone awry. Dan could just imagine this man in prison dealing in stolen soap or toilet paper— survival of the fittest.

"Anything's possible where money is involved, Mr. Flaherty." His grin still locked in place.

"Obviously in your line of business, Geno, I would say that is an understatement."

Geno envisioned having his slate with Luther wiped clean, even leaving a little extra change for a wager on the Yankees game. *And to think I almost didn't pick up the phone when the caller ID revealed it was Luther,* thinking it concerned his gambling debt.

The excitement was clearly evident in Geno's voice. "For $5,000 I'm even going to throw in social security cards free of charge, Mr. Flaherty. If you could just provide me with the passport pictures and any special names you want, I can go to work right away."

Dan handed over the pictures and a list of names he'd like to use. "One hour, right? I don't want to be hanging around here all night. I have some other matters to tend to."

"Just grab a chair in the living room, and give me a chance to do my thing. I work alone in the basement to speed things along. I don't want anyone disturbing me at my work. Now, if you like baseball, the Mets are playing the Phillies on channel 42, and beer is in the fridge. Help yourself. I don't have any of that Irish beer," he said, making a play off his accent. "But I have the regular domestic beers."

"Thanks, but I'm not in the drinking mood just yet," Dan replied. "And I absolutely deplore your American baseball. I think I'll just read some of your magazines on the coffee table and unwind a little while you work your magic."

DAN HEARD GENO re-enter the room.

"These are works of art, Mr. Flaherty, if I may say so myself, real friggan Picassos," he said, tossing the rubber-banded packet of IDs over to Dan for his inspection.

Geno returned to the kitchen to grab a beer. Upon re-entering the living room, he eyed Dan already hunched over the coffee table with a jewelers magnification piece covering his right eye, performing a detailed inspection of his work.

After Dan appeared satisfied with the passport stamps, he held the paper up to the overhead light to look for the watermark on the individual pages.

*This joker certainly knows his business*, Geno thought, waiting a few more minutes before he spoke. "If everything is in order, Mr. Flaherty, can we discuss the payment issue? We did agree to five grand?" He knew Luther would want his customary cut by weeks end.

Dan placed the rubber band back around the packet of passports, satisfied with the high quality of work.

"Yes, we did, Geno, five grand," Dan said. Looking up at Geno, he reached into his sports coat pocket and extracted a Beretta 9 millimeter, silencer already mounted on its barrel, now aimed at Geno. A sly grin was evident upon Dan's face as he delivered two clean shots to Geno's head, the shots force propelling Geno back into the kitchen, slamming him against the refrigerator door.

Dan looked at the lifeless body slumped against the base of the refrigerator, his eyes still wide open, mouth agape.

"Sorry, but no witnesses," he said.

Dan quickly searched the immediate area for something flammable before locating a pint of turpentine under the sink. Gathering old newspapers and magazines, he built a pile on the kitchen floor next to Geno's body. Taking great care, he poured a measured portion of the turpentine onto the papers. Next he walked to the basement where Geno kept his records and equipment, dousing the records with the remainder of the turpentine. Satisfied with his work, he tossed a lit match on top of Geno's meticulously compiled records of customers, waiting a few seconds to make sure the records caught fire.

"Geno, you old geezer," Dan said aloud. "You were going to blackmail a lot of people with your detailed records, weren't you? On the other hand, was it double duty for the cops to save your skin? Oh well, I guess it really doesn't matter now, does it?"

The fire in the basement office quickly spread as Dan returned to the kitchen and then lit the pile of papers next to Geno's body.

Satisfied, he slipped out the houses rear door, navigating his way down a darkened back alley and around a side street to his awaiting taxi.

"My business here is complete my friend. You can drive me back to where you first picked me up, Luther's Pawn Shop, West 82$^{nd}$," Dan commanded. He casually looked from side-to-side to see if any of Geno's neighbors were out and about.

The cabbie was delighted to be chauffeuring around such a well-paying customer. "No problem, Mon," he replied.

"If you don't mind my friend, I'm going to take a little nap." Dan mentally replayed the whole process to make sure no mistakes were made. Satisfied there were, as always, none, he drifted off into a fitful sleep.

# THE VATICAN's LAST SECRET

"YO, MAN, WE ARE here my friend," the cabbie said, the smile still evident upon his face, the hundred-dollar bill still working its magic. "Shall I wait again, boss?"

Shaking off the effects of his nap, Dan checked to make sure his gun still lay in his jacket pocket. "Are you kidding? After tonight I'm going to have to deduct you from my taxes," he said, smiling. "This will be a quick visit. Give me two minutes. I have to drop something off."

He quickly exited the cab and bounded up the two concrete steps leading to Luther's storefront, he burst through the door as if he owned the place, taking care to lock the door after he entered.

"You back already, Danny boy? You just left a couple of hours ago," Luther said, puzzled at the grand entrance and Dan's' locking of the door. "Everything work out okay between you and Geno? You look a little pissed."

Dan held up a wad of hundred dollar bills as he strolled passed Luther. "Sort of, Luther. Can we talk in the back about something private?" He looked around to make sure they were alone.

Luther squeezed his mass from behind the glass counter and followed Dan into the back room. "What other of my vast services do you require for that type of money you're waving around, Danny Boy," Luther said. "And why the backroom bit? I usually conduct all of my business outside at the counter. The cops don't bother this place. I pay them decent money."

Dan pulled out his 9mm for the second time in an hour. He quickly raised it to Luther's head. "I hate to do this Luther," he said sympathetically.

"Danny…don't…we go back a ways," Luther shouted, searching for anything that could be used as a weapon. "We are friends. I have a wife." He stumbled over a stack of racing sheets stacked high on the floor as he backed up, falling on his ass. "Here, take my money. Is that what you want?" He waved a thick bundle of bills in front of him as he struggled to get up.

Dan's reflexes took over. It was something he had performed many times before, not that he enjoyed doing it. *He had to.* "Its business, my friend," he said, before he shot him once between the eyes.

Luther fell back heavily against a rack of used CDs, crushing the table they were stacked on.

"I have to cover my tracks," Dan mumbled to the dead body as he walked over to where he lay, callously placing yet another bullet into Luther's head.

He grabbed several portable radios dating circa 1980, and tossed them on the shops floor to make it appear as if it were a robbery. Finding Luther's wallet, he pocketed the Visa and $870 in cash, dropping the now-empty wallet on the floor at Luther's feet. As he stared at his friend laying in his own pool of blood, a flood of memories suddenly rushed over him. Dan closed his eyes in silent prayer, performing a sign of the cross over his deceased friend's body.

Outside, he stood on the shops stoop and performed a cursory check of his clothing for any obvious sign of bloodstains. Satisfied there was none, he stepped down and into the cab. "All right, my cabbie friend, please take me to the Empire Hotels parking garage on 32$^{nd}$ Street," he said casually.

Looking in his rear-view mirror, the cabbie was still grinning. "Are you in town for long? If so, I can be your personal cab. It won't cost you much." This was a cabby's dream, to only have one passenger for a few days and not have to desperately search the streets for a fare.

Dan laid his head back to rest, obviously not wanting to indulge in small talk. He took no pleasure in his actions, especially in the killing of a friend. "No, I will be leaving for Europe tomorrow, but thanks anyway."

After mentally reviewing his actions for any signs of error, he once more drifted off.

# THE VATICAN's LAST SECRET

IT TOOK ONLY twenty minutes to navigate through the nighttime traffic.

"Excuse me, my man. This is the Empire Hotel," the cabbie said. "You want me to park in the Hotels garage or drop you at the front door?"

Dan opened his eyes, not realizing where he was for a moment or two. Panic soon ensued, looking from side-to-side until he saw the familiar orange and green neon lights of the Empire Hotel.

"All right, just pull into the garage. Drive up to the second level, and park alongside the wall furthest from the elevators. I have one last errand to run."

"You're the boss," the cabbie replied, driving up and around the garages concrete turn shafts.

Dan slowly extracted his Beretta for the third time that day, the driver not noticing his actions. He waited until the cabbie reached the second floor and pulled alongside the wall. "This is good, my cabbie friend. This will be my final destination," he said, looking about for any potential witnesses.

With the cabs meter turned off since Dan presented him the hundred-dollar bill, the cabbie was mentally compiling the bill.

"Well, with the tip that will be another one hundred seventy-five dollars on top of the hundred you gave me earlier, boss," he said, half-turning to face Dan, only to see the Beretta pointed in his face. "Shit, don't rob me. I need the money for my family. Give me a break. I didn't see what you did," the driver pleaded, his hands up.

A soft thud was the only noise heard as the bullet stuck the cabbie between the eyes, blood spraying against the front windshield.

"Sorry, friend, but no witnesses are allowed in my line of work."

# CHAPTER 16

**EMPIRE HOTEL - NEW YORK CITY**

Long considered more of a very large bed & breakfast, The Empire Hotel contained *only* 45 rooms. *A boutique Grandma's house stuck in the Victorian era,* stated the New York Times in its last travel section review. Its interior tended to run rampant with heavy velvet drapes, velvet floral wallpaper, dark cherry wood floors that squeaked when walked on. This made the hotel a virtual magnet for the German and English tourist trade who relished every detail of its Victorian "yesteryear" interior.

At the front desk Dan found an envelope waiting with his recently ordered airline tickets and a key card for his room. Written on the envelope was the suite number Jim had arranged for them.

On his way to the room Dan decided to stop by the hotels gift shop for a bottle of scotch—something to settle his frayed nerves.

Fingering his plastic key card as he walked to his room, he shook his head and grinned at the thought of having to pop three people. "I'm getting too old for this shit," he whispered aloud.

Dan slipped his card into the electronic door lock repeatedly only to have it rejected time and time again, the door finally opened from within.

"Where in the hell have you been," Jim shouted. "I have been worried sick that you were dead somewhere. You're three hours late. You said you would meet me at five o'clock. Well its eight o'clock."

Dan held his hands up, almost dropping the bottle of expensive Scotch. "Calm down, boy. You sound like somebody's wife, and I must say an ugly one at that. The job got a little complicated. Then I had to visit some friends. So it took longer than I anticipated. Everything is okay. Trust me. Pour us a drink from the mini-bar and we can save this good stuff," pointing to the bottle in his hands, "for the next round."

Jim walked over to the mini-bar, pouring them a drink from the airline-sized bottles that lined the counter. "You're right. I am a little rattled."

Dan relieved Jim of one of his glasses. "Relax. It even happens to someone like myself. Let me take a shower and put on some fresh clothes so we can go to dinner."

Jim raised his glass to Dan in a silent toast, realizing he was right. From his Navy SEAL experience, he should have known to never bother someone upon returning from a mission. They required time to decompress. He decided to change the subject, if ever so slightly.

"Did you have any problems getting our passports and credit cards?"

"No trouble at all," Dan shot back. "Not only that," he said as he walked toward the bathroom, taking off his shirt as he went. "But I also had time to buy two Air France tickets to Paris departing tomorrow evening. You can check out the merchandise on the coffee table."

# THE VATICAN's LAST SECRET

Jim removed the paper tickets from the envelope, hoping Dan was joking about Paris. He knew damn well the farm was four hours east of Frankfurt. "I don't believe this," he said aloud as he tossed the tickets back onto the coffee table. "What do you mean, Paris?" he yelled to Dan through the closed bathroom door. "My father's farm is outside Weimar. That's in Germany...*not France*. That's got to be a few hundred miles away from Paris."

As he shaved, Dan eyed the image in the bathroom mirror, trying not to cut himself, laughing aloud in response to Jim's comments. "I see you're also an intelligent lad and are familiar with your geography," he replied sarcastically. The door opened to reveal Dan's face laden with shaving cream on one side, the other side shaven clean. "Let me ask you something, Jim. Have you ever been hunting?"

Jim knew he was being set up, wondering where Dan was leading him. "Sure, my dad took me hunting for deer when I was kid, but it was also about the ability to survive in the great outdoors."

Dan wiped an excess of shaving cream from his metal razor onto the towel draped over his shoulder. "Right you are my boy. Now, when you would approach a deer in the woods, what's the best direction to do so?"

"Everybody knows it's downwind so the deer can't pick up your scent," Jim replied smugly.

"Give that man a prize," Dan said, as if teaching one of his high school students. "That's exactly what we are doing — going in downwind to surprise the prey."

Jim paused for a few seconds to allow the meaning to sink in. "You really believe there's going to be trouble after all of these years?"

"You can bank on it, my friend. Now, let me finish so we can eat, drink, and then hit the sack early. We need to get some rest. I have the feeling we're going to need it."

# CHAPTER 17

**VATICAN CITY**

"I have just come from a meeting with his Holiness," Perluci began, his voice resonated off the thick concrete walls of the bunker. "I informed him of our progress with the missing gold and documents. His Holiness stated to me that he wants them retrieved at any cost."

"Would you like me to activate the Action Team, or would you prefer to wait?" Father Lester asked. He already knew the answer would be a resounding no, but decided to pose the question anyway.

"We can still wait and see how the operation progresses," Perluci replied. "We can always track them through the usual credit cards and other means, but if that fails then…"

"Are you still planning on going it alone?" Father Lester quizzed, wondering why he was answering to Perluci and not vice versa. Wasn't he the supervisor? Of course, he was also upset at having not been invited to Perluci's one-on-one meeting with his Holiness.

"But of course I am," Perluci shot back. "Our man Flaherty *is*," pausing for a moment, "*was* very good. I'm sure he has become 'soft' and lost his touch being in America all these years. I know it is a little late in the game, but I recommend you have some of our people at the American Military Veterans Center in St. Louis pull the military records on this James Dieter. We can have him checked out thoroughly since time permits," clasping his hands together in anticipation.

"Let us see the enemy unmasked."

THE VATICAN's LAST SECRET

# CHAPTER 18

**PARIS, FRANCE**

From the comfort of an airport cab, Dan eyed the weekday crush of people making their way to walk along the Seine and its bustling cafes before turning to face Jim. "Is this your first time in Paris?"

Jim took several long seconds to respond, viewing the passing Parisian women dressed in their ultra-chic finery. "I have the pleasure to say that this is my second visit. First time I was a military attaché at our U.S. Embassy. That job lasted for six glorious months. And the place hasn't changed a bit."

"You were a military attaché?" Dan asked, now intrigued. "Your father never mentioned you were an attaché. Do you still keep in contact with any of your French counterparts? They might come in handy down the road."

"As a matter of fact, the new Chief of Staff for Technical Affairs is Jacque Batiste, a former navy captain. He was my liaison at the French Ministry of Armed Forces. I haven't talked to him in over three months, but we remain in touch, bouncing ideas back and forth. I'm sure he could help in a pinch."

"Excellent," Dan replied. "One more duck lined up for us. We can keep this in our back pocket for now," assuming a more serious tone. "How much money are we down to? We have what, ten grand apiece for expenses?"

Jim nodded. "Yes, and after paying for our two first-class tickets, we still have about fourteen grand left between us."

Dan slapped the cabs leather seat. "What the hell was I thinking?" He looked over to Jim for confirmation. "We each have two credit cards that Geno the forger manufactured for us. Ten grand stacked on each one, and you don't have to pay back a single dime, for a total of maybe thirty-four grand between us. Damn it, I love American ingenuity, even if it is illegal!"

Jim managed to laugh at Dan's exuberance. He also saw an opportunity to raise an issue that had bothered him since New York City. "One thing on my mind, Dan," he began, half-turning in his seat to face him. "The next time you go visit one of your local contacts, I want to string along. Believe me, I can handle my own."

Caught by surprise, Dan took a few deep breaths as he allowed the seconds to tick bye. He gazed out the window at an argument evolving between a shopkeeper and a tourist, probably over the inflated price of a postcard the tourist held in his hand.

"Let me fill you in on my side of the action," Dan said, still looking out the window. "When I approach my business transactions it's not your typical exchange of money and everyone's happy like some dime store novel ending."

Jim nodded. "Exactly what happened in New York City?"

Dan paused once more, searching for the right words, now facing him. "I guess you could say it was a dirty operation, my friend. Let's just say that everyone I had contact with in New

York is now visiting one of their long-lost relatives in a very hot climate, and I don't mean Mexico."

"Jesus Christ, I knew you ex-IRA types were ruthless but damn it, Dan, just how many people did you erase? One, two…?"

"Now listen to me and listen well. I'm only going to say this once," he replied, changing his demeanor as quickly as a chameleon, shocking Jim in the process. "Don't even think about talking to me in that tone again. I'm involved in this situation because of your father. He had the foresight to realize you would need a little help from someone with my obvious kind of talent. Now think with a clear head, boy. Anyone of those people in New York could have dropped a dime on us for something. Then some clever detective, who was bucking for a promotion, only had to put two and two together and figure out what we were up to."

Jim sat for a moment shifting his gaze between Dan and the bustling sidewalk cafes of the Left Bank as they drove past. Tourists intermingled with ordinary Parisians acquiring their daily fix of caffeine, sitting side by side at quaint cafes. He was taking his time to digest what Dan had said before choosing to respond.

"Deep down, I realize you're right, but can we keep the killing down to a minimum?" He paused, looking about. "And to finish my earlier question—just how many in New York are looking for their lost relatives?'"

Dan realized Jim had performed a full 360, now resigning himself to the aspects of the mission. He had hoped for as much. This was not the time to be a Boy Scout. "Only three and I have to warn you that won't be the end of it. If this is getting to be too hairy for you, I can back out now. You can take your chances alone if you prefer. No hard feelings."

The words had no meaning. Dan would surely see the project to its end.

Jim sat pondering the simple notion of going to pick up the gold and returning. Nobody gets hurt. Then again, Dan was an expert in this type of business. At least that's what his father had relayed to him.

"No, you're right," Jim replied, trying to disarm the situation before it spiraled out of control. Each required the cooperation of the other in order to complete the mission. "I can't do this alone, but damn it, I want to be part of the operation when you hit the streets again. I don't concur with cold-blooded murder, but I guess you're using what you perceive as necessary force."

"Let me ask you a serious question. Have you ever seen someone killed? I don't mean someone far off in the distance or hit by a car. I mean in person, close up, a shrapnel or bullet wound, intestines hanging out, body parts missing?" Not waiting for Jim's response, he continued. "Let me tell you from first-hand experience it's not a very clean operation like those portrayed on TV or the movies. The people don't get up after the screen shot is complete, wiping off the remnants of an exploding ketchup pack as the director yells cut."

Jim held his hand up to stop him. "Before you go on, it's my turn to ask you a question."

Dan gracefully conceded the floor, or in this instance the back of the cab.

"Exactly what did my father say I did in the Navy?" allowing a smile to escape, knowing the whole story had not been told.

"He said you were a shipboard officer on a frigate or a destroyer. You were busy dealing in a load of, as your father would say, '*administrative bull shit*.' He also showed me the exotic postcards from Tokyo, London, and Berlin. Hell, you know better than I do. He said you were sort of a playboy with a girl in every port, and enjoying the service way too much to get out."

"That's all? He didn't tell you anything else about my job?"

"Oh yeah, that you had almost gotten married five or six times," Dan replied, allowing a deep hearty laugh to escape.

"Yeah, that sounds about right for dad," he said. "I guess he was just trying to protect me."

Now it was Dan's turn to be intrigued. What if the boy had a checkered past like himself? Wouldn't that be interesting? He sat back in the seat wondering if the cab driver spoke any English, knowing he would have one hell of a story to relay to his friends after work.

"All right, you have me. What did your father have to protect you from?" Dan inquired. "Are you telling me that you weren't just an admin shipboard officer?"

"Hold onto your socks because the old man kept a whopper from you," he replied. "He neglected to tell you that I was a Navy SEAL for almost twelve years: Afghanistan, Iraq, and way too many small places thrown in for good measure. So in getting back to the question you posed earlier, the one when you asked me if I had ever seen anyone killed close up, guts in hand. Well, yes, Mr. Flaherty, I have seen too many of my men killed to have kept count, and have in turn killed many men. I have had friends killed in missions that the government says never happened. Killed in so-called traffic accidents or training missions, trying to cover it up for the TV newscasts or the internet. The poor families never knew what really happened to their fathers, husbands, or sons. Their heroics only known to those who accompanied them on their missions, or, in too many cases, accompanied them in death."

"I do believe I've opened up a can of worms," Dan replied. "I think it's time we go and grab a bottle of something and have a little talk before we proceed any further."

Jim nodded. "You must be reading my mind."

# THE VATICAN's LAST SECRET

## **Dockside, St. Florentine, France**

THE SMALL TOWN of St. Florentine sat on the lush border of Burgundy and Champagne, in the heart of France's wine country. The town's history dated back to ancient times, when it served as a fortress outpost on the fringe of the Roman Empire. Through time, it adapted and experienced not only an Italian influence in its stone and fresco architecture, but also some of a Germanic nature. It also had the dubious distinction of serving as a "backdoor hub" for vacationers, both wealthy and working class, eager for a barge vacation and waterway access to travel throughout Europe.

The night before, Jim and Dan had talked well into the morning hours, consuming large quantities of scotch. Both learned a great deal, and in the future would take care not to underestimate the other.

"I'm still at a loss," Jim said as he shook his head. "Why in the hell did we have to take four different cabs to get to this place when one would have done the job nicely? I could have slept off this horrible hangover in peace instead of shifting to a new cab every thirty minutes."

Dan waited until Jim emptied the remainder of his water bottle. "Now, don't you think the Paris cabdriver, if questioned, would remember a fare he drove for almost a hundred kilometers? Think about it, lad. That would have been a big payday for that bugger. He would have returned to his garage bragging about the exorbitant fare he charged two foreigners for such a long ride in his cab. I'm only trying to help our cause. My lifelong experience will hopefully get us through. As we agreed last night, in certain circumstances we will just listen and learn my friend. Then, and only then, shall we acquire the knowledge of a true professional."

"I bow to the master," Jim said in reply.

"Now, enjoy this," Dan said, pointing over to the canal, its various yachts and pleasure craft in residence. "Its beauty does something for the soul, the mind, and the body. Wouldn't you agree, Jim?"

"Beats me, I'm still trying to reacquire my sense of smell, that along with the rest of my senses after last night."

Dan proceeded. "Proverbs: never try and consume beverages for the purpose of drinking someone under the table, especially an Irishman.

"How about Ezekiel: 17.5? Never drink water downriver from the latrine," Jim fired back.

"A battle of wits — I like it," Dan said. "If we can keep up with humor for the remainder of our trip, things will pan out. They say humor is a key ingredient for following through on tough operations."

"Right you are. But maybe you can fill me in on the rationale for our being in the middle of a dinky town in France, at its docks to boot, and whose overwhelming fish stench is not helping my hangover."

Dan pointed over to where a group of three, twenty-five-meter long steel barges lay tied parallel to and against the towns dock. The barges reminiscent of its larger cousins that plowed the canals of Europe for some fifty years, giving way to tandem trucks in the late 60s. These barges were of the smaller variety used to off-load cargo from the larger barges and the cargo delivered to destinations on the shallower rivers. Most of the smaller barges eventually made their way into the lucrative tourist trade.

"We need a boat my boy, not just any boat, a barge, a river barge," Dan said. "We can basically float over to the farm using rivers and canals, and sneak back out the same way. There are no custom checkpoints between France and Germany, hasn't been one for years. Plus, we can enjoy the scenery and have a vacation on the side."

Jim looked first to the parked barges, then to Dan as he allowed a smile to creep across his face. "You truly have a devilish mind, Dan. I would have never approached the operation with an idea like this. One question though. After we remove the gold and documents from the farm, how do you plan to get the gold from the barge and across the Atlantic?"

Dan already started to walk away, allowing Jim's last comment to hang in the air for a moment before he turned back on his heels. "One trip at a time, my boy," he said, holding up his index finger for emphasis.

"One trip at a time."

# CHAPTER 19

**VATICAN CITY**

Father Brandon Wetzel, Chief of Vatican Internal Affairs, sat patiently through the one-hour update, choosing to politely refrain from comment until Perluci and Father Lester's closing remarks.

Short in stature, his skin pasty white in color, head shaven bald, Father Wetzel resembled a chemotherapy patient whose prognosis was not encouraging. He also despised the Vatican's discrete use of personnel such as Perluci, but he realized world events necessitated their presence.

Father Wetzel handpicked Monsignor Sims and Father Lester to oversee Perluci's *Sodaitium Pianum* or Special Action Team. It was his duty to make sure that the strict Vatican guidelines were always followed to a "T" during its various missions. If it were up to Father Wetzel, he'd throw the whole lot out on the street, but he was only following orders from above.

"What do you mean we've lost our contact?" Father Wetzel yelled. "Are you telling me that this Flaherty character has left us high and dry, and he has not communicated with us in over a week?" He tossed his plastic coffee mug against a slate board containing maps Perluci had carefully hung up. He turned to face Perluci, his puffy face now crimson in color. "Didn't you inform me that we owned this Flaherty person? That he damn well knows the routine? They were your words, not mine. He is your responsibility, Mr. Perluci. Now what are you going to do about this?" He turned toward Father Lester, disappointment in his eyes but realizing Perluci was mainly to blame.

Standing in front of Father Wetzel's Spartan desk, Perluci was at a loss for words. After all these years of loyal service he was being hung out to dry because of one lousy screw-up. Looking back at Father Lester then to Father Wetzel, he knew he had to admit fault, even if it were to a jerk that had no idea how hard it was to work the streets for information.

"Yes, when I am wrong, I will admit it, sir," Perluci said meekly. "I do believe your assessment of Flaherty a fortnight ago was correct." He formed a tight fist with his aged calloused fingers, slowly opening his hand to reveal his palm for Father Wetzel to view. "I thought I knew our Irish boy, but he slipped through my fingers. As you suggested earlier, I will activate our special action teams. I will call our offices in London, Paris, Madrid, and Berlin and assign a priority code red to this assignment. Eventually we will know every detail on these gentlemen. Where they sleep, crap, and shave. We won't care how our people get the information or whom they have to use. They will just complete their mission.

Father Wetzel handed the well-worn file to Perluci. "What's your personal take on this, Mr. Perluci? Why do you think Flaherty has turned on us and hitched his oars to this man?"

The tone of the meeting had changed, evidently, in his favor. This was significant in itself. Possibly his position was safe for the moment.

"In the dealings I've had with Flaherty, I found him to be a retread from the knightly ages of the past, sir. He's a most eloquent man who could charm you to wits end, and then simply stick a dagger in your back. In addition, you would not feel the sensation until it was too late. So you can see why this Flaherty can be a tough man to figure."

Father Wetzel pointed back to the file Perluci had handed him. "According to your report," he took the file, opening it, "when this man Flaherty bombed that Irish hotel in Londonderry, he could have eliminated all traces of the Protestant families involved. In the process, he could have killed all twelve Protestant children staying there. He chose to wait until most of the children were out of the building before he destroyed it."

"Yes, sir. That would be the knightly part of him," Perluci replied. "He does have a weak spot in his heart. However, he is ex-IRA. I think his motivation is greed. That could be the only logical excuse. I almost feel sorry for the other gentleman he is traveling with."

"I don't understand. Why would this," he referred to his note pad for the full name, "James Dieter worry about Flaherty? Aren't they friends? Wasn't he also a friend of the father?"

Perluci nodded. "As I understand Flaherty, this is a man who will not leave any witnesses for his ugly past deeds. He will not allow himself to be apprehended by the authorities, most of all not our people. Him leaving behind witnesses only increases that chance. I know this type. One thing I am certain of, he will kill Dieter when he no longer has any use for him."

**Canal side, St. Florentine, France**
JIM AND DAN STRODE ACROSS THE barge's topside teak deck. "This is a beauty," Jim said to the salesman. "This boat resembles a fully loaded motor home only she's lacking the wheels." Dan and Jim then followed the salesman as he moved on to the kitchen.

"And as you will notice," the salesman said snootily in flawless English, only a slight French accent detectable, "this kitchen is outfitted to satisfy any chef. It contains many amenities, all *Top shelf.*"

Jim opened the sub-zero glass double-door refrigerator, then admired the stainless-steel quad-burner stove.

"All of our vessels meet the highest French Maritime standards in accommodation. Our corporate office recently received three stars from your American Mobile Guide for excellence. This model in particular earned extensive praise in that booklet." Not missing a beat, he continued with the tour, one of many he had clearly provided. "This barge has two bedrooms, each with in-suite private Jacuzzi baths."

The salesman offered Dan and Jim a quick glance in the area before hastily pushing on.

The salesman continued. "As you can see, the galley and dining areas make extensive use of elegant cherry wood. Each of the areas are also equipped with the latest in the Sony surround-sound entertainment equipment. I must also note that they come with an impeccable array of music I have personally selected."

Jim and Dan exchanged brief glances. Obviously new music would be in order.

"And notice the floors. We have modest oriental carpeting located throughout the barge protecting the fabulous teak wood floors."

The salesman moved on as if he had another appointment waiting. "If I can direct your attention over here," he said, pointing to an elaborate digital control panel the size of a paperback book mounted on the wall. "You will notice our central air-conditioning system. It is rare for the European environment, but we think it's a requirement that should be afforded to our, shall we say, *higher echelon clientele*. Now, over here is the fully stocked bar area. All beverages would be included in a signed rental package agreement."

# THE VATICAN's LAST SECRET

Dan eyed the liquor selection with obvious disdain. He walked behind the bars solid walnut veneer, picking up a blue bottle of liquor by his forefinger and thumb as if it had some type of fungus growing on it, placing it back on the shelf.

"Let's get something straight. Irish Whisky and Irish Mist. You can toss the rest." He casually turned to Jim. "Would you prefer a few bottles of Canadian Club to go along with my selections for the ride?"

"Canadian and Irish whiskey should do nicely and throw in a few cases of Beaujolais and Burgundy wine for our dinners," Jim replied, smiling at the salesman before looking back at Dan. "You did say the trip should take two weeks—right?"

The salesman lips quivered in apparent disapproval of Jim and Dan's tastes. "Very well, sir. If you decide to rent our product, I can clean out the bar area and restock it with several bottles of your selected whiskeys and your vintages. Now that we have the bar selections, we can complete the tour."

In a hushed tone, Jim said. "I do think we offended the snot—wouldn't you say?"

"Just a tad," Dan replied.

The salesman walked toward the middle of the barge with Jim and Dan in tow. "And as you can see, the top deck is also richly appointed in teak and mahogany woods. Only the best for our clientele. And, gentlemen, unfortunately this is where I conclude the tour." He pointed to the barges aluminum gangway.

Dan removed a crisp, new, one hundred-dollar American bill from his wallet, admiring its off-center picture of Ben Franklin as he held it up to the light to observe its watermark. It also had the desired effect of catching the attention of the salesman.

"Thank you, Monsieur Dobet, for an excellent tour," Dan said, casually slipping him the bill. "You have quite a majestic product here. I think we may want to procure for her for several weeks' time."

The salesman had an uneven smile upon his face. He was accustomed to most people simply thanking him and walking away. Especially after they heard the rental price.

"Our terms are simple. I will provide you with a cashier's check for full payment in Euros by 11:30 a.m. today," Dan said looking at his watch before continuing. "That's about two hours from now. We will expect to shove off around noon. *That is 12:00 noon today.* Do you foresee that to be a problem?"

Taken aback at such rudeness, the salesman stubbornly crossed his arms in response to such a foolish request. He could expect such a demand from the American, but from an obviously educated and refined Irishman, there could be no excuse.

"But, sir," he spat out. "That is only two hours from now. I cannot possibly have the liquor and food delivered by that time. The logistics of such a request is too incredible. I simply cannot do it."

It was a fishing expedition, surely, on the part of the salesman. The first tip received, he now required a bit more bait. Dan had planned for as much.

"Monsieur Dobet, I apologize for the short notice," Dan said. "We would not dream of inconveniencing someone of your stature." Dan looked around to see if they were being observed. "Maybe we could achieve some type of understanding." He removed five, American one-hundred-dollar bills from his wallet, placing them one by one into the salesman's now open palm. "Would this tend to move things along at a more ambitious pace?"

The salesman withdrew a white handkerchief from his pocket, wiping the perspiration from his brow. "I will personally see to the operation, sir. You can count on me. Should you require anything else, anything at all, please let me know. *Yes*?"

# THE VATICAN's LAST SECRET

"If I need anything else you are the man, Monsieur Dubet," Dan said. "Thank you for your time."

The salesman patted his pocket as he watched Dan and Jim walk down the gangway.

Once clear of the salesman Jim turned to Dan. "Do you believe that guy? He changed his mind pretty quick when you produced the big bills."

"That and then some," Dan replied, gauging the remainder of his billfold. "Ah, yes, and how about that tour? That look on your face was priceless. For a while, I thought you were going to die when you viewed the accommodations."

"Are you kidding me? I would have done forty years in the Navy if we had ships outfitted like that. Just mount a couple of fifty calibers, and we would be in business." Jim paused for a few seconds before he continued: "I am curious about one thing though. You seem to know your way around a boat. You ever do a little sailing in your day?"

Dan steered Jim over to the canals edge, him wanting to get a full view of the barge from afar.

"Your observation skills are still in excellent form, my friend," he responded. "You are right. I have done a little sailing in my time. In what seems to be another life and another time, I had the opportunity to utilize boats similar to this one for operations in Ireland."

Moving closer to Jim's position by the canals iron railing, he looked around, satisfied no one was about, before proceeding. "Back in the 70's the British Army patrols were very efficient in closing the roads, searching vehicles for weapons and such back. It was then that the river rose up and spoke to me."

*"Use the pleasure boats as a way to move about".*

"A bloody brilliant idea that was just waiting to be unearthed. I took a few basic boating courses. After that, I was able to move more product to the boys up north via the inland waterways. For some reason, the Brits didn't pay much attention to the river areas. I guess they thought the Irish bastards couldn't learn to sail. On the one occasion that they did happen to patrol the river and chose to board my boat, I had secured the perfect place for hiding my illegal cargo. I had placed twenty AK-47s and five pounds of C-4 explosives, all enclosed in shrink-wrap, mind you, in the boats shitter before I left the dock. Using this particular mode of operation, I was able to ferry in weapons up and down the river for various operations."

Jim shook his head. "You really have a checkered past, a regular man for all seasons. I'm surprised you agreed to go on this little operation my father dreamed up. You could be taking a chance."

"You mean with me being a wanted man in, what, three or four different countries? Dan replied.

"Exactly. I didn't want to put it that way, but yes."

"Well, it's only four if you count my newly adopted homeland of the good old USA," Dan said. "But have no worries. A little bird informed me they only have one photo of me, and it is from 1978. I was thirty pounds lighter, and my hair was a bit browner and thicker. It makes moving about a lot easier since I have been in hiding for forty years. You can say I have turned into one of the forgotten few. And that may be one of the reasons your father asked me to assist you with this operation. He knew if anyone could perform an operation such as this, it would be someone just like me, a ruthless bastard when needed."

Dan pointed back to the barge, wanting to change the subject. "Who would suspect two tourists to be transporting illegal cargo on a vacation barge? More importantly, we are also covering our tracks from any snooping souls. Who would expect us to be boating on a luxury barge through the rivers of France and Germany to our Weimar destination?"

"Only someone who thinks like yourself," Jim replied.

*Only someone like yourself."*

# THE VATICAN's LAST SECRET

# CHAPTER 20

**MI-6 HQ – LONDON**

A rare day to be associated with London in the month of June: sunny and mild. Two words that never seemed to click in the London weather vocabulary. The kind of day that could seduce office workers to leave the office a little early for a round of golf, or perform some long overdue gardening.

For most office workers in London, this would have been an acceptable notion to consider, the exception being the staff at MI-6. National security was a twenty-four-hour-a-day mission for Britain's Intelligence Service.

Most of the MI-6 workforce suffered from what the British commonly referred to as the "coal miner effect." Workers who entered their workspaces before the sun rose and left after it set.

One such employee who suffered from the "effect" was Roscoe Hopkins: tall and gangly, pale skin the sun had rarely kissed, bald as a cue, cauliflower ears from his amateur boxing days.

## THE VATICAN's LAST SECRET

His office lacked windows due to his boss's level of importance. Another measure put into place in a constant effort to improve security. This prevented any sort of eavesdropping or assassination attempts from street level nine floors below.

Employed as an executive assistant to Sir Robert John, Director of MI-6, Hopkins was intimately associated with most of the top-secret operations and events that transpired not only in the United Kingdom, but also worldwide. Even the Prime Minister was not aware of most active operations.

Hopkins nodded to the morning duty officer who delivered the overnight message traffic. After the duty officer had departed Hopkins arranged the messages by operational theater, just the way his boss preferred: Europe, the Americas, and so on.

The duty officer had also delivered a red folder with *Top Secret, Director's Eyes Only* stamped across its face. The normal color for interoffice correspondence was blue. The significance of the red folder marked this as a sensitive issue, usually involving a terrorist incident or a political assassination of some kind. Hopkins immediately picked up the red folder, walking up to Sir Roberts's office. He straightened his tie before knocking lightly to announce his presence, waiting until his director had looked up from his old-fashioned newspaper before entering.

"Sir Robert, sorry to bother you, but you have a red message," Hopkins said. He walked over and laid the folder on Sir Roberts's desk. "I took a peek, sir. Evidently, one of our communication stations outside of Cheltenham intercepted a message indicating one of our Irish hooligans has surfaced on the continent—possibly Paris or Berlin."

Sir Robert John provided Roscoe Hopkins "carte blanche" on reading message traffic, allowing him to review all messages no matter what level stamp, thus weeding out all of the unnecessary and trivial traffic before reaching his desk. Sir Robert leaned back in his chair, wondering what could possibly make his day even more interesting. "Come now Hopkins, we are down to only what, fifteen brethren still out of touch? Is it someone I know personally?" He said, not bothering to open the folder.

"It's an old timer, Sir Robert. Flaherty, Daniel Flaherty," he responded efficiently. "Flaherty disappeared over thirty years ago after destroying a hotel in Londonderry. We suspect he went into hiding in either Canada or the States. Nothing has ever been confirmed."

Sir Robert sat back casually puffing on a fresh Cuban cigar, one supplied by a private source in the Cuban Embassy. "Flaherty, yes I remember that bastard. A rather ruthless one if my memory serves me. He totaled the whole damn hotel, but not until all of the children had vacated. How could I forget a person like that? The papers had a field day, calling him the terrorist with a heart."

Most found Sir Robert to be a gentleman's gentleman. Balding, tall and fit, ruggedly handsome to most, along with a touch of old English charm, with an elegance long forgotten. Well respected in the circles he moved, both professionally and personally. He had recently celebrated his forty-third year with MI-6 since recruited out of Oxford University by the legendary Sir Newton Clive, former head of the MI-6 Overseas branch, long since departed.

After readily accepting Sir Clive's rather generous offer for employment, he was quickly put to work. First was the breaking of codes or ciphers, as they were then known, before being sent to a posting at the new communications complex outside Cheltenham. After ten years of mind-numbing deskwork duty, he received an assignment to work in the former West Germany. He infiltrated the "Iron Curtain" on eleven separate missions culminating with the turn of an East German Army General whom he personally escorted across the border. This led to a real intelligence coup for the western powers. For that distinction, he received the honorary title of "Sir" by the Queen. Moving up through the ranks rapidly, he naturally assumed the directorship of MI-6 when the sitting director retired several years back.

"Yes, I would like to get my hands on that bastard and bring him home" Sir Robert said. "What or whom is the source of our information intercept?"

"The Vatican in Rome sent out the equivalent of an encrypted all-points bulletin on our boy Flaherty, which we easily intercepted and broke at Cheltenham," Hopkins replied competently, his boss not having to search for information. "If the information is to be believed, they say he may be in Paris or Berlin. There is also a side note that may be of some importance, Sir Robert. He was also known to be traveling with an American, one James Dieter from the State of New York."

"Ah, one of our Irish lads has taken up company with an American traveling partner. I do not like it one bit, Hopkins," Sir Robert said. "See what our cousins in the CIA have on this American. Then get Rufus Sneed to pay me a visit in thirty minutes. I think we can arrange a nice reception for our prodigal son who has obviously come home to do no good. Also, I think we will have to call in some favors from our military friends on this one. See if General Parker can alert the Special Air Service Team for possible action, either here or across the channel."

Sir Robert then leaned back in his chair. "Hopkins, we are going to nail this bastard to the wall once and for all. I only hope I'll be there to see it."

**Paris, France: Vatican Counsel Mission Office**
IN AN INDISCREET townhouse situated in the 11th arrondissement, Father Francis Jenkins sat keenly reviewing the days message traffic, sipping on his third cappuccino of the morning. He picked up the nasty cappuccino habit when he was a special assistant at The Vatican some fifteen years ago, something now of an addiction to complete his customary ten- to fourteen-hour shifts.

A studious 55 year-old whose hair had already turned prematurely gray, his doctor pleaded with him to put some weight on his six foot, 130-pound frame.

He sat staring at his computer screen for several minutes, digesting what he had read, re-reading the short email text several times yet again. "I can't believe it. The Vatican has sent us a priority red. This is highly unusual," he said aloud. After re-reading the message from The Vatican for a sixth time, he looked over at his lay assistant. "I have not seen one of these since 1983, when our Holiness was shot by the KGB in Vatican City.

Standing up in order to gather his composure, he walked away from his assistant before quickly turning back and allowing his trained reflexes to take over. "We have to act quickly on messages like this. I will need you to call Interpol and the local police who are in favor with us. See this message gets the proper attention it requires. You will inform them of our need for a full electronic search, meaning credit cards, airport tickets, banks, and the other assorted areas. Inform them The Vatican has provided us with a list of, looking back at the email for confirmation of the names, "one Mr. James Dieter and one Daniel Flaherty, their credit card numbers and recent photos. I want copies of these distributed to all of our friends."

Father Jenkins' young assistant looked a bit perplexed before responding. "I will be happy to oblige. But can you explain to me what exactly a priority red is? I am casually aware of the priority yellows and greens, but not a priority red. This is new territory for me."

Turning slowly toward his young apprentice, placing a paper copy of the message on the table in front of him, Father Jenkins nodded. "Yes, we are still in the early stages of your training. You are obviously too young to remember how hectic it was with the assassination attempt on the Pope in 1983. You have only been exposed to our typical business here for two months? Much has changed from that troubling time in 1983."

# THE VATICAN's LAST SECRET

He motioned for his apprentice to sit down. "As you are still in training, let's reminisce with the codes shall we? Only this time, I will enlighten and expose you to one additional color in our system. Our priority codes are assigned three colors, not just the two that you were previously exposed to. As you are already aware, yellow translates to a low-level search, usually indicating a robbery of church property with only local assistance required. Green is for crimes committed against a member of the church's faculty. This would involve our council offices in the general area of the crime. Priority red means find at all costs. We use every office and person at our disposal, worldwide. It is only used when one of our higher-ups are affected, usually a bishop or cardinal, but it could even involve his Excellency, the Pope.

It was a little overwhelming for the young apprentice as he sat up from his prone position. "You must forgive me Father Jenkins, I am only used to dealing with the local police," he said. "You say we retain a worldwide capability and capacity to actually locate people such as this? How can this be?"

Father Jenkins enjoyed returning to his former role as an instructor, if only for the moment. "We have people in such places as the local police, Interpol, American FBI, and various military personnel who are friendly to our religious cause. They all work together to complement our own security services at The Vatican. We place a call, the operation goes into effect, and we usually have our suspect within a few days, a week at tops.

"I understand the sensitive nature of the business, and the information stays with me," the apprentice said. "But does it always work?"

"I would say nine times out of ten. That is a percentage better than the American CIA, the Israeli Mossad, or the British MI-6. Our targets tend to slip up somewhere, whether it's using a credit card or a money transaction via a bank in their own name. You know how everything is recorded on the computer nowadays. We also recently started working hand in hand with the Israeli Mossad to expand our intelligence into Arabic countries, thus providing us with a more global resource."

The young apprentice picked up the message, "So I contact this number at Interpol and our part of the operation just goes into effect?"

"Just contact that person and relay our message with our code number and the network goes into action," Father Jenkins said, pointing to the name listed at the top of the page. The same message is being sent to all of our networks in Berlin and London. After you contact Interpol, then call this number in the military and this one at American Express. We will cover all of the bases."

"So the net is being cast," said the apprentice, admiring the simplistic nature of the system.

"Yes, it is," Father Jenkins replied. "We are the fishermen—let us reap the bounty."

# THE VATICAN's LAST SECRET

# CHAPTER 21

**ABOARD THE SAILING BARGE "JACOB"**

The barge was traveling at its rated speed of six knots, putting them at a distance of twenty-five kilometers downriver of St. Florentine as they approached the farming village of Tonnerre.

As they were still on the "shakedown" portion of their cruise, they were getting used to the barge and its eccentric quirks. The only inconvenience to surface so far was the engines tendency to "hiccup" a dark plume of exhaust every thirty or forty minutes.

Jim sat enjoying the scenery from the top deck, reclining on a chaise lounge, sipping whiskey from a short frosted glass. Leaning back, he raised his glass in salute to where Dan stood in the pilothouse.

"Dan, if someone had told me about this type of luxury boating years ago, I would have gone out and bought my own barge by now. Hell, after getting out of the Navy, I promised to never set foot on another boat, but this baby is something else."

Dan decided to dock the barge alongside a line of beech trees that ran parallel to the canal bank. Easing the beast into a position was easier said than done, reversing its engine three times in order to maneuver out of the main waterway. Satisfied, he yelled down to Jim. "And to think this morning you thought I was crazy suggesting we go by barge. I think your exact words to me were," *'you're not getting me on the damn water again. I did my time in the Navy.'* But alas, then I showed the amenities to you."

"I didn't realize it was like traveling by a floating hotel with a full bar to boot. I feel as though we are on vacation instead of searching for something in my father's past."

With the barge safely secured to the canal bank, Dan withdrew from the pilothouse and sat down on the chair next to Jim. "But we *are* on a vacation, my friend, so just enjoy it. By the way, this is the low end of the vacation barges if you can imagine that. They even have one with a Jacuzzi, a sauna, a chef to cook, and a captain to pilot you downriver."

Dan proceeded to pour some whiskey into a glass for himself, offering to top off Jim's before replying. "I'm sure anything could have been arranged with enough notice."

"How long did you say we would be renting this tub? One week or two?

Dan took a sip from his glass, enjoying the view for a few seconds before choosing to respond. "I have the pleasure to announce that we are booked for three weeks. It's only going to take about two for a round trip, and that's if we proceed at a snail's pace. That would leave almost one full week of leeway for us to enjoy. So to make this trip pleasurable, I would suggest we pull in wherever we fancy and be the proverbial tourist."

Jim raised his glass in toast. "Dan for a rehabilitated terrorist you really know how to travel in style."

"I'll take that as a compliment," he said as moved on from the whiskey and popped open a bottle of a local burgundy, skipping the glass and sipping it straight from the bottle.

A slight grin indicated it was to his satisfaction. "To tell you the truth, I don't like the word terrorist — *I prefer renegade*. It sounds more romantic then terrorist. He raised his bottle.

"For I am the last of the true Irish renegades."

## Lyon, France: Office of Interpol

INSPECTOR LOUIS JACKO's large girth was comfortably ensconced in his well-worn Moroccan leather chair, his legs lay propped up on his imitation Louis XIV desk as he calmly spoke on the phone.

"But Father, I am busting my back working sixteen-hour days on petty cases trying to cover for someone who is out on vacation. I also have my own work piling up, and you expect me to drop everything to start a search for these two people," he said, awaiting the response.

After a slight pause, he seemed to understand the severity of the situation, nodding.

"My apologies, I did not realize it was a priority red. I will assign a detective to work the situation full-time on my end, with others available in a part-time role. I will personally lead the hunt. The net will be cast as soon as I get off the phone. I can also activate highway and airport police using the guise that two terrorists are on the loose. That should have everybody up and on the alert. If they are here, you have my assurances that we will find them. Count on my organization, Father."

## Aboard the "Jacob"

AFTER SPENDING A dreary, rain-whipped night at their impromptu canal side docking space, Jim and Dan arose to find a brilliant sunrise greeting them. The previous night's activities could now be felt in earnest. Even with this unfortunate factor working against them, they were able to start motoring by 9:00 a.m.

Dan resumed his post of steering the barge while Jim stood beside him consulting a maritime map and drinking one of Dan's *"hangover specials,"* consisting of tomato juice, egg whites, Tabasco sauce, and horseradish.

Jim savored the last of the drink, actually enjoying the bite it provided. "How did you ever come up with a concoction such as this? He inquired, puckering his lips at its unique taste. "Somebody's bar room no doubt."

Dan steered around a log floating in their path, looking ahead at the narrow lane his barge had to traverse before answering. "A bar room is it now? Would you believe the recipe was from an old Benedictine Monk?"

"With you, anything's possible," Jim responded.

Dan ignored him as he continued. "I was on a religious retreat back in the late nineties, trying to get rid of some old demons that pay me a visit every blue moon or so. I happened to be walking the plush grounds of a monastery when I stumbled across this old monk in a brown robe who resembled Friar Tuck of Robin Hood fame. You know the type: short, stout, hair clipped as if someone placed a bowl on his head. He was on the losing end of a struggle with a wheel barrel full of barley. The old guy was having a hard time emptying its contents through a basement window into the cellar. Of course, I gave him a hand. In appreciation, he showed me his private beer vat and provided a little tasting of the vintage he had already brewed. Well let me tell you, the old monk and I drank from the conclusion of evening vespers until breakfast the next morning, a good nine hours. Then he drinks this "hangover special" mixture, and the old goat was as good as new. He was like a recharged battery."

"Coming from anyone else but you, I wouldn't believe it," Jim said. "So I guess you are sober enough to take control of the wheel then?"

Focusing through the pilothouse window, Dan pointed down the river to what appeared to be the end of the waterway. "I think we have a much bigger issue looming."

Jim dashed out of the pilothouse in time to view a canal lock coming up fast. "Damn it, this lock was supposed to be ten kilometers further downstream," he said aloud.

Dan reversed the diesel engines to slow the barge. With their forward progress slowed to an acceptable speed, Dan switched off the engine and allowed the barge to glide.

Jim eyed the lockkeeper swinging his arms wildly. No doubt he thought the boat was obviously going to miss its mark. A feeling of déjà vu hit Jim as he sensed he was watching a football referee signaling a series of penalties, only in slow motion.

"You've got to be kidding," Jim shouted back to Dan, him still watching the lockkeepers spastic fit. "Are you sure you can park this baby in the locks opening? It looks really narrow to me. Maybe we should allow the lockkeeper to come aboard and have a go before you do some real damage."

Dan ignored Jim comments as he glided the barge forward on a slight angle, gently bumping into the ring of car tires neatly strung across the locks' now-open wooden doors.

The lockkeeper appeared frustrated at Dan's lack of boating skills. "If that damn clown cannot dock his boat, I'm climbing aboard to guide it through myself," he mumbled aloud, allowing some stress to creep back into his life.

As a lockkeeper for the French Maritime Commission for fifteen years, Arto Juneas had spent all but two years at the Forte Locks. Approaching his 55th birthday, short and slender, white hair buzzed to within a half inch of his scalp, he had his second retirement clearly in sight. He chose to enjoy each day as it presented itself. Good or bad. He learned this lesson the hard way with his first employer. A heart attack at age 40 forced him from a regular police beat in the Paris Gendarme to this humble position.

A traditional pensioner, he also maintained a small garden beside the lockkeeper's cottage, selling fresh vegetables or flowers to the tourists who did happen along. It also helped to supplement his police pension and meager pay from the French Maritime Commission.

As an experienced police officer from the beat, Arto never allowed his policing skills to languish. He kept them fresh by guessing the line of work of the boaters who came through, perhaps even their country of origin.

The one operating the bow ropes, obviously an American by his accent, either military or ex-military due to his muscular build and eyes that did not seem to miss a beat. The Irishman was of a different breed. Arto had seen this type before. He had a ruthless air about him. A bastard of many colors. A regular chameleon. *He was also a jackass from the way he kept thinking he could steer the boat.*

"That's it, Dan. You're allowed one more attempt, and then it's my turn."

The barge having lost its forward momentum, Dan restarted the barges engine, having no choice but to back it up.

"Monsieur," Arto yelled to Dan, "when you approach the lock you need to swing the rudder to the left and then full right, then shut down your engine when you pass the set of doors." Arto used his body motion to assist. He watched as Dan once again maneuvered the barge into position. "Yes, that is good," he said, now directing him with his hands. "Okay, good, that's it, now straight into the mooring point."

Dan yelled down at Arto. "Now what do you think I am trying to accomplish?" It's this damn French boat. She doesn't want to respond to an Irish master."

Shaking his head at such unpleasantness, Arto chalked it up to the man's frustration. He chose to focus on the docking, hoping the lock wouldn't suffer any serious damage from this rank amateur.

"You've got it, sir, cut the engine and glide in," Arto yelled above the motor, the barge clearing the lock with a half meter to spare on each side.

Arto turned his attention to Jim. "You, on the bow, toss the rope over here, and I'll tie you up," pointing down to a small metal post at Jim's feet.

"Good job," Jim yelled sarcastically to Dan. "I was hoping you would make it by dinner time." He tossed the rope across to Arto, him effortlessly tying them up as if he were working the docks of London.

With the barge safely in the lock, the lock now filled up with water to lift their barge up to match the next portion of the canal. Dan joined Jim and Arto standing by the lockkeeper's garden.

All seemed forgiven as the lockkeeper provided him a friendly nod before turning to walk amongst his crops.

Never one to lose an audience, Dan reverted to the poet that seemed to reside in all Irishmen. "This is a beautiful countryside, so peaceful and full of serenity," he said. "The land is a gift of bounty, the mother of all to see, the reflections of her wonderful beauty, from bouncing on a knee, the young all are weary, 'til time slowly passes by."

Still trying to profile this mysterious man, Arto loaded carrots and tomatoes into a cheap wicker basket, using an old paintbrush to casually brush the dirt off the carrots. "I see you enjoy poetry, sir," he said.

"Not just any poetry, a poem by Mr. Yeats himself. The one and only decent poet of our time," Dan replied.

"At what college or university would you have learned that, sir?" Arto said, probing for additional information as he tried to ascertain Dan's background.

"Not really college, my new friend but bar room 101," he replied, realizing Arto's probing was intentional. The last thing they required at this juncture was a meddlesome lockkeeper. "My father was fond of Irish poets and had me recite line and verse in his establishment. We made the locals feel like landed gentry."

Easing towards the barge, Dan was eager to put some distance between himself and Arto. As he walked past Jim, he whispered out of earshot of Arto. "Let's pay this kind man and be on our way for we have many miles to travel and the sunlight is dwindling."

He had no intention of committing yet another murder.

*At least…not today.*

# CHAPTER 22

**OFFICE OF INTERPOL – LYON, FRANCE**

The desks appeared to be government issue, gunmetal gray, all neatly arranged in two rows of ten. This allowed Inspector Jacko to view "his subjects" from the comfort of his glass-enclosed office.

As the hour was fast approaching 5:00 p.m., the office assumed a natural posture for this time of day, its workers winding down from yet another long one.

Since its founding, Interpol steadfastly earned a reputation as one of the premier policing agencies in the world. Their success rate of arrests and convictions hovered around 90 percent, considered one of the best in the business.

Its personnel were considered the crème de la crème for criminal investigative work. The Paris office contained an equal mix of English, German, and French detectives. Each detective selected by their respective governments to represent them on the Interpol team.

The day began quietly enough with the standard robbery and murder cases crossing the desks for most of his employees to review. Events changed mid-day when Inspector Jacko received a phone call from his Vatican contact, setting in motion a frantic search that involved several of the offices most trusted employees.

Now standing in front of the desk of one of them, his lone female detective, Inspector Jacko wheezed heavily due to the short walk from his office.

"Mrs. Lenine, how many false leads must we follow before somebody locates these clowns? He slammed a old fashioned paper fax down on her desk. "Can you explain to me why I have highly paid and educated people following every tour group that contains a male American and a male Irishman? This has been our tenth check in five hours. That is not the worst of it, Mrs. Lenine. The last pair turned out to be a black American, and the supposed Irishman wasn't Irish but Canadian."

Rebecca Lenine was constantly compared to a young Elizabeth Taylor by her co-workers: lithe, long black hair, and stunning violet eyes. With this combination, her third-degree black belt came in handy from her many unwanted suitors.

The only woman in her class of 75 men attending the Marseille Police Academy, she not only graduated, *she was its valedictorian.*

Only six years out of the Police Academy, she had already compiled a long list of commendations to her credit. With this in her portfolio, she easily moved up through the police ranks until achieving the rank of detective. This enabled her to be appointed to one of the highly coveted Interpol positions.

Rebecca rose up from her desk, index finger pointing at Inspector Jacko mid-section to stress her point. "You may be my boss but I don't appreciate you speaking to me in that manner, or throwing things in my direction. I too have been working hard on your little case and deserve some respect.

Now if you wish to receive the latest information, I suggest you calm the hell down."

Inspector Jacko raised his arms in surrender, then simply nodded.

Satisfied this would be the extent of his apology, she proceeded. "We have another sighting of the two possible suspects being sought by the Vatican Council.

"Another sighting? No, don't tell me," Inspector Jacko said. He removed an index card from her desk and applied it to the side of his temple as if he were a mind reader in a famous television program. "They were both midget carnival workers speaking in a foreign tongue, so they were automatic suspects." He flung the card across the room. "Give me a break."

He walked back to his office with Rebecca fast on his flank. "I should have never taken on this case," he said aloud.

"But this one is from a reliable source," she replied. "A retired inspector from our office is manning the Forte canal lock down by the town of Tonnerre," thrusting his already open file onto the inspector's desk. "Mr. Arto Juneas."

She continued to speak as the Inspector mindlessly looked out his window. "I was going through this man's file to get some background information. I wanted to make sure he was not a crackpot like some of our past informants. Well, he's not. He retired on medical leave after he experienced a heart attack. Before that he had received numerous awards and was a valuable source in breaking open several major cases in his day, including one in which you were prominently mentioned, the Paris Slasher case in 2006."

Looking up at her, the Inspector said not a word, now intrigued.

Rebecca continued. "To me he sounds like a viable source who knows exactly what he is doing. He received our all-points bulletin and two hours later came into contact with our suspects on a pleasure barge."

"Arto Juneas you say?" Inspector Jacko leaned back in his chair as if in deep thought, memories flooding over him, both good and bad. "That old coot taught me a thing or two when I was a Paris beat cop back in the 90s. He saved my life not once but twice. I will not bore you with the stories but let me just say this man was one of the best. Now, you say he sighted them at Forte Locks? What was Arto Juneas doing there? Is he on holiday?"

"No sir, not quite," she replied. "He is evidently the lockkeeper. He received our *All-Points Bulletin.*"

The inspector envisioned himself receiving a medal from the Pope for his capture of the two suspects. "I think we should pay Mr. Juneas a visit as soon as possible. This sounds like a solid lead to me."

"Do you think we should dispatch the local constables further downriver to the town of Montbard to pick them up?" She asked. "Or maybe provide the Vatican Counsels Office with a copy of the information we have just received. They might want us to back off, allowing their own personnel to capture the suspects."

This would not do. It would not fit into Inspector Jacko's grandiose plan. *Afterall, How could he receive his award from the Pope?* This was to be a feather in *his* cap, not some lowly constable.

"Just what information would we provide the local constables, Mrs. Lenine?" he stammered, thinking fast, searching for the right words. "The Vatican wants them to apprehend an Irishman and an American for some mysterious crime? I cannot share with you as to the extent of the crimes because the information is of a most delicate matter. We are working on a case with the Vatican. You know, hush-hush. We would appear to be fools. No, I will personally pick up our two misfits and escort them to the Vatican Office. Please book us a car from the motor pool. We will be leaving first thing in the morning."

"*We*, sir?" she said, feigning surprise, knowing how much the inspector seemed to despise her presence as the only female in the office. "You said *we*, as if both of us were proceeding on the same assignment."

"Yes, you will be covering my proverbial ass on this one," he spat out. "I suggest you inform your husband that we will be out of town for several days on assignment. Please make all of the necessary arrangements."

"But, of course," Rebecca said, hoping her performance would somehow change his opinion of her. "Do I also have permission to check out a semi-automatic from the armory for my personal protection, sir?"

"I would highly recommend it, Mrs. Lenine. From the information I have on these two, they will not come lightly. We may have a fight on our hands."

## **Vatican Intelligence Office, Rome, Italy**

SITTING IN HIS office deep in thought, Perluci stared intently at a younger picture of himself taken in a post-war Germany. It also happened to be when he was first assigned the Dieter case; many years of working in one fashion or another on this high-profile case. A light tapping on his office door by his assistant, Father Martin, startled him for a moment.

Father Martin gingerly deposited a folder in front of Perluci. "Mr. Perluci, sir, this is the military record on Mr. James Dieter from our contact at the United States Military Records Depository in St. Louis, Missouri."

Perluci quickly opened it, scanning its contents for Dieters military skills. *Now he could finally view his new adversary.*

Father Martin continued. "It seems that when our operative first inquired about Mr. Dieter's service record, her attempts were rebuffed. He evidently maintained a top secret stamping on his file, this indicating his personal importance or the nature of his work to which he was previously assigned. Being denied access to his record via their online system, she had to bribe someone in the records room to perform a manual search."

Perluci was visibly impressed. "It seems our Mr. Dieter was a Special Forces lad stationed with the SEALs in Dam Neck, Virginia. I know from internal reports that this unit participated in the U.S. operations against hostile forces in Iraq and Afghanistan."

He paged through Dieters record until reaching its awards section. "It also states that he was wounded twice and had been awarded the Silver Star. This man obviously knows how to perform missions without fail. I think the teaming of Dieter with Flaherty now makes for a lethal partnership that must be stopped."

"More like a Molotov cocktail, would you not agree?" Father Martin said, turning to exit from Perluci's office, pausing at the door.

Perluci nervously tapped his fingers on his desk, deep in thought once more. "I don't like the idea of an American SEAL and a former IRA member forming a partnership. I want you to activate three men from our Swiss Guards to go along with me for our little operation. Make sure it's Team Two, they have the most recent experience."

Father Martin nodded. "Yes, sir, Mr. Perluci, but from what you just read maybe you would prefer an armored car instead."

Perluci smiled graciously to his assistants comment, the man not realizing how close to the mark his arrow had struck.

### Aboard the "Jacob"

THE BARGE CRUISED along at a leisurely pace of six knots through the Burgundy region of eastern France.

Dan enjoyed piloting the barge, reluctant to let Jim have a go.

# THE VATICAN's LAST SECRET

"Are you going to hog the wheel, or can you take a break and let an old sea salt like myself have a try?" Jim inquired.

"Are you kidding me," Dan replied. "I'm having a grand old time and trying to enjoy this sensation for as long as possible."

"Well, when you're ready for a little relief, just yell. I'm going down below to start opening a few bottles of cabernet from that vineyard we visited this morning."

"Now that's not playing fair, my friend. You tease me with the opening of a good case of wine." Dan waited several seconds before backing away from the wheel, performing a courteous bow from the hip. "All right, I'll tell you what. You can drive this grand old lady, and I'll open the vintage. A younger person such as yourself might destroy such a delicate creature."

Dan quickly descended the wooden ladder leading to the bar area before Jim could change his mind.

Jim took charge before it ran aground in the narrow confines of the canal. "You act as though the wine is comparable to a child or a dear family member," he yelled down to Dan.

"Ah, but it is, Jim," he said leaning his head out of the main cabins window, holding up a bottle for Jim to see. "This is something of the earth, something that provides me great pleasure to enjoy. Now you drive, I'll open and pour."

With the dinner hour fast approaching, Jim decided it was best to moor for the night and join Dan. "I have a better idea," he yelled down to the galley once more. "Let's park this baby and go over the so-called plan of attack, that way we can enjoy the wine together."

"Good idea my boy," Dan yelled back in response. "Plot and drink. A devious man you are."

*A soft pop signaled the opening of the first bottle.*

# CHAPTER 23

**FORTE LOCKS – BURGUNDY, FRANCE**

Arto Juneas probed about his garden with a small metal spade, removing the never-ending weeds that were trying to overtake his small plot of ground. He hoped to finish most of the work before the days humidity triggered his arthritis and possibly sideline any future activities. It would also slow his pace around the waterway, hindering his handling of the Locks' gears.

Approaching in silence from the main road where they had parked their government issued vehicle, Inspector Jacko and Detective Rebecca Lenine tried not to startle Arto at his work. They chose to sit on a worn wooden bench by the main house, awaiting Arto's inevitable success in the weeding process.

Having already heard them approach via the gravel footpath, Arto took his time in paying them any notice. *At least they were polite about it.* Out of the corner of his eye, he could view a rather attractive woman with well-tanned legs sitting next to a portly gentleman, both admiring the scenery. He wondered who the hell would be bothering him on such a fine day, having a little free time to handle his chores and now these people show up. It's probably tourists wanting him to take their picture or open the locks just to see the mechanical wizardry of how they operated.

Arto gently cleaned the dirt from his spade before placing the tool in the back pocket of his worn jeans. *Oh well, I guess I might as well get this over with,* he said to himself, rising up, brushing the dirt off his pants. He walked over to where they sat.

Eyeing Rebecca appreciatively, Arto missed nothing in his head-to-toe gaze, ending with a slight smile, albeit missing a few teeth. "Bonjour. What may I do for you on this fine day?" he said to them in greeting.

The inspector nodded to him. They both stood up. "I assume you are Mr. Arto Juneas, formally of the Paris Gendarme?"

A look of surprise spread over Arto's weathered face. These strangers not only knew his name but his former occupation. "Why, yes sir, I am," Arto said in reply. "I take it that you are no ordinary tourists?"

The inspector smiled in response. "No, we are not, Arto."

"Then would you allow a kind old man to guess your occupations? It's a little game I play to humor myself." He waited until they nodded in agreement before he walked around both of them in order to gain their full profile.

*He required a second walk around for Rebecca.*

"From your conservative dress, the obvious mismatch of this beautiful woman by your side, and the weapons bulge in your sport coat, I would say you are both police officers. Am I right?" he said, slapping his hand against his thigh knowing his assumption was correct by the inspectors expression of surprise. "I still take pride in being able to deduct a person's profession or skill. Now, you must be responding to my message of the Irishman and American who passed through here yesterday evening."

The inspector nodded. "Yes, I would have regarded the message we received lightly, but when I was told it was from you, the great Arto Juneas, I knew this had to be reliable information. Allow me to begin the introductions. I am Inspector Jacko, and this is Sergeant Lenine. Both of us represent Interpol."

Inspector Jacko looked away shyly for a moment before continuing, "Mr. Arto, you probably do not remember me but…"

Arto stopped him with a wave of his hand. "I remember you. Yes, I never forget a face." He tugged at the whiskers on his chin, a smile spreading across his face in acknowledgement. "Didn't I save your ass twice in the late '90s when you were a beat walker like myself? Yes, it is you, isn't it?" Not waiting for a response, he proceeded. "The first time you slipped on a patch of ice and shot yourself in the ass with your pistol. You would have bled to death if it were not for me. The other time you..."

"That's enough, Mr. Arto. No need to reminisce with stories from our past," Inspector Jacko said, obviously not wanting to expose his past deeds in front of a subordinate. He looked over at Rebecca, his crimson face revealing his embarrassment.

Arto laughed aloud so hard that he even startled himself. "I can't believe they promoted you to inspector, one for Interpol at that. Are they desperate for people? Maybe I should come back." An even heartier laugh followed. "I could be in charge of the whole damn force by now, don't you think?" He elbowed the inspector in his ribs, enjoying his own barbs for all they were worth.

Rebecca took the cue from Arto, unable to contain her own laughter, eyeing the inspector and covering her mouth. "I'm sorry, inspector, it was just the way he worded it."

"All right Mrs. Lenine, please contain yourself. We have a job to perform," the inspector said, extracting a note pad from his suit jacket, hopefully signaling a change in the direction of the conversation.

The inspector continued. "I was hoping you could provide us with additional information about the two suspects that passed through here yesterday, Mr. Arto."

"Yes, yes, by all means. Where are my manners? Let us go inside where I will prepare us a light lunch. We can discuss the two foreigners of yesterday and maybe my possible reemployment, yes?" he said, winking at Rebecca.

Limping back into his house with his arm around Rebecca's waist, he led her along the uneven brick path, secretly hoping she would trip so he would have to catch her.

"Quickly now, Miss, let's get into the house before I have to rescue him again. Maybe this time from drowning in the canal!"

**Aboard the "Jacob"**
THE NEWLY PURCHASED case of wine was now missing three of its brethren as Jim and Dan hunched over the dining table along with a block of farmers cheese and the remnants of what was, at one time, a half-meter-long crusty baguette.

Pouring himself yet another generous helping of Bordeaux, Dan scanned the NATO ordinance map spread along the length of the dining saloon table. The ordinance maps were a remnant left over from the Cold War, providing precise topography details down to every stream, ridge, road, and hill. The maps were originally intended for artillery strikes in the event of war, now used by tourists on holiday.

Dan lifted his glass in a toast to Jim. "I must say this vintage is an excellent one, my friend. Chalk one up for you."

Jim simply nodded, having selected it earlier in the day from a two-hundred-year-old family owned winery.

# THE VATICAN's LAST SECRET

Dan applied small metal calibers to the map, measuring off the distance on the ordinance map. "If we can keep our present pace and make close to forty kilometers per day, we should be able to approach our target by Tuesday night."

Jim shook his head. "I think you should slow down on the wine, because you're making a slight miscalculation with choosing Tuesday. There's no damn way we can cover 350 kilometers by Tuesday. Do the math. Three days at forty kilometers per day still equals 120 kilometers. *We're still short by 130 kilometers.*

"Damn, you're good," he replied sarcastically. "Yes, it does add up. I see your math skills are still strong. Your father always said you were a smart one. Those private schools really paid off." Dan held up his glass of wine to the light as if he were a professional vintner, looking at its clarity, the pause planned. "Okay, we are now entering phase two of my schedule.

Jim opened his mouth to protest.

Dan raised his hand to silence him. "What you are not aware of is that I have already arranged for a mid-sized truck to meet us just a few kilometers from the German border. The person driving that truck will be one of my relatives with an affiliation from my early IRA days. He will stay with the barge as our guest while we drive the truck to your father's farm in Weimar."

"How come you didn't mention anything about this earlier? I should have been consulted?"

"Jim, I did it for your own safety. The less you knew up to this point the better. If caught, you would have nothing to disclose to the police or anyone else. And, I also did it for my own safety. These are my contacts, my family. I will not endanger them. But most of all I wanted to maintain a vacation aura about us until we cleared the majority of towns along our water route. It's just something from my bag of tricks I learned in the old days; protect your friends and try to throw as many obstacles in the path to make the hounds lose the scent."

Jim simply nodded. "It's my turn to bow to the master, for you truly know how to run an operation. *A thorough one at that.*"

**Forte Locks, Burgundy, France**
THE LUNCH ARTO promised was more of a processed food banquet with smoked meats and cheeses along with a local bakery's assorted breads. The French are famous for their farmer's lunches, and this was to be no exception.

With the meal now complete, Arto cleaned the plates of his guests, scrapping the leftovers into a bin for recycling into his garden.

Arto turned to his guests. "Enough business talk. Would you be so kind as to provide me with the plain truth? So my Irishman and American sound like the ones you are looking for, ah?" He looked to both for confirmation before deciding to proceed. "Good. Then I see my eye for suspicious characters is still in working order." Arto paused a few seconds. "Is there a reward included? My pension doesn't buy what it used to anymore with inflation and all."

The inspector avoided eye contact with Arto. "Sorry, Arto, you will just have to accept the humble gratitude of your former employer as thanks."

"Yes, yes, the humble gratitude speech. But it does not pay the bills—does it, inspector? Arto replied angrily. "I was kind enough to invite you into my home and provide you with a lot of solid information for which I receive nothing but your humble thanks." Arto turned and spat on the kitchens cobblestone floor in disgust.

"I think it is time for us to depart, Mrs. Lenine," the Inspector said, seeing how agitated Arto had become. "Again, thank you for your information, Arto, and good luck in your position here."

Inspector Jacko made an effort to shake Arto's hand, but Arto turned away with his arms folded in disgust.

# THE VATICAN's LAST SECRET

"Adieu, Arto," the Inspector said.

Arto slowly turned to face the inspector, a smile creeping across his face. "But inspector, you forgot to ask me one important question. Do you want to know which way they were going through the locks? Or how about the destination they inquired about?"

Inspector Jacko feigned surprise to Rebecca before confronting Arto. "I cannot believe you, Arto," he stammered, "a former policeman soliciting money for information. This is not only unprofessional behavior but also highway robbery."

Arto resumed brushing aside the remnants from lunch. "Yes, it is a shame what society has done to us poor, hungry, retired policemen."

Inspector Jacko lowered his voice in whispering to Rebecca, "Do you have a hundred Euro…."

Overhearing the meager request, Arto relished his being in control of the situation. "No, not a hundred, let's make it more like *two hundred*," he said. "For I am just a humble lockkeeper."

"That's highway robbery. I will not pay it." the inspector responded.

Returning to his sink, Arto tended to the dishes, laughing aloud at their obvious predicament. "I guess if you both split up with one going east and the other west, you will eventually run into the people you seek."

"Damn you, Arto," Inspector Jacko stammered once more, shaking his fist at Arto before turning to face Rebecca. "Mrs. Lenine, could you lend me two hundred Euros until we get back to the office so I can pay this lowlife of a man?"

Arto smiled as he watched their reflection in one of his cooking pans hanging over the sink.

# CHAPTER 24

**MI-6 HQ – LONDON**

The executive offices of MI-6 were anything but traditional. From the Chippendale desk to the extravagant use of imported American oak panels and brilliantly waxed cherry wood floors. The expensive yet tastefully decorated offices were intentionally meant to convey an impression of greatness and power, to intimidate all that entered. It usually had the desired effect on anyone exiting the elevator, overwhelming them with old world English charm.

Of course, the most elaborate office happened to belong to the Director of MI-6, Sir Robert John.

Besides the heavy use of expensive woods, the director's office contained a museum quality assortment of antique weaponry, each a gift from various heads of state that were aware of his passion. This, along with six, oil-on-canvas paintings of his predecessors and one of Winston Churchill, hung about the room.

Presently seated around the director's cherry wood oval conference table were Rufus Sneed, Head of the Northern Ireland Office; General Anthony Parker, Head of the Special Air Service (SAS), and their various administrative underlings, totaling ten in all.

Sir Robert John stood up from his desk to address them. "Gentlemen, I am glad each of you could accommodate me on such short notice. As my executive assistant, Mr. Hopkins, briefed you earlier, we evidently have a terrorist who has come back to roost."

A wide screen television displayed a grainy, thirty-year-old black-and-white photo for all to view.

"His name is Daniel Flaherty."

"Next picture, Hopkins," Sir Robert barked to his assistant operating the screen's remote. "Mr. Flaherty blew up a hotel in Londonderry, pictured here after the bombing," walking up to the screen before standing no more than a meter from its base and using his index finger to emphasize the dead bodies, one by one. "Killing ten of our Ulster allies in the process."

"Next picture please." *A white brick with the name of an arms manufacturer appeared on the screen.*

"He used Czech made Semtex smuggled in through his Libyan connections. Next picture."

A middle-aged, paunchy male, photographed from a distance, flashed on the screen. "This is Omar Seri, someone whom we are all very familiar with, the former Libyan Deputy Intelligence Officer, and Mr. Flaherty's primary source of explosives."

Sir Robert leaned over, his fists resting comfortably on the conference table. "Now for the good news. He has resurfaced with an ex-US Navy SEAL by the name of James Dieter just outside of Paris, this information originating from a transmission we monitored between a canal lockkeeper and the main Interpol offices. Since the last message we have refocused additional assets in the area to monitor future transmissions."

"Gentlemen, now is the time to rid the world of this type of bastard," he said, pounding his hand on the table for full effect. "General Parker, would you be able to work with my office and provide us with some assistance? I would require a small team, say only three or four of your SAS lads, to visit the area of the last known transmission and pick up the trail and start the hunt for this bastard."

"What about his American partner, sir?" General Parker inquired. "The Americans won't take too kindly to us offing one of their own."

"Well, if our Irishman has this American as a traveling companion, I would say he is guilty by association. Wouldn't you agree, General?" Sir Robert replied.

"Loud and clear, Sir Robert," knowing from experience that Sir Robert just signed their death warrants. "Stop me if I am off base, but as I see it, we can have the operation done cleanly in a matter of days. If I may, I would like to provide some details of what a typical operation of this magnitude would look like."

Sir Robert nodded. "Any help you can provide our office would be greatly appreciated."

General Parker smiled in return realizing he was now gaining a future card he could use anytime he wanted with Sir Robert. "As you are aware, we always keep a Special Air Services team on alert 24/7 for situations that could potentially arise. I can have a four-man SAS team on the ground in the Forte Locks area less than a few hours from the word go. They will travel incognito with civilian clothes and go via the Chunnel. Once our team is on the ground, we can expect to interrogate the owner of the home where the transmission took place and pursue our leads from there. The team leader for this operation will be Captain Robinson, a veteran of the Iraq – Afghanistan War. He has over 17 years experience performing this type of nasty work for us.

Sir Robert nodded once more. "Thank you, General. Can you keep me in the loop as the operation unfolds."

"Yes, Sir Robert, can do. I will personally see to it and contact your assistant, Mr. Hopkins, with the requisite information," the General replied.

"Excellent. And another thing, General," Sir Robert said. "This IRA rogue is a scoundrel who evidently is very good at what he does."

"Sir Robert, I don't think there will be a problem with Captain Robinson. He actually lived in the Iraq desert for two months. He survived by living off the land similar to our old Eighth Army "Desert Rats." Between the U.S. Navy SEALs and his SAS team, they pinpointed a majority of the Iraq communication positions for air bombardments. He is ideal for this type of operation. He actually relishes it."

Sir Robert casually extracted a cigar from his desktop humidor, cutting one end with a modified 7.62 mm bullet before lighting it. "Well, the American traveling with Flaherty is an ex-U.S. Navy SEAL, also a veteran of the Iraq War. Hopefully he didn't work together with your Captain Robinson, or this operation will be shot from the start, eh, General? Thank you all. This meeting is now adjourned," he said, casually dismissing them with a wave of his cigar.

**SAS Training Facility, Herefordshire England**
FOR YEARS THE British Government found it necessary to maintain a Special Air Service (SAS) commando team on alert 24/7, used primarily as a small quick-response team. They stood ready to deal with any type of worldwide conflict. SAS teams participated extensively in the Irish troubles and Iraq/Afghanistan Wars, responsible for damage so substantial that it was once compared to an Army division.

They are also known to work silently in most countries with or without the host country's knowledge.

# THE VATICAN's LAST SECRET

Seemingly a relic left over from the Cold War period, they now seem to dovetail nicely with the recent rise in worldwide terrorism.

CAPTAIN ROBINSON EYED his twelve recruits as they prepared to jump off a cinder-block retaining wall used to simulate parachute landings.

"You are supposed to be professionals," he bellowed.

At 38, Captain Robinson was the "old man" of his SAS troop. Most of his own graduating class had already moved on to command positions in brigade or battalion levels years before. He would have nothing to do with a desk job. Captain Robinson preferred the field. At the end of the day, he wanted dirt in his nails to prove he put in a full day's work.

"Stop your bitching and jump off the goddamn platform. Christ sake, its only five meters to the ground. The way you are complaining you would think it was a hundred damn meters." The Captain picked up his MP5 submachine gun, inserting a full clip, slamming it into place with pure military efficiency.

"You would not have a problem if the damn aircraft were on fire now, would you?" he shouted.

Captain Robinson knew somebody would hesitate at the platform. One or two of the first week recruits always did. Hell, he had hesitated himself. But he grew to learn that you perform as ordered with no hesitation. It could be a matter of not only yourself being killed but also the troops with you. *They will learn that lesson the hard way*, raising his weapon at the recruits.

He walked down the line of recruits sneering at each one. The eighty pound packs they had on their backs didn't help with the jump. "Let's get one thing straight. When I order you to jump, *you damn well jump*! Do you hear me?"

He approached one recruit standing only inches from his face. "You never, ever, question what I say! Questioning what I say in the field could get you or me killed, *and I would not like that very much*. Do you understand what I'm saying?" He removed the safety from his weapon for all to see before pointing the weapon menacingly at the startled recruits. "I will give you all until the count of three before I fire this weapon."

A shout from his aide, Corporal Bellows, saved the men for the moment, his aide holding aloft a cell phone. "Captain Robinson, you have an emergency call from General Parker. It sounds like you are a go within the hour for a show."

Captain Robinson smiled. "Damn fine day it has turned out to be. I guess we better get cracking."

"Corporal, could you please take over this operation for me? Make sure these lads keep jumping off this wall until at least one of them breaks something, I don't care what, a leg, arm, wrist, it does not matter. Understood?" He purposely said it loud enough to be overheard by the young recruits.

"Perfectly, sir," the Corporal replied.

Each recruit nervously eyed the other wondering if joining the elite SAS was such a brilliant idea after all.

# CHAPTER 25

**ABOARD THE "JACOB"**

The wind picked up, gently rocking the barge from side-to-side at its mooring point alongside the bank of the canal.

Dan had decided to end the sailing day at an early hour in order to perform a thorough review of the maps one last time. They were once again hunched over their NATO ordinance map, sharing its space with dishes left over from their evening meal.

"As far as I can tell, we can tie up about fifty meters from this point here," Dan said, pointing to a blue line on the map that indicated a distant portion of the canal only a few kilometers distant. "From what this map states and according to my sources, there is a small dirt road that runs parallel to the canal. Looks like a road only locals and tourists similar to us would probably use."

Dan pointed to a predetermined spot on the map marked by a bright red cross before continuing. "If we moor up here, we won't be noticed by anyone unless someone is actually searching for us. If you notice the terrain, it's isolated, with several farms on both sides combined with a natural bend in the canal. There should also be enough shrubs and trees to provide perfect cover for us and this big tug we have here."

Jim allowed his finger to traverse the map to the town of Weimar trying to gauge the distance from the canal. "What do you estimate the time frame for our travel to the farm?"

Dan used a metal compass to measure the distance from that nights mooring point, to the town of Weimar. He then applied the distance to the legend at the bottom of the map. With pencil in hand, he performed a quick calculation.

"If we hit no traffic and average about ninety to a hundred kilometers per hour, we should be there about midnight," he replied confidently. "And if we immediately get to work, we could be out of there by 4:00 or 5:00 a.m. Then if my calculations hold-up we should be back here five or six hours after that."

Jim looked over to Dan, seeming to concur. "We need your man to come through for us," he said.

Dan's expression turned serious at Jim's off-hand comment, rising slowly, allowing the map to roll up unaided. "I assure you on my life, young Dieter, we can depend on this man. He is a cousin on my mother's side, God bless her soul. He owes me a great deal for some work I performed for him a long time ago. It's another one of those stories that I could tell you, but someone with your American attention span would probably get bored very quickly."

Jim could sense he hit a nerve and knew it was a subject to drop right then and there, nodding in acknowledgment. "Sorry, Dan, I didn't mean to insinuate anything by my comment."

Dan proceeded to the bar, withdrawing a bottle of Irish Mist, pouring two generous shots. He wiped the rim of the glasses with a freshly cut orange piece, He then provided one of the filled glasses to Jim, raising his own glass in toast. "To our families, wherever they may be. May they always find solace in our conversation and eternal presence."

*In his own way, accepting Jim's apology.*

"To your health," Jim replied, raising his glass accordingly, drinking its contents in one quick swallow. "You Irish are so damn poetic. Can you just say cheers and let it be?"

"But I need to drink to the success of my cousin," Dan said, a slight grin evident upon his face. "That was a solemn blessing in disguise."

"Sorry, it just sounded so poetic," Jim replied.

Dan poured two additional shots of Irish Mist. "Allow me to provide dignity to the author and finish the toast," he said, repeating the same process of sliding an orange piece around the rim of each glass before raising it in the air.

"And if they do not, may they die a painful and lonely death."

## Vatican Special Action Team, The Vatican

THE VATICAN SPECIAL Action Team job description essentially mirrored that of the U.S. Secret Service, to give their lives, if need be, for their charge. The Action Team also had one additional assignment added to its tasking during the late '90s: to act as an elite, mobile, fighting force.

The bunker office was now operating at a feverish pitch. Since the news broke that Dan and Jim were going for The Vatican's treasure, five additional personnel had been added to Perluci's team. They were each busy working phones and computer networks looking for any possible leads and scouring all friendly sources for relevant information on Dieter and Flaherty.

The Vatican hierarchy also called in favors culled from years of service in order to locate them, making this a true priority red.

"Mr. Perluci," shouted one of the new office staff, a rather large woman in her early 30s who reeked of garlic. "One of our people in the French office of Interpol has just contacted us. They have located two possible suspects in the Burgundy region on a sailing barge called the *Jacob*."

Perluci clasped his hands in exaltation. "Excellent. Fine work, Miss Aniti," he said. "Acquire all of the details and send them our deepest thanks."

Turning to his left, he observed his military assistant, Lieutenant Lern of the Swiss Guard, having just arrived. "Lieutenant, you are just in time. I want you to call the airport and make preparations for our jet to fly in the morning."

Perluci consulted one of the many detailed maps on his office wall before continuing. "From Burgundy to Weimar should take three to four days by barge if they go full-out, motor ten to fourteen hours a day. I want our team to be there ahead of schedule just in case they have something up their sleeve. This is our big break. If all goes according to plan we should be in the area of Dieter's farm by 5:00 p.m. tomorrow."

Lieutenant Lern was familiar with Perluci's tact for planning an operation without consulting its members or its executive officer. *Who knows better than Perluci, than Perluci?* It was a running joke in the bunker. Having been his second-in-command for several years, he relished the day when Perluci would simply retire so he could take command and employ newer-style tactics.

"Mr. Perluci," Lieutenant Lern replied. "I have been familiarizing myself with the area surrounding Weimar and would suggest we concentrate all of our resources down by the river. If our subjects are due to approach by barge, it would be easier for us to locate and then follow them in. We could allow them to depart the barge unmolested, locate our product, and return with our product to the barge. They would be performing all of the work for us. We then confiscate the product and in the process capture our suspects.

# THE VATICAN's LAST SECRET

Perluci pondered the man's modest suggestion for a moment.

"Excellent idea, Lieutenant. Why should we divide our forces in the town of Weimar when they must sail up the river? We could then choose to follow them to the farm or wait on the boat and allow them to bring the gold and paperwork to us," he said as if it were his own idea.

"You are a wise man. I can see that with you in control, this operation should proceed smoothly," Lieutenant Lern replied, turning away, knowing who would receive credit for his suggestion.

## French Interpol along the Canal Road

THE BOXY CITROEN auto requisitioned from the government carpool suffered from a common compliant typical of most low-end European autos: it was small and drastically underpowered. The car would be a perfect choice for a trip around a crowded city, but not built to handle rough country driving, especially off-road driving. The car was no match for the small, winding, pot-hole-laden roads prevalent throughout the rural regions of France, where a secondary road could still consist of dirt or crushed stone.

Rebecca had the dubious distinction of scanning the canal for their prey as Inspector Jacko drove the auto at a steady 25 kilometers per hour.

"Inspector, we should have rented a powerboat instead of chasing them in this car," she said, appealing to the inspectors better judgment

"Wrong, Mrs. Lenine. This is the way to go," the inspector snapped in retort. "I know it has its drawbacks, but the auto is faster and more maneuverable for this type of operation. Plus we could lose the element of surprise. The people we are trailing would undoubtedly hear a powerboat from over a hundred meters away. No, I think this is best. That is why I am the inspector and you are the detective. You could learn from me, Mrs. Lenine. Now stay in your pay grade and watch the canal."

Rebecca rolled her eyes in response to the inspector's comments, *not wanting to antagonize the beast any further.*

If not for a flat tire and then an unfortunate encounter with a herd of sheep blocking their route, they quite possibly could have caught up with their prey in the light of day. Now, with the evening hour fast approaching, they would have to apprehend their subjects in a nighttime environment, never an appealing prospect in police work.

"Mrs. Lenine," Inspector Jacko said, "If our friend Arto was correct in his assessment of the boats maximum speed and course, we should be able to overtake them in a few hours."

He looked to her for confirmation.

She smiled curtly in response.

"Damn it, Mrs. Lenine, I just love the idea of an attack in the dark. We will have the element of surprise on them."

Rebecca Lenine pondered her boss's comments for a moment—*wondering who would be surprising whom?*

# THE VATICAN's LAST SECRET

# CHAPTER 26

**FORTE LOCKS – BURGUNDY, FRANCE**

The Euro Star's short journey under the English Channel arrived on schedule, to the minute. Upon reaching Paris, the SAS team switched to a nondescript rental van for travel to the Forte Locks.

A few hours' drive on the main highway enabled them to cover the distance in a relatively short time, pulling into the Forte Locks' parking area by late afternoon.

"I want you three to stay with the van, and let me talk to the lockkeeper alone," Captain Robinson said to his men. Exiting the van, he walked to where the lockkeeper was busily performing his duties.

Two, wooden, seven-meter pleasure craft were presently in the lock. Aligned side-by-side, they demanded the full attention of the lockkeeper as he prepared to open the doors to the upper level of the canal and allow the boats to be on their way.

# THE VATICAN's LAST SECRET

The Captain waited until Arto had the lock doors fully opened and the passengers had reboarded before approaching him.

"Good day, sir," the Captain said in impeccable French, garnered from his years at Sandhurst. "I am trying to gain information on some company you may have had recently."

Arto untied the small boats port lines thus enabling both boats to get underway at the same time. "Just give me a second, young man, while I cast this rope off," he said, tossing the ropes onto the departing boats deck.

Arto turned slightly to the Captain as he spoke in a hushed tone, waving politely to the now-receding figures. "These damn tourists are an impatient lot and tend to get a little mad if I do not devote my full attention to getting them on their way. Can you believe those people? They would not even look at my flowers or vegetables for sale." He pointed to his neatly arranged wooden boxes of brightly colored roses and fresh produce situated alongside the canals towpath. "How do they expect me to survive at this job without selling something on the side?"

The Captain simply nodded.

"My apologies. I sometimes go off on a tangent. Must be old age getting to me. Now you were saying something about the company I may have had recently?"

Having practiced his ruse for the past hour with his troops on the drive down from Paris, the Captain stood ready to play his role. "Yes, sir. My brother said he was going on holiday with an American friend of his. He mentioned something about renting a barge or some kind of large boat. I honestly wasn't listening at the time, but I did pick up that he would be motoring on about this region of France. Unfortunately, my mother has suffered injuries in a terrible car accident in Ireland that has put her close to death.

Arto tapped the Captain on his arm before speaking. "You say that you are related, eh. Why don't you do us both a favor and cut the bullshit and tell me the real reason you require information on the Irishman and the American? I can tell by your accent you are not Irish." Arto stepped back, surveying the Captain from head-to-toe. "Also, by the look of you, I'd say you're either a cop or in the military, possibly anti-terrorist or SAS if my wits are still about me. Let's start again with a second introduction." Arto extended his hand in greeting. "My name is Arto. I am a retired policeman from the Paris Gendarme."

The Captain looked slightly embarrassed as he shook Arto's hand, taking time to wave to his cohorts in the van, a prearranged signal that indeed everything was okay.

"A retired policeman? I should have known better. I apologize for trying to deceive you. Let's give it another go." He produced his British Military identification for Arto to inspect before continuing. "I am tracking a possible terrorist. And those gentlemen in the van behind me are my team members," pointing over his shoulder to his anxious mates.

Arto waved to them before focusing on the Captain's identification badge, fingering it for any alterations that could prove it a forgery.

"If we could get some basic information, we will be on our way," the Captain said.

"You are the second group to come through here inquiring about my visitors," Arto said, realizing his comment would raise the Captain's interest and possibly up his expected generosity. "Interpol came through late this morning, and I only told them what I will tell you, that the suspects are on their way toward Dijon," pointing past the lock towards the canal. "They were using the barges motor at a good speed when they came in and when they left. In my best judgment, they should be a good 50 kilometers from Dijon—that is if they stuck to the main canal and are still operating at full speed."

Arto started to rearrange his assortment of carrots and tomatoes, in doing so calling attention to his produce. "They were also kind enough to buy some of my vegetables for their reefer and flowers for their table," he said, waiting for the Captain's expression to change from serious to one of understanding.

"Would you be offering any type of reward for this type of information?" Not waiting for a reply, Arto continued. "Interpol, those cheap bastards, provided me nothing for my information." He spat on the ground in disgust.

The Captain realized Arto was holding back on something else, waiting to throw his trump card down if it were lucrative enough. "Yes, I think that something could be arranged, Mr. Arto."

Turning toward the van, the Captain yelled to his second-in-command. "Sergeant, please bring 500 pounds over here for our new-found friend," he yelled. "I wish to reward this man for valuable information to her majesty's government."

Arto eyed the sergeant as he jogged to where they stood, a bundle of notes wrapped in a paper band from the Bank of England in hand. "Thank you, kind sir," he said to the Captain, grateful for his generosity. "The English have always been my best customers through the locks. They are always so kind and generous. They usually purchase all of my flowers when they are in season." Arto eyed the sergeant hand over the new bills to the Captain who in turn handed them to Arto.

Arto placed them in his vest pocket. "You know what else, sir? He continued. "Since you were so kind with your reward, I would like to provide you with something else that may assist you in your mission."

The Captains hunch was correct. The little man was holding back on some valuable information and just wanted a little money to pry it loose. This was one of the first lessons he learned at counter-terrorism school, money or booze will prompt even the most faithful to talk. *The bait having been provided, it was time for the fish to jump into the boat.*

"Any information that you could provide would greatly benefit us," the Captain said, casually dismissing his sergeant with a nod.

Arto pointed back over to the Captains van. "Well, the French police are driving down that side road," he said. "And it runs parallel at most points to the canal where it provides you with decent enough coverage to see below. The possibility still exists that you could drive past the barge if it were, say, nestled in a grouping of trees or scrubs."

He paused several seconds before continuing in a slow deliberate tone. "What if I told you there is a way for you to catch up to the barge at about the same time as the French Police?" Arto searched the Captains face for some sort of understanding.

The Captain looked at the canal where a boat rested on the banks, its bow protruding from under a tarp.

"I told them the longer way because they were so cheap. And I was not going to show them my boat, or they would have confiscated it in the name of the police," Arto said, laughing aloud.

For the moment, Arto turned serious, attempting his best sales technique. "But for you, I will lease the boat for only 200 English pounds and throw in a full tank of gas." He led the Captain over to where his twenty-foot 1998 American Chris-Craft was resting half in the canal, half on shore. "Isn't she a beauty? I bought her from an American serviceman over in Germany. She purrs like a kitten and has a top speed of twenty-two knots to boot, faster than what you could achieve on that damn dirt road with all of its twists and turns."

The Captain stepped into the boat to gauge its condition. "Would the barge hear our approach?

"Not necessarily, Captain. They would only hear you if they were docked for the night. They are operating an old eight-cylinder Detroit diesel that happens to make a lot of noise if you know what I mean," covering his ears and whistling aloud. "But you could sneak up on them while they are still moving and await their night stoppage point, overtaking them under the cover of darkness."

# THE VATICAN's LAST SECRET

Captain Robinson turned back to the van, motioning for the rest of the team to join him. "You are a gentleman, Mr. Arto. It looks like we are taking a river cruise."

# CHAPTER 27

**ABOARD THE "JACOB"**

"That's our signal, two quick red flashes," Dan said, slowing the rate of speed on the Jacob, maneuvering close to a spot where the light had originated.

Dan flipped a switch in the cabin in order to shut the engines down as Jim moved forward to assist in the barges mooring.

The stillness of the night was deafening as the engines grumbled to a halt.

With the trees' dense canopies spread over the canal and dusk already an hour past, Jim probed the water's edge with the flashlights beam.

A slight fellow stepped out from behind an overgrown holly bush no more than fifteen meters from the barge. In a thick Irish brogue, he yelled. "Hello to you on the Jacob. May I approach?"

Jim searched the woods for the mysterious voice, his flashlights beam probing left to right. "Only if you show yourself and put your hands where we can see them," he said in reply.

"I'm in the open for all to see my American friend. Just switch off that bloody torch," the stranger said. Satisfied he wasn't going to take a bullet, he moved toward the Jacob to assist in its docking. The stranger then tied the bow and stern ropes to the nearest trees to secure for the night.

Satisfied, the stranger approached to where Jim was busy lowering the wooden gangway.

Dan brushed past Jim, pulling the man aboard with a sturdy grip in the same instant.

"Sean, you old bugger, how is my favorite cousin," he said in greeting, holding him at arms' length before hugging him.

"Favorite cousin is it now? Sean said in reply. "Well that's a change from the last time we met. I must say you are a man blessed with the words, Dan, or should I just call you Father Dan?"

A select few of Dan's family were privy to the occupation he had assumed while he hid in the Americas.

Dan led Sean toward the barges dining room, Jim close on their heels. "I see my exploits are still making the family proud, something to talk about at the holiday gatherings," he said.

"They always have," Sean said. "And we'd still talk about you anyway."

Sean handed Dan a green canvas duffel bag, one that would have pushed the airline requirements for fitting in an overhead aircraft compartment.

Dan laid it carefully by the gangway as if already aware of its contents.

"You're a sight for sore eyes, Sean," Dan said. "Let us have a short nip to celebrate what will, unfortunately, be a brief family reunion." He waited for his cousin's grin to fade as he viewed the comfortable accommodations aboard the Jacob.

Sean whistled before blessing himself for having such luck.

On the bar, Dan had poured three generous shots of Bushmills. "I apologize in having to make do with just a wee dram, but you know the rationale of why you're here," he said, serious for the moment. "The only other information I can disclose is that Jim and myself have a long distance to travel tonight.

As he raised his glass, Dan wondered if either man truly realized the danger they were in. "Cheers, slancha, my friends," he said. The drink complete, Dan patted his cousin's shoulder in affection. "Sean, my dear cousin, we are about to see if the proverbial pot of gold truly does exist at the end of the rainbow."

**French Interpol, Somewhere along the Canal Road**
ARTO's DETAILED INSTRUCTIONS and well-known shortcuts turned out to be a case of one mistaken turn after another. This allowed a bitter source of frustration to exist between the Inspector and Rebecca. They decided it best to discard Arto's shortcuts and stick to the canals path.

They expected to overtake their prey in four to six hours if everything proceeded according to plan. Unfortunately for them, the drive now approached its eighth hour.

To their surprise, the canal had a steady clientele of holiday boaters and vacation barges. The roads vantage point above the canal didn't always provide them with an unobstructed view. They had to stop and check each and every barge along the way for the elusive Jacob. This only added precious time to their journey.

The Inspector looked over to Rebecca, his frustration clearly mounting. "I thought the objective of a shortcut was to save time not add it," he said sarcastically. "If that bastard purposely gave us these shortcuts to slow us down, I'm going to make sure his police pension check is lost in the shuffle."

"Slow down, Inspector," Rebecca implored, ignoring his last comment along with the previous ones he had dispensed during the torturous ride she had to endure. "I think there is another barge just ahead. Look off to your left-hand side at about a hundred meters," her arm crossing his field of vision.

"Mrs. Lenine, I can't see the damn road while your arm is waving in front of me," he scowled at her, brushing her arm away. He slowed the car down to a crawl, looking for a place to park on the narrow road before maneuvering the car to a clearing.

"I think you may be right, Mrs. Lenine. This could be our subjects," he said. Darkness hindered an actual reading of the full name on its stern, only a large "J" visible to the naked eye. "Use the infrared scope and give us a read on the name while I consult the map for our exact location."

Rebecca aimed the bulbous scope at the barge. The night's full moon only aided her, allowing her to focus on the barge with extra clarity. She professionally adjusted the dials mounted on the unit, maximizing its magnification. "Yes, sir, it's the Jacob alright," she said in exhilaration. "We have finally caught up with them."

The Inspector looked up and down the dirt road. "Mrs. Lenine, I say we park 500 or so meters from the barge and approach from up along the riverbank. We can use all of this overgrown shrubbery as cover. I also want to double check and make sure that this is our Jacob and not some vacationers on their honeymoon when we burst in. This tricky bastard could have painted the Jacob's name on another barge just to throw us off."

"Inspector, don't you think we should wait for full darkness instead of this fading light for our approach?" she replied. "We don't want the possibility of making our prey skittish, do we? From the looks of their docking ropes, they should be tied up for the night."

"You may have a point, Mrs. Lenine," he said.

"I think we passed a small bistro about two kilometers back. We should probably grab something to eat and inquire about the local police presence."

"No local police involvement," the Inspector spat out, not intending on sharing his spotlight. "This has been a carefully laid-out plan from the beginning. A fine bit of detective work I'd say. No common officer will share in our moment of triumph. Besides, there are only two of them, and we shall have the element of surprise. What could possibly go wrong?"

**SAS Group, along the Canal**
Approaching its sixth hour, the seven-meter Chris-Craft motorboat churned at its maximum speed of 22 knots. With dusk passing two hours before, the night's darkness would only aid them in their assault.

"I'm slowing down, Captain. Barge dead ahead, 500 meters, starboard side," the team's youngest member, Private Crumfield said. He wore an awkward fitting night vision gear strapped to his head, its single lens presenting him with a clear image bathed in an eerie green and white. "She looks to be moored for the night to some beech trees, sir."

"All right, Crumbfield," the Captain replied. "Have a look on 70 magnification and slow us down to five knots so we don't startle the buggers.

Adjusting the unit's magnification, Crumbfield scanned the deck for any evidence of movement. "She's the Jacob, sir. You can see her white lettering on the stern," he replied.

"Okay, sergeant, take the helm from Crumbfield," the Captain said. "I want you to motor past but slowly. I want to get a positive ID on the boat and check out the territory we have to traverse tonight. We can't afford to screw this one up, not on French soil."

The Captain turned his trained eye back to the barge, looking for any weaknesses as their Chris-Craft slowed to almost a crawl. His assessment complete, the Captain then ordered the boat to shore no more than a hundred meters in front of the barges mooring point, just out of view of the barge. Once on shore, they quickly unloaded their gear.

The Captain focused his tripod-mounted night vision unit on the moored Jacob. The tripod scope differed from the head-mounted unit in that it also came complete with a built-in microphone that was capable of picking up sounds up to 200 meters.

With everything checked and ready to go, the team assembled around Captain Robinson for the final brief on their mission.

"All right, gentlemen, from the record we have on this bugger, he prefers to indulge in a few drinks after his main meal. Based on this information, we will attack the subjects after they've had their nightcap and a little time to settle in." He looked at his luminescent Swiss watch for the correct time before proceeding, "which should be in about an hour or so."

The Captain removed his canteen, taking a drink, passing it around to the others, before continuing. "I want Crumbfield and you, Sergeant, to perform our classic vessel attack. Take the boat and use its wooden paddles to glide up to the port side of the Jacob. Verify my position, then board, sweeping from bow to stern. I will enter from the starboard side via the land route and sweep from stern to bow. Private Swift, you will stay here with the equipment and monitor our progress."

Each nodded in understanding.

The Captain continued. "We have practiced this maneuver many times on our hostage course. Now it counts for the money boys. One thing in our favor, we don't have to worry about hostages being onboard, so shoot to kill if they don't immediately surrender.

"Gentleman, if all goes according to plan, we should have our two trophies back home in time for breakfast."

### Aboard the "Jacob"

SEAN McMINN ADMIRED his cousin's generosity, having left him the keys to a luxurious barge and close to fifteen thousand American dollars to boot. Too bad there was a hint of danger or he could have brought along the wife and kids.

The barge itself came stocked with filet steaks, prawns, and plenty of booze. Dan even instructed him to keep the barge out for as long as he wanted, *forcing* Sean to have a free vacation in the sun. He did realize a slight danger was to be associated with the job. His cousin briefed him on that particular aspect prior to his accepting the job. But what the hell, with Belfast unemployment approaching ten percent, he'd take any work he could lay his hands on.

Using the full amenities the gourmet kitchen provided, Sean cooked himself a lovely steak dinner before moving in on a bottle of whiskey. Adjourning from the kitchen, he settled into a leather chair situated conveniently next to the bar—pouring himself another generous glass.

Sean sat contemplating how many days to stay in the area when a noise startled him, not a noise that would normally be associated with the everyday workings of a barge. It sounded something along the lines of a champagne cork popping.

The barge tilted ever so slightly from side-to-side.

Sean grabbed his Meisser semiautomatic that lay beside him.

"Dan and Jim can't be back already," he said aloud, deciding it would be best if he sought safety behind the heavy wooden bar.

# THE VATICAN's LAST SECRET

"**MRS. LENINE, YOU** take the stern and walk around midship, I'll take what appears to be one of the bedrooms and walk forward," the inspector whispered. This being his first operation involving weapons in years, his nerves were a bit frayed. "And put your silencer on that damn weapon. We do not need the locals reporting a shootout. We have to do this as quietly as possible."

Rebecca was moving just ahead of him. She tried to screw the silencer on in the dark, but dropped it to the deck of the boat creating a loud metallic pop for all to hear. She recouped by efficiently scooping it up and professionally screwing it on in a matter of seconds.

Inspector Jacko was furious, slowly shaking his head.

Rebecca had hoped for this to be her big moment. Now he would return to make crude jokes to her teammates about her ineptness. *I'll show that chubby bastard.*


**SEAN DETECTED THE** movement of at least one and possibly two persons who had come aboard. He leaned heavily against the bars mahogany, switching off the bars light in the process, plunging the galley and lounge into darkness. But not a total darkness. The night's quarter moon streaked in just enough through the open window blinds on both sides of the salon.

Fingering his weapon, he once again checked to ensure a full magazine. Sean quickly thought of three possibilities as he removed the weapons safety. The most obvious would be Dan and Jim have returned. Second would be thieves coming aboard to rob tourists flush with cash. Or, lastly, his cousin's enemies he had warned him about.

He was hoping for the third.

**REBECCA EASED HERSELF** along the barges portside walkway, the walkway no more than one-half meter wide, careful not to slip into the canals murky waters to her left. Moving silently, she passed what appeared to be the galley area, its metal pans hanging from overhead racks. She noticed a door ajar three meters ahead. She allowed her weapon to lead the way as she eased it open. She paused several moments, allowing her eyes to adjust to the staterooms darkness. Moonlight streamed in through the window blinds' narrow slots, providing the rooms only source of light. Pushing forward, her heart raced, looking from left to right, out of the corner of her eye, she noticed movement.

**SEAN KEPT PEAKING** out from his confined space, pinned between the end of the bar and a floor-to-ceiling wooden post, his attention directed toward where the Inspector slowly crept forward.

**REBECCA FOLLOWED THE** moons narrow beams of light that formed paths in the room's darkened interior, the light seemingly urging her forward. With this as her guide, she crept to within five meters of Sean's position. She could now hear his rapid breathing, her own breathing increasing in time so loud she was sure it would give away her position.

Rebecca pulled her gun up to her lips, kissing it softly, saying a silent prayer. After many years of practice on the gun range, never having fired her gun in anger, she felt that streak was about to end.

**SEAN WATCHED THE** Inspector creep toward his position. Being presented with a somewhat large and clear shot, he brought his gun up to fire.

# THE VATICAN's LAST SECRET

**INSPECTOR JACKO** pushed forward, finger on his weapons trigger.

Rebecca stood up boldly declaring: "Police. Drop your weapon," aiming her weapon at the dark shadow in front of her, "and put your hands in the air."

Inspector Jacko moved within three meters of Sean's position, now leveling his own weapon in the same general direction as Rebecca, still searching for a target.

Sean could see the portly man in front of him producing a silver badge that glistened in the nights moonlight.

Sean quickly crossed off robbery as a motive. "Well, at least you're not here to take my valuables," he said, still greedily fingering his weapon, its steel barrel pointed at the Inspector.

He would not go peaceably with the police. They would only turn him over to Scotland Yard, and he would be in an English prison for a long run.

"Bastards," Sean cried aloud, diving to the floor, firing in front of him at the Inspector, his three shots missing wide left.

The Inspector in turn emptied his gun in Sean's general direction, missing widely, most of the shots impacting the wooden bar with a series of sharp cracks.

Rebecca watched as Sean dove for the floor, keeping her poise and waiting for the Inspector to shoot the man practically at his feet.

The Inspector hastily tried to reload his weapon as Sean leveled his own weapon, laughing aloud at the Inspector's predicament.

Rebecca fired instantly in response, killing Sean with two well-placed shots to the upper torso. Moving in quickly, she stood with her arms extended, her weapon leveled at Sean. After a few seconds, she searched for a light switch.

With the lights now on, the Inspector appeared as pale as a piece of Gambian ivory, mopping his brow with a handkerchief.

"Mrs. Lenine, I must commend you on your shooting," he said, turning the body over with his foot.

"But enough of this, we still have one more," he said, quickly gaining his composure, scanning the area once more. "By the deceased's accent, we have our Irishman. Now let us concentrate on the American. He has to be around here somewhere."

# THE VATICAN's LAST SECRET

# CHAPTER 28

**AUTOBAHN, FRANKFURT GERMANY**

Jim assumed the driving duties since their departure from the barge. No need for their being stopped for a traffic citation at this stage of their mission. A nosey traffic cop was just as dangerous as anyone else possibly on their tail.

"You drive like a bloody old woman on Prozac, you know that?" Dan said, amusing himself as he tormented Jim on his cautious driving. "Now, can you step on the gas and do 120 like everyone else who is passing us? Hell, that old man in a BMW just gave you the finger for driving so slow. *And it was his arthritic finger to boot.*"

Jim smiled. "Hell, if you want to drive then you take the wheel. Be my guest little man. I've had the wheel for going on three hours now, and by my calculation we should still be there on schedule."

Dan brushed aside his comment, looking out the window at the passing scenery, obviously bored. "Come on, Jim, can't you take a little ribbing? I was just, as you Americans are fond of saying 'pulling your chain' and keeping you awake in the meantime. Don't be so uptight."

Dan looked out the window for several minutes, deep in thought before he turned to Jim. "I hope my bloody cousin is taking care of the boat and not having any wild parties."

Jim increased the speed for Dan's sake. "I'm sure he can take care of himself. He's a big boy."

Dan mimicked an old-west gunfighter by drawing two imaginary weapons from the hip. "And pretty good with a gun, I might add. I taught him myself. But you're right. He's a big boy and will do just fine."

## **SAS Team, along the Canal**

THE BRITISH SAS TEAM had been monitoring the Jacob for close to an hour. They now sought permission from headquarters for the next phase of their operation to proceed.

The Captain dialed a number into his secure satellite phone. Several seconds elapsed before the call was routed through Cheltenham's secure communications network and forwarded to General Parker's cell phone.

The General picked up on the second ring.

"General, the team is in place and ready to proceed," the Captain said. "We have detected movement by our subjects onboard the barge. Repeat, we have movement by our subjects." The Captain once again eyed the target with his night vision gear. "General, it has to be them. I have to admit our glimpse of the subjects was quick before they ducked into the galley, but it's definitely the barge, and there are two subjects onboard. I say we are a go, sir."

General Parker brushed his corgi dog off his lap, sitting upright in his bathrobe, the room about him dark with the exception of the glow from his computer screen. Having left the base hours before, he chose to monitor the operations progress in the comfort of his home office.

"All right, based on your recommendation, you are a go Captain. Make it count. And you better bloody well cover your tracks."

"Thank you, sir. You can count on us," the Captain replied. Turning to face his men, they eagerly awaited his orders.

"Show time, gentlemen."

**"INSPECTOR," REBECCA SAID,** "I searched this barge from top to bottom, but found no evidence of Dieter or anyone else on board. Do you think he went out for a walk and could be on his way back here as we speak?"

"He could be," the Inspector replied. "I think it's best if we just sit and wait for our little American friend to come back and then we can nab him. "We are going to plan a little…

"Did you hear that?" Rebecca interrupted him. "I think someone just came on board. Dim the lights and take cover."

**CAPTAIN ROBINSON ANTICIPATED** as much as he adjusted his night vision goggles for the low-light environment. "I think we have our pigeons, boys," he said, speaking into his helmet-mounted microphone as he apprised his team members of the situation in the salon area.

"Private, I want you take the bow door. Sergeant, you take the starboard side. When I give the signal, rake the entire salon with machine-gun fire before entering, but for God's sake do not hit any windows. Aim for the wooden area if you can. The windows make too much noise. We are using silencers for a good reason. Now let's go."

# THE VATICAN's LAST SECRET

**"INSPECTOR," REBECCA SAID** peering out into the darkness by the salons side door. "I see more than one shadow out there, and they look to be armed with machine guns."

"It has to be our American friend Mr. Dieter, who has evidently come back to roost with a few friends of his own," the Inspector replied.

"Should we identify ourselves as police officers now or wait until they've found us?" she replied sarcastically.

"I believe we should stay in hiding and find out how many of his fellow terrorists are out there before we make a move."


**"I'M FOUR METERS FROM** the salon door, gentlemen. Are you in place?" Captain Robinson queried.

"We are in place, sir, on the starboard side door and out of the way of any possible friendly fire from your angle," the sergeant replied.

All right, on the count of three open up on full automatic, repeat full automatic and remember to aim for the areas that are absent of glass," the Captain said.

"Okay. One, two, three…

# CHAPTER 29

**AUTOBAHN, OUTSIDE OF WEIMAR**

"We should be there in close to 30 minutes by my calculations. Do you agree?" Dan said.

Jim nodded. "Barring any unforeseen traffic tie-ups, I would say you are, pardon the pun, *right on the money*. Maybe another 30 kilometers, tops."

Several kilometers passed by before Jim broke the silence, his curiosity getting the best of him. "So Dan, do you have any plans for your share of the money? Or do you intend to donate all of it to charity?"

"Funny man, aren't you," Dan said, propping his feet up on the dash, contemplating his response. "My share of the money will fund a nice retirement, a stylish one at that, my friend. After all these years of living this false life, I have a chance to start over, a completely new life with no strings for someone to pull. Then, my boy, I'm going to up and vanish to the Florida Keys."

Jim smiled. "Up and vanish, just like that, eh?"

"Look at me with a straight face and say I can't," Dan replied. "I'm the proverbial wanted man. I have done it before. This wouldn't be the first time," closing his eyes as if already contemplating his new life. "Sweet Jesus, I can see me now."

Jim laughed aloud before responding. "What would someone like you do in the Keys: Fish? Chase women? Play cards? I can see you with a fishing pole laying back on your yacht drinking a nice margarita while dealing a hand of poker with a nice-figured blond on your lap."

"Check, check, check: correct on all of the above except for the drink," he said. "A nice cool glass of the Irish if you must but I could become accustomed to one of those Margaritas they fancy down there. I don't want to seem anti-social."

"My apologies. Drinking a nice, tall glass of Irish," Jim shot back.

"You paint a nice picture, boyo. But enough of me, what are you going to do with your share?"

"I haven't really given it much thought," he said, studying the road before him, reality hitting him for the first time. He stood to gain more money than he could possibly spend in his lifetime. "You know with me inheriting my father's fortune, I just might become one of those philanthropists like Bill Gates and give most of it away."

"Give it away you say?" Dan sat up rapt with attention, a look of surprise crossing his face. "You're truly a virtuous man, Jim Dieter, a man of dignity. Yes sir, a man of dignity." Dan pondered his partner in a completely new light.

"That's me, the dignified man," Jim said, enjoying his new title. "Speaking of being the dignified man, could you tell me where we are? Because the next exit looks to be Weimar."

"Right you are, Mr. Philanthropist," Dan replied, consulting the hand-drawn map for directions. "Exit at Weimar and make a right turn at the fork in the road. Then go straight for 10 kilometers before taking a dirt road turn-off named Bukberg Strasse."

"I can't believe that until last month I wasn't even aware this farm existed," Jim said, anticipating the arrival at something his father held in secrecy all of these years. "We are almost at my father's farm, his hidden pride and joy."

"Wait a minute, Jim. With your fathers passing, don't you mean *your* farm," Dan said, correcting him.

The thought took Jim by surprise. With his father's recent passing, all of the Dieter's properties were indeed legally his.

"You're right, Dan. Let's go to *my farm*," he said, the words lacking any genuine enthusiasm.

"Let's go to my farm," he said once more, the words trailing off into the night.


### Aboard the "Jacob"

"GENERAL," CAPTAIN ROBINSON said into his secure satellite phone, his voice remaining calm considering the circumstances. "We have mission failure, repeat, mission failure." He looked over at the bodies as they lay side by side, a white sheet covering their outline except for an exposed female foot. "We have taken down one male and one female, who according to their IDs are attached to Interpol. Repeat, we have removed two police officers. We have no sign of our subjects. There was already one dead body on board, and he was most likely killed by one of our deceased. I suggest we get a cleaning crew over here straight-away and immediately shut our operation down."

General Parker moved about his homes darkened hallway, struggling to tie his flannel bathrobe, having been awakened from a sound sleep by Captain Robinson's phone call. Making his way downstairs to the study as to not arouse his wife, he brushed aside the fog of having only one hour's sleep. "You have no idea where they went? He said, attempting to light a cigarette. "There was no visible sign at all?"

The Captain once again eyed the two dead bodies, suppressing the sudden urge to be sick. Even someone like himself could still become faint at the sight of a dead body. *The ones that were on your side were especially hard to take.*

"Zero idea at this point sir," he replied. "My recommendation at this juncture is to cut our losses and regroup at home base."

General Parker gave up on lighting his cigarette as he placed the half-empty pack on his cluttered desk. "I concur with your assessment, Captain. I'll get some people over there to assist, but it's going to take a few hours to assemble a team so stay onboard and don't let anyone see you. We don't need a diplomatic incident especially with the damn French."

"Will do, sir," the Captain was quick to reply. "Over and out."

**Vatican Special Action Team, Weimar**
THE VATICAN SPECIAL Action Team arrived the night before via a private jet at a little used auxiliary German military field, five kilometers southwest of Weimar. They were quickly spirited away by the local police chief, yet another member of the Vatican's extensive network of sympathizers. They lodged at his private home near the river. By sheer coincidence the same river the barge was expected to arrive on.

After a nights rest, the Vatican team spread out along the banks of the River near the outskirts of town. The barge would have to pass by their position in order to reach the Dieter farm. Posing as fisherman on vacation, they awaited the arrival of the "Jacob." The ruse was a simple one since the area was known for its abundance of trout. The team attracted little attention because of the popularity of the sport in the area. Based on information they received before departing Rome, the barge would arrive by early afternoon.

One of the Vatican Special Team members cautiously approached Perluci. To anyone seeing them from afar they were two fishermen discussing bait tactics or fish stories.

"Mr. Perluci, sir. I mean no disrespect, but don't you think it would have been more beneficial for you to stay in Rome, leaving the mission details to your younger men?" asked his executive officer, Lieutenant Lern. "We have performed this type of operation on numerous occasions."

"Yes, I am aware, Lieutenant. In my position as a supervisor for Special Operations, I am most familiar with everything that goes on in my branch. Thank you for your concern, but I've been doing this for over sixty years. Now please just shut up and take any orders that come your way. Understood?"

The casually clad lieutenant betrayed his military bearing, snapping to attention to Perluci's order, potentially undermining the operation if anyone happened to be watching them. "Loud and clear, sir. I did not mean to imply…"

"Yes, you did, Lieutenant. Now re-deploy those two men opposite us another 300 meters further down the riverbank and await further instructions."

## Dieter Farm outside of Weimar

BUKBERG STRASSE WAS a street in name alone, one that mapmakers tended to drop due to its *'rural attributes.'* The rut-filled, rock-laden dirt road could barely accommodate the width of their truck, making for slow going, especially at night. Tall hedges grew wild on each side, scratching the sides of the truck as it maneuvered down the narrow road. But the combination of night and hedges did provide one benefit: they hid the truck from onlookers. For Jim and Dan they couldn't have requested a better location.

With Dan now driving, Jim concentrated on his father's hand-drawn map.

"Do us a favor and don't hit anything like you did with the barge back at the canal. Okay?" Jim pleaded, extracting sweet revenge for some of Dan's earlier barbs.

The hedges on both sides of the road brushed against the trucks side mirrors as Dan struggled to keep the truck on the narrow road.

"Jocularity, young Dieter. Never lose it," Dan said as the truck swayed from side-to-side. "You have a keen eye and a good sense of judgment for detail. As you have so kindly noted, I try to apply myself a hundred percent for all tasks, whether it's screwing up on piloting a barge through a lousy French canal lock or finishing a bottle of good wine. My father, god rest his soul, always told me, *'If you're going to accomplish anything in life, do it all the way through and not half-assed. Leave that for the everyday man.'* He was a man of few words yet profound ones at that."

"Hold up here," Jim said excitedly. They both followed the dim light afforded by the trucks headlights as they viewed an opening in the hedges, a graveyard just beyond it. "This is it, my friend," he said as he consulted the directions that his father had provided. "Yes, this is definitely it. My father said you could not miss it because it was the only graveyard along this stretch of road. I think we have arrived, Dan."

Within minutes, Jim had guided Dan into a tree-covered location with the aid of a flashlight he had located in the glovebox. They had to make sure the truck was entirely off the dirt road and hidden from direct view if anyone were to pass at this early hour.

Dan exited the truck's cab, surveying the area for a quick escape route if need be. Even at this early hour he was constantly on guard. "Now, young Dieter, I would expect you have a rationale for parking in the back of the farm along the darkest road I have ever seen in my life."

"My father said it would be best to park near the gravesites. And I think we have located them." He used the flashlights beam to focus on a group of twenty or so tombstones, they surrounded by an ornamental iron railing. "We can thank Dad for the directions down these dirt roads that are no more than a cow path if you ask me."

Jim directed Dan over to the graveyard with the flashlights beam leading the way. "Now for the fun part, my friend," he said, pausing at the graveyards entrance, its Victorian style Iron Gate slightly ajar. "I'll give you one guess as to where he buried the gold."

"I knew there had to be a reason for our coming in the back way," Dan replied. "That old bastard buried it where nobody would suspect. He buried the gold in the damn graveyard, didn't he?"

Dan relieved Jim of the flashlight, him now probing about the meticulously maintained gravesite.

"That was the main reason my father asked you to leave his room when we visited a few weeks' back. He wanted to discuss the location with me and me alone. For some reason, he didn't want you to know the exact location until we actually arrived."

Jim followed Dan as he maneuvered in between the well-tended stones.

"I'm going to make this real easy for you, *even if you are Irish*," Jim said, looking about the unfamiliar area for what his father said would be the largest stone. He paused upon seeing the majestic stone rise into the night air.

Dan shone the flashlight upon a familiar name engraved on the stone.

"Excellent guess, my friend," Jim said.

Both touched the stone to acknowledge the person buried beneath.

Jim tapped the stone with his forefinger as he turned to Dan. "The gold and documents are buried two meters under the marker on Goot's grave. My father, in all his wisdom, thought that Goot should have the gold as long as possible. One final salute to him. "

"Who would have thought to bury it in a grave?" Dan said. "Especially in Goot's grave—his friend from the war. Brilliant. Bloody brilliant. Yes, it all makes sense now."

"I was just as surprised as you were when Dad disclosed the location. That was the poker player in my father. Let's bluff the world until the end, *then call*."


JIM AND DAN alternated between thirty-minute shifts, one digging and the other resting, this in order to keep fresh for the return drive. After two hours, a grave-sized trench suddenly took shape. They were making excellent progress with almost a meter of dirt having been extracted.

It was Jim's turn in the hole when Dan noticed movement in the woods off and to the left of their position.

Dan dropped a small stone into the hole, hitting Jim's shovel with a soft metallic click, one not audible outside of the hole. Jim looked up to see Dan indicate they had company.

Jim calmly extracted himself from the hole.

"Don't look now, but I think we are being watched," Dan whispered.

"Where?" Jim replied.

"From the direction the sounds originated from, I would say about 10 meters to your left— one o'clock position," Dan whispered. "Whatever you do, don't look. Make them think we haven't noticed them yet."

Jim searched for his weapon, cursing that it wasn't on his person, having left it on another headstone. "Shouldn't we at least prepare to defend ourselves?"

"Every once in while you have a good idea," Dan said, eyeing possible locations where others may lay in wait. "Yes, that might be a good idea, my friend. Slowly make your way to your weapon. When you reach it, dive to your left, and I'll break right. That should draw our company out into the open."

Dan watched until Jim was no more than a foot from his weapon. "Break now, lad."

Jim dove for his weapon rolling for cover behind Goot's tombstone.

The motion by Jim and Dan drew the lone figure out from behind a tree, a burst of semiautomatic fire exploding the earth around them.

"Jesus, who are you? Identify yourself," Dan demanded, slamming a round into his guns chamber, leveling the weapon at the last sighting.

The mysterious figure replied in near perfect English. "I have one question for you both. Would one of you happen to be Mr. James Dieter?"

Jim had sought refuge behind a tombstone whose writing had been obscured by age, looking over awkwardly to Dan.

The mysterious figure waited several seconds before he proceeded. "By your silence and sudden appearance on this property I will assume as much," he said in near perfect English. "Allow me to provide you with some information before we potentially kill one another. Approximately six weeks ago, I received a call from an old friend of mine. The old friend happened to be Hans Dieter. It was right before he died. He informed me that his son would be coming within a few weeks for a visit. Well, if you are him, you sure took your time getting here, didn't you?"

The mysterious figure emerged from behind a tree, his hands up. "I mean you no harm, gentlemen," he said politely, laying his weapon on the ground in front of him as a sign of good faith.

Jim walked toward where the man stood with his hands in the air, still pointing his weapon at the mystery man. If you are a friend of my fathers, why in the hell did you fire at us?"

"Me, fire at you?" responded the older man, a wisp of gray hair covering his head, slightly stooped. "Why did you make such a sudden move? You scared an old man like me. You left me with no choice."

Dan emerged from the shadows, his gun pointed at the mysterious figure. "Sounds like a pretty reasonable excuse to me," he said as he moved closer to inspect the man. "Now that you know who we are, could you please identify who you are?"

"Yes, but of course. Gentlemen, my name is Axel, Axel Schmitz. I have been the caretaker of your father's farm for 70 plus years."

Jim paused for a moment. "Schmitz? I just heard that name used in a story my father told me." The memory of his father suddenly flooding over him. A smile creased his face. "You wouldn't happen to be the same Schmitz that my father helped escape from Berlin during the war?" Not waiting for his reply, he walked over with his arm extended, wanting to shake Schmitz's hand.

"The one and only, Mr. Dieter," replied Schmitz as he grabbed Jim's hand in a bear-like grip. "I owe your father a debt I will never be able to repay. I was sorry to hear of his passing. He was a great man. You should be very proud of him."

Jim fought to control his emotions at finding yet another rock of his father's past overturned. "Thank you. That means a lot coming from someone who knew him from his younger days," he said.

Dan looked to Axel for a moment wondering if the man spoke the truth. "Mr. Schmitz, you mean to tell me that you have been working here for 70 years and you had no idea what lay buried here?"

Axel walked over to the freshly dug grave and peered in to see the progress the two men had made, admiring their work. "Mr. Dieter informed me of the gold only when he called several weeks ago. I had no idea before that."

## THE VATICAN's LAST SECRET

A genuine look of shock spread across Dan's face. "He told you a few weeks ago?" Dan asked. "Why didn't you steal it yourself and run off?"

Axel performed a slow gracious turn from his position near the open grave before he walked over to where Dan stood. "Who said I didn't?"

Dan fell for Schmitz's gag before realizing the joke was on him. "Oh, I like this man, Jimmy," Dan replied, having met someone just as sarcastic as himself.

"No, no, just joking with my new-found friends. I don't need the money," Schmitz, replied. "I am happy with whom and where I am. The gold is not mine to begin with. I just stood guard over it for the past few weeks until you came to pick up what was rightfully yours, Mr. Dieter," pointing over to Jim.

An awkward few moments elapsed before they all laughed aloud at the silliness of the moment, Jim and Axel patting each other on the back.

"Well, I don't mean to interrupt this little midnight garden party, but I must insist we get moving before daylight," Dan said, pointing back to the grave.

"Yes, you're right. We're wasting time," Jim said, turning to face Axel. "Mr. Schmitz, allow me to introduce Mr. Dan Flaherty, a friend of my family. He is also a major player in this little adventure my father cooked up."

"Any friend of your father's is a friend of mine," Axel said, shaking Dan's hand with the same bear-like grip he had provided Jim.

Schmitz pointed over to where a yellow tractor lay secreted beneath an old WWII vintage green and brown camouflage net. "I moved my backhoe down from the barn a couple of weeks ago to assist in your dig," he said. "But don't worry, the townspeople, they won't hear you digging. We are a good half kilometer from the nearest farm, and we are located in a valley where sound will not travel far. Even if they do hear something, they will just think its crazy old Schmitz up working early again."

*Luck had once again raised its glimmering head.*

# CHAPTER 30

**VATICAN SPECIAL ACTION TEAM – WEIMAR**

Perluci's subordinate tossed a small pebble into the river below, obviously angry at the handling of the operation. He turned to face Perluci, his rage boiling. "We have been in position for two days with nothing to show for it. Nothing even resembling a barge has crossed our path."

He allowed Perluci the luxury to run the operation with no questions, but no longer. The time was ripe for a change.

"Mr. Perluci, I don't want to second guess your decisions, but don't you think the time has come to split our forces into two teams? This would enable us to keep surveillance on both the farm and the river."

The Lieutenant realized a decision should have been made a full 24 hours before.

Perluci turned to face the young lieutenant, his face drained of all color, looking through him as if he were part of the background. This act of defiance amounted to a cold slap in the face for Perluci. Was it truly his fault? Maybe the Lieutenant was right. For the first time in his life, Perluci felt powerless. Maybe his superiors were right to insinuate that he was getting too old for this type of operation. In his youth, he would have trailed Flaherty from New York instead of playing the waiting game on the receiving end.

"Excellent idea, Lieutenant. We should split our forces," Perluci's voice trailing off. "I think you should take two men and reconnoiter the farm. From our intelligence, they should have already arrived. When you approach the farm, I want you to check all areas front and back, then split up with one man in front and the second in the rear of the property," his voice lacking the authority it once brandished.

"Yes, sir. I will notify you if we encounter any activity at the farm," the Lieutenant replied.

"Yes, excellent idea, Lieutenant. And another thing," said a visibly shaken Perluci, scrambling for the appropriate words. "Upon our arrival in Rome, I am going to recommend you take my place. You are ready for the job. The time has come. I am going to retire after this one. No more Perluci to kick around."

The Lieutenant concealed his delight.

*If only he realized the higher ups would have relieved him after bungling this job anyway.*

## **DIETER FARM OUTSIDE OF WEIMAR**

With the aid of an aging backhoe, the remaining work moved swiftly. Jim was now in the trench providing guidance to Axel when a loud wooden crack punctuated the night. He signaled for Axel to withdraw the backhoes shovel.

Jim used his flashlight as a probe, quickly pushing aside the wood debris, withdrawing a single bar of gold, waving it in the air triumphantly for all to see. "We did it. We did it, baby," he said, handing the heavy bar up for Dan to scrutinize.

# THE VATICAN's LAST SECRET

Dan held it up for examination under his own flashlight, eyeing it appreciatively, allowing Axel a peek. "Let's not screw around now that we've found it. Let's move it along, Jimmy. We have a schedule to keep."

The backhoe aided considerably in the retrieval of the heavy wooden crates from their entombment. Jim maneuvered each of the twenty by ten-inch crates from the bottom of the earthen hole, placing them into the backhoes bucket, the backhoe then lifting the crates up to the rear of the truck where a waiting Dan removed them and carefully slid each box to the front of the trucks bed.

Thirty minutes elapsed before the last box was removed from the trench, revealing the simple wooden coffin of Goot. Upon seeing the coffin, Jim stopped the men, offering up a moment's reflection for the guardian of the gold.

"This man has performed his last watch," Jim said, executing a near perfect salute. "And may he rest in eternal peace." He tossed a symbolic handful of earth onto his coffin.

Dan performed a sign of the cross, mumbling a simple prayer.

With the retrieval complete, Schmitz used the backhoe to backfill Goot's grave, taking all of five minutes to perform a job that had earlier taken Dan and Jim almost two hours.

They reconvened in the rear of the truck where Dan had rigged two Coleman propane lanterns to provide a well-lit working area.

Jim now fingered a solitary gold bar, having pried open one of the wooden crates with the claw of his hammer. "Look at all this product, and I can't believe how well the wood held up after all these years," allowing his hands to run along the smooth surface of the wood.

Dan shook his head, a devilish smile appearing on his face. "Listen to yourself would you now. You have tens of millions of dollars' worth of gold in front of you and all you want to talk about the quality of the wood on the crates. It must be nice to have so much money that this haul doesn't even faze you."

Jim ignored Dan's comment, focusing on one of the gold bars before him. A puzzled look creased his weary face. His initial view had been in the darkened trench, trying to maintain a balance between a flashlight, shovel, and the gold bar. The well-lit area now afforded him a better view.

"Axel, stop me if I'm wrong here, but didn't the Nazis stamp their German Eagle on everything, especially their gold bullion?"

Axel adjusted the lantern's dial, coaxing some additional light. Satisfied with his efforts, he took the bar in question from Jim and withdrew a pair of bifocals from his overcoat pocket. "You are correct, Mr. Dieter, everything from bullets to gold. Why do you ask?"

Axel moved the bar closer to the light for his inspection.

"Because that is not the symbol for Nazi gold," Jim said, holding up another bar for all to inspect. "This is the symbol for something else, possibly some other country, but definitely not the Nazi government."

Dan realized the time had come to inform his young protégé of the depth of his knowledge. *But how would Jim respond? Would he take the information in stride as with his recent IRA disclosure?* He didn't feel right withholding critical information from his young friend. The twenty-year deception with his father was unfortunate enough. It had to end here and now.

"You're right, Jim," Dan said, picking up a bar of gold to inspect it for himself. Then he held the bar up for all to see. "But to answer your question, the emblem you refer to is the Vatican seal. It was designed hundreds of years ago by some obscure priest lost to time. I know it well," whispered Dan to no one in general. "It's affixed to all official Vatican correspondence or product, which is basically what this shipment was all about."

# THE VATICAN's LAST SECRET

"You mean this gold is church property?" asked Schmitz.

"No, not at all. It was stolen from Jewish concentration camp victims by the Croatian government and then *'transferred'* to the church's possession for safekeeping."

Jim sat back. A look of shock graced his face. The man never ceased to amaze him. He searched for the right words to respond. Taking a deep breath, he proceeded. "That brings up two possible questions, Dan. The first obviously would be how do you know the history of this gold? And secondly, is this the reason why my father was so worried, the church getting wrapped up in a Nazi gold scheme and somehow sharing in its blame?"

Dan felt uncomfortable sitting in the back of the truck, tugging at his shirt collar as if it were a noose about his neck. *So this is what it felt like sitting on the proverbial hot seat*. He eyed Axel and then Jim, both anxiously awaiting Dan's response. "Jim, I told you of my history a few weeks ago, so I won't bore you with the details. Let us get down to the, as you Americans say, the nitty-gritty. I work," stopping to correct himself, "*worked* for the agents of the Vatican. Yes, past tense. Up until two weeks ago, I worked for them before I stopped reporting our operations progress. Before that, I provided them with up-to-date information on our location. They, in turn, used this information to set up a retrieval team, a team that by my best guess is still by the river waiting for our barge to come sailing in. Most likely they were going to allow us to retrieve the gold from the farm and then confiscate it on the way out. But they also had a bigger interest," he said, pointing to the rear of the truck near the makeshift propane lantern workstation. Continuing, he said, "That crate behind you, you may have noticed, is the only oversized crate among the others. That is what the Vatican is really after. In the wrong hands that particular crate would cause untold problems for the Vatican."

Jim looked behind him at the crate Dan spoke of, resting his hand on its wooden surface, knowing his father last touched this same crate some 70 odd years before. "So this would contain the documents my father referred to when he said to *retrieve the gold and documents?*" Not waiting for an answer, he started prying open the case.

"The one and only," Dan replied.

"Mr. Flaherty, you have some explaining to do," Jim said, straining to pull a stubborn slat of wood from the box held securely in place by rusty nails. "Would you be so kind to fill us in on the rest of the storied history that goes along with this collection of gold?" Jim reached into the box, his reward, a worn leather pouch containing a wealth of Nazi stamped documents and photographs.

Dan rapped his knuckles on one of the wooden boxes in front of him as if a judge presiding over his courtroom. "I was waiting for the appropriate time and that would seem to be now. Just the good parts. Bear with me, the story is as old as I am, and it's second hand at best. It was September 1944. The war was proceeding badly for Yugoslavia. Germany had first invaded in 1941, and now the Russian army was advancing on its borders. Early in September of 1944, the Croatian leader, Ante Pavelic, approached his close friend, Gestapo Chief Heinrich Himmler, with a plea for help. Pavelic had millions of dollars' worth of gold stolen from Jews and the Croatian Treasury, but it needed to be moved before the Russians or Partisans overran their positions to some place safe from prying eyes. Himmler immediately realized how the gold could aid them to possibly escape persecution after the war, maybe even be used to buy their way to South America. Soon after, they approached the Vatican with a deal to store the gold in the Vatican Bank. The Vatican agreed based on the condition that the Germans and the Croatians stopped the genocide of Serbs and Jews in their concentration camps.

*In effect, bartering gold for lives.*

The Germans and Croatians had no choice but to agree. Their backs were against the wall. The Vatican then had the gold re-poured in a local Croatian foundry and re-stamped with the Vatican seal." Dan paused for a moment, reaching over to see a gold bar for himself, viewing the Vatican Crest emblazoned on its top, before continuing. "The Germans wanted this operation to seem perfectly legal, so they forced the church to sign receipts for the gold. Not just any clerk would do. They had the Pope flown over in a Luftwaffe Junkers to Osijek, Croatia, and personally sign the receipt. They also had him pose for pictures with Pavelic and Himmler with the gold in the background. After the dignitaries left, the gold was then held at a Catholic Monastery in Croatia until early 1945, and then transported out under guard of the German Army and Vatican guards."

A gasp was heard from Axel as he crossed himself realizing the far-reaching consequences of the Pope's action. Nazi ghosts had risen once more to claim yet another innocent victim.

Dan continued. "Of course, this is where Jim's father comes into play. His father's unit attacked one of the gold-laden trucks that had fallen behind the rest of the Monastery's convoy, mistaking it for the enemy."

"The truck was on its way to link up with a train that would take some of the loot to Germany and some of it to the Vatican. But this was not just any ordinary train. It was known as the *Gold Train*. It contained cargo looted by the Nazis from all across Eastern Europe."

Jim pondered the story for a moment wondering where the connection lay. "Why should the Vatican have to worry about something that happened over 70 plus years ago?"

The same thought had occurred to Dan when first told the story many years before. "There were no witnesses to say the Pope signed under duress. Those documents and pictures you hold in your hands could be turned against the church. People could say they cooperated with the Nazis the entire time, and stole the gold, and allowed the Jews and Serbs to be killed. Remember, Jim, it only takes a single match to start a raging fire."

Jim wiped the perspiration from his brow, nodding in agreement before speaking. "I can see why the Vatican would want to keep this secret hidden, to retrieve the documents and the pictures if only just to burn them and get this episode behind them."

"Bingo, my boy!"

Dan leaned back, satisfied the story was now out in the open. "Well, now you know the whole story and the reason why we should be getting this show on the road. It's only going to take the Vatican team a few more hours before they realize they've been double-crossed."

"I see your point," Jim said. He placed the documents back into their original box before turning to Schmitz. "I must apologize but as you can see, we are in a bit of a rush with some rather nasty people on our tail."

Jim tuned back to Schmitz. "I have one nagging question. Is it true that you worked for my father for almost seventy years, running this farm while he was in the states?"

"Yes sir, Mr. Dieter," he replied proudly. "It's hard to believe that so much time has passed. Of course, he tried to visit us whenever he could."

Jim contemplated what his father had achieved in total secrecy, looking up at Axel, a single tear sliding down his cheek. "He never told me, or from what I know, my mother, about his visits to the farm."

"Another secret that death's door opens, eh, Jim," Dan said. "We learn more about a person in death than in life."

"There are probably a lot of things your father did not inform you about, Mr. Dieter," Axel said. "He was a brilliant man who did not want to burden anyone with its many details."

"You're right, Axel. My father had a way of thinking things through. But there is one thing he didn't get a chance to complete and now I must finish." Jim looked to Axel, resting his hand on his shoulder. "Your years of loyal service to my father and to our family must be rewarded. The Dieter farm is yours. I really have no attachment to this piece of land. I only just learned of its existence a few weeks ago. Yet, you have spent your entire adult life here. It would be unjust to keep such a place that is really your home and not mine. Since I am now the official owner of the farm with my father's passing, I can rectify this situation easily enough. I hereby decree the farm to you, Mr. Schmitz, for all of your hard work and dedication to my father."

Schmitz was taken back. "I don't know what to say, Mr. Dieter," he stammered. "I'm speechless. All I can say is, yes, I accept. Thank you very much. Your generosity is most kind. Deep down I have always thought that in the end I would get to keep this wonderful piece of land. Now it has come true. I think your father realized you would make this grand gesture and the reason why he wanted you to come here in person."

"Axel, I have one additional question," Jim said, his curiosity peaking. "Are you the only one still alive from the group of children who lived on the farm after the war? My father spoke of a large group of children who had taken up residence here at one time or another."

Axel shook his head. "No, sir, some of the others are still alive," he said. "They moved to America, Australia, or Canada many years ago. As far as living on the farm, it is only my wife, Inga, and myself. We still hear from the others around Christmas or when someone dies."

"Your wife, Inga?" Jim inquired, yet another name from his father's past playing out before them. "Would this be the same Inga who used her own savings account at the end of the war to help fix up the farm?"

"The same beautiful lady, Mr. Dieter," Axel replied, the pride evident in his tone. "Yes, I know we had some bit of an age difference."

"My father implied she was in her early 20s in his story. That would put her in her early 90s by now. Am I right?"

"You are correct, 97 this past May," Axel said. "It took some time, but I finally convinced her I was the only man for her. Of course she waited a few years after your father left, hoping he would eventually send for her," looking away awkwardly, "but we both realized that was never to be."

"Yes, my Dad said he left pretty quickly with the wars conclusion, his new business taking priority."

Axel pointed over to a silhouette of a farmhouse in the distance. "You passed Inga's former home as you came down this back road. Your father and Inga grew up on adjoining farms. When they were teenagers, your father would sneak over after sundown, meeting in the barn or back here by the creek, talking for hours on end. This went on for years until your father went off into the Army. Of course, he returned on leave whenever he could, one time even promising to marry her. When your father was released from the prisoner of war camp, their agreement suddenly changed, with him leaving several months after that. I don't know if it was out of spite or true love, but Inga finally gave up waiting for your father, marrying me in 1950." His smile almost lit up the night. "I am indebted to your father for three things Mr. Dieter: escaping from Berlin with my life, the privilege of working this farm, and my wife Inga."

Dan, quiet up to this moment, allowed the two to reminisce before choosing to speak. "I'd say that's a lot to be thankful for, Mr. Schmitz: life, livelihood, and a partner."

"I truly am, sir," Axel replied, now looking over to Jim. "When your father first returned to the farm," pausing to ponder the date for a moment, "it was a good nine years after the wars conclusion, and he was already married to your mother," smiling, patting him on the shoulder. "Your father never once forgot us. Since the end of the war, we have received yearly checks for the upkeep of the farm and to provide for our every need."

Jim nodded. "One day you must allow me to visit under different circumstances and meet her, if I may, since it is now your farm. We seem to be under some major time constraints right now." He pointed to Dan readying the truck for travel. "Well, enough of this. More importantly, I will have my lawyer send you the deed for the farm when I return to New York."

"I understand, Mr. Dieter," Axel said. "Good luck in all of your endeavors. Gentlemen, until we meet again," he said, his hand extended. "It's beginning to turn light, and from the weather forecast it should be good driving weather for you. When I return to the house, I will tell Inga I have met the son of Hans Dieter, and he is just as generous and caring as his father. My wife Inga will take great joy in knowing that. She always carried a torch in her heart for your father."

*"Now she will carry one for you."*


## Vatican Special Action Team at the Dieter Farm

AS ORDERED, THE Lieutenant maintained his position by the farmhouse since early afternoon, the only activity he noticed being the occasional farm animal wander by.

"Our targets have not, repeat, not shown up, Mr. Perluci," the Lieutenant said into his credit-card-sized cell phone. "Maybe we should interrogate the owners of the farm to see if they have any information concerning our friends."

"Absolutely not," Perluci replied angrily. "You will not harm the workers nor the owners of the residence. We have no quarrel with them. That is not our way. Do you understand me? Times have changed. Our people no longer perform such actions."

"What I meant to say is maybe we could just flat out ask," the Lieutenant said. "If they do not want to answer, that is up to them. The farms owner may not even know a Hans Dieter."

"Point well taken Lieutenant, but let's not bother them until we get clearance. I will call back to the Vatican and explain the situation to see what actions are to be recommended. We must also alert them to the possibility that our property has already been removed."

The Lieutenant paused, pondering an idea that crossed his mind at the river. "Did anyone ever think that Dieter's son may want to keep this under wraps as long as we allow him to keep the gold?"

"Yes, it was discussed once or twice," Perluci said. "But my desire is still to have a simple exchange, their lives for our product. Everyone just walks away from this little bit of history."

The Lieutenant nodded. "Mr. Perluci, may I suggest we try and restart this operation in the United States? We know where this Dieter lives and he most likely will be with our man Flaherty, that is, if Flaherty hasn't removed him from the picture first."

Perluci pondered the idea for a moment before responding. "No, at this juncture of the mission it would not be Flaherty's style. If he were going to kill Dieter, it would have been right after the property was located, meaning Dieter would be dead at the farm somewhere and displayed prominently. I do believe you would have noticed something along those lines."

"So what do you suggest, Mr. Perluci?"

"If we don't get clearance to interrogate the farms owner, then we can meet in the United States with Mr. Dieter to discuss options. Of course, we always have the choice to hurt him financially, but that will be a decision for a later time. For now, I will join you at the farm in 15 minutes."

# CHAPTER 31

**AUTOBAHN – OUTSIDE OF FRANKFURT**

Jim exited the autobahn west of the city of Wiesbaden. He searched for one of the popular gas station/cappuccino businesses that seemed to be springing up all over Europe.

"How about a quick shot of some caffeine?" Jim asked. "I think we could use it before we hit the road again."

Dan rubbed his eyes. "Agreed," he said. "Now do I want the large or super-size cup of coffee? No — how about a keg?"

"The super it is," Jim replied.

"And some donuts."

Dan watched Jim disappear into the store portion of the gas station. He casually glanced about the parking lot for any suspicious cars or trucks. If they were being followed, the attackers would probably wait until the truck was about 30 kilometers west of their current position. It would be more isolated and conducive to a hijacking, but that's only if they were being followed, and if Perluci knew the lay of the land.

*Perluci was a smart bastard. I'll give him that.*

Right about now, his boys were either a few meters behind them lurking in the shadows or on their way back to Rome, tails between their legs. God forbid if they were behind them. Dan was ready for a fight as he fingered his Mac 9 machine pistol he kept secured under the passenger seat, another gift from his cousin. If they were an intelligent bunch and chose to return to Rome to regroup, it was only a matter of time before they would meet up.

"Here we go, the big cappuccino and a box of crawlers," Jim said rather loudly, tossing the box of donuts down beside Dan, and handing him his coffee.

"I like it," Dan said. "The jocularity persists even at an ungodly hour such as this. Now switch sides. It's my turn to drive, for we have a schedule to keep."

"No problem there friend," Jim replied, walking his way around to the passenger side, allowing Dan to slide across to the driver's seat.

Jim settled into the passenger seat, trying to locate a comfortable spot to place his coffee cup, finding none, settling on the spot between his legs.

"So do you have any boats picked out yet or just the location?"

Dan casually opened the box of donuts, choosing a cinnamon one. "I have everything down to the color of the boats rug in the bathroom, or the head as they call it on boats," he replied, satisfied with his choice.

"You are a man for detail, Dan. I must say that. I suppose the boat is around 50 feet in length with an onboard Jacuzzi the size of Lake Michigan."

"Jimmy, in my dream it's 54 feet long with both a sauna *and* a Jacuzzi, I'll have you know," he said before selecting yet another from the box to satisfy either hunger or nerves, never able to distinguish between the two. "But first things first." A look of mischief crept into his eyes as he looked about the parking lot. "I would now like to inform you about the rest of my plan. That is, if you agree?"

Jim sipped his coffee. "Do I really have a choice?"

Dan turned the truck west towards the autobahn. "We have a rendezvous in five hours just outside of Paris with a converted Boeing 777. The jet is a rental from a Dublin company that I've done business with in the past and should be well equipped for both comfort and cargo. The person making the airfield arrangements is also doubling as the pilot for this leg of the journey. He also happens to be another cousin who is a corporate pilot and happens to have a little time off. Of course he will be rewarded handsomely for working during his vacation time."

"But of course, naturally," Jim said, nodding at Dan's take on events.

Dan continued, ignoring the sarcasm in Jim's comment. "He's well versed in the Atlantic Ocean route, frequently flying his company's president between the home office in the U.S. and France. So our route home should not be a problem. After our journey across the Atlantic, we then land at a small airport in Millville, New Jersey. It's located equidistant between Philly and New York. Once we land at Millville, we off-load our cargo before the United States Customs Agency is even aware we are on the ground."

Jim propped his feet up on the dashboard, shaking his head in awe of Dan's plan. "Damn it, Dan, remind me to never get on your bad side."

"You have nothing to worry about, my friend. I took an instant liking to you from the get-go. I could immediately sense your integrity. My grandmother, god rest her soul, used to call it *Irish intuition*."

Jim smiled. "Let's get back to the more pressing issues at hand. How do you propose we land at Millville? If I remember correctly, don't we have to make prior arrangements for U.S. customs to be present when we land?"

"Details, details my friend, but luckily only minor ones. To answer your question, yes, you are correct. *We normally do*. Now, this is where I scare even myself with my dastardly planning. We prearrange for the U.S. customs' agents to meet our aircraft at Newark International. This would appear to make our flight legitimate. Now, if we were to, say, declare an in-flight emergency as we approached the New Jersey coast, we would have priority to land at the closest airport, which at that particular moment would be Millville," looking over at Jim for a response. "Pretty clever, eh?"

"And we conveniently happen to have a truck already there to off-load our gold and whisk it to an undisclosed location. Right?"

"See, now you're catching on—easy as one, two, three," Dan said, snapping his fingers before he shifted the gears to adjust for the straightaway. "You better watch out. I think I am beginning to rub off on you."

"I have the funny feeling this isn't your first time arranging an operation like this," Jim said, seeking a comfortable position.

"Well, now that you brought it up…"

# THE VATICAN's LAST SECRET

# CHAPTER 32

**MI-6 HQ – LONDON**

Sir Robert John was summoned to the Prime Minister's residence at the ungodly hour of 5:30 am, being the PMs first appointment of the day, this in order to explain the debacle of him involving one of General Parkers' SAS units.

Upon returning to MI-6 Headquarters, he asked his secretary to locate General Parker and see if he had time to meet with him within the next hour.

Once back in his office, Sir Robert picked up an antique wooden golf putter, a birthday gift from his wife, and angrily tossed it into the oil painting of Winston Churchill.

"I never liked that bastard looking down on me anyway," he said aloud, making a crude reference to Churchill.

General Parker winced at the crashing of the putter, silently striding unnoticed into Sir Robert's office, easing into a seat at the conference table. He sat there watching Sir Robert inspect the damage to his Churchill painting.

# THE VATICAN's LAST SECRET

Several seconds transpired before Sir Robert noticed General Parker out of the corner of his eye, turning on his heels to meet his steady gaze.

"I understand you nor your people work directly for me. But your goddamn people screwed up royally, General Parker," Sir Robert screamed, thrusting his fist in the air. "Do you want to know how badly, General?" Sir Robert walked around the conference table in order to stand beside him, index finger in the General's face. "I had to meet with the Prime Minister this morning where I promptly had my butt chewed off. If you think I enjoyed it, you're sadly mistaken."

Sir Robert straightened his tie, trying to achieve some sense of calm. "But, that's not the big problem. I can handle the simple details with the PM. Do you want to know what really burns my ass? Just five minutes ago, I had a phone conversation with the commanders of both the Paris Gendarme and Interpol. They asked me if I knew anything about our people operating in the area of Surie, France—a simple enough request, director to director. It happens all the time. They proceed to inform me that two of their police inspectors are missing. Now this is the kicker. They were presumed to be operating on the same case and in the same area as our team. Do you believe this coincidence? How the hell did they even know our people were in the area?" He walked over to his in-office bar, searching his mini-fridge for something substantial, settling on tomato juice but feeling more like a scotch.

"I have no idea how the French found out about our operation in that area, Sir Robert," General Parker replied coldly. "Its quite possible there was a leak on our end. We did have a great deal of people involved. Upon my return to base headquarters, I will personally question the team members."

Sir Robert poured himself a glass of tomato juice, not offering General Parker so much as a glass of water. "I despise having to lie to people, especially when I know damn well we screwed up."

"Sir Robert, if I may, Captain Robinson is one of the best we have in the business. If he chose to act in the way he did, I can only say it was out of necessity. From our initial debriefing of Captain Robinson, the team was operating with night vision goggles at the time of the incident. They viewed what appeared to be our two subjects moving about on the barge. They approached the vessel using standard sweep procedures with two on the bow and one from the stern. They noticed two subjects moving in the salon area of the barge. Not wanting to take any unnecessary chances, they raked the entire area with silencers."

"May I be so bold as to interrupt for a second, General?" Sir Robert said, obviously displeased, putting his glass down on his antique desk, spilling some of its contents in the process. "Why did your men rake the entire area with machine gun fire when they did not positively identify the targets? At least see what they were firing at."

General Parker had no desire to escalate the conflict into a shouting match. He wisely allowed several seconds to pass before responding. "But, Sir Robert, the team identified the correct barge and had what appeared to be the two possible subjects on board. Don't you find it peculiar that Flaherty and Dieter were not on board, but that the French police were? This was an extreme case, a million-to-one shot. It could never happen again." He searched Sir Robert's face for any sign of understanding. Finding none, he continued. "As you are well aware, its policy not to take chances where terrorists are involved. The safety of our troops is foremost. And it has always been my personal creed since I first took this job, and it will remain so until I am removed."

Sir Robert pointed to the door. "I thank you for your assistance in this matter."

### **278 Kilometers SE of Paris**
DAN MANEUVERED THEIR truck around a slow-moving Fiat, passing it with a half meter to spare. "I hope my cousin is having a dandy time on the barge. He is going to need one hell of an excuse trying to return that thing. Come to think of it,

that bastard won't return it. He'll sell the damn thing for scrap if he can get a few bucks for it."

"I thought you said he was trustworthy, a man of his word, totally loyal to his family?" Jim replied, amused at Dan's sudden shift in attitude toward his cousin.

"And he is all of that, my friend, but he's not stupid. Before we departed, I told him to have a little fun with the barge. Translation for people like yourself: *We basically stole it*, and it's his if he wants it. Hopefully the cops don't pinch him before he has some fun."

"When your family gets together for a holiday they must love the stories of your exploits."

"We go on into the night, my friend, as long as the beer, whiskey, and bacon sandwiches abound, so does the bullshit. One goes with the other, wouldn't you say."

Jim leaned back in the cab, placing his feet up on the dash. "You know what? I'm going to hate for all this to end. I've really enjoyed this little adventure we've been on."

"Don't enjoy it too much. We're only half done, and it might get a little hairy before we reach the states."

Jim wondered what else Dan had up his sleeve to aid in their escape. "You caught me off-guard with the barge switch and then the truck. I wasn't ready for that one, so I have complete confidence in your future plans."

Dan mustered a heavy Irish brogue. "Ah, a vote of confidence from the big man. I thank you from the bottom of my heart."

Several seconds elapsed before Dan reverted to a tone of seriousness. "Just one thing bothers me about our operation so far. I know I'm not perfect, but think about the barge we rented. Even though the names and credit cards we used were fictitious, what if anyone got a sniff of an Irishman and an American renting a barge? What if that salesman that rented us the barge talked to someone? Usually people who take a vacation reserve those things a couple of months in advance, not on the day of sailing."

"You're right on that one. We stood out like two dogs at a cat convention," Jim said.

"And another thing, I don't want you to get paranoid or anything, but my cousin didn't rent this truck were driving in. *He did the Irish borrow on it*," Dan said, passing yet another slow moving car.

"Translation for the amateurs: *it's stolen*."

# CHAPTER 33

**VATICAN TEAM – DIETER FARM – WEIMAR**

After a series of wrong turns and over an hour of driving, Perluci reached the Dieter farm, adding a bit of complexity to what should normally have been a 15-minute drive. Upon his arrival, he met with the assembled team members. After a few minutes of discussion, Perluci and the Lieutenant agreed it would be best to directly question the owner of the farm.

Perluci knocked on the farmhouses wooden door. He had already positioned the remaining Vatican Special Team members by the farms barn.

*No need to overwhelm anyone at this point.*

After several anxious moments, the door opened to reveal Axel Schmitz. Jim Dieter had warned Schmitz to expect additional visitors. Schmitz decided it best to play along. "What can I do for you, gentlemen?" First eyeing Perluci, then the Lieutenant.

Perluci removed his hat, placing it in his hands out of nervousness, not respect. "Good morning, sir. My name is Mr. Perluci, and this is my adjutant, Lieutenant Lern. This may sound a little ridiculous to you, or it may not, depending on your situation. We are hoping to ask you a few questions regarding some church property that could be located on your farm." He turned to indicate the plowed acreage behind him with a sweep of his arm.

Schmitz tried his best to look dumbfounded. "Is this some type of joke, or are you really trying to sell me something?"

A forced smile creased Perluci's face. "No, sir, we are looking for something that was apparently lost around the closing days of World War II."

"I don't know what you are talking about, sir," Schmitz feigned. "I have lived here for over 70 years and have never seen nor heard anything about church property on this land."

"I really don't want to play games with you, Mr. Schmitz," Perluci said. "I don't have the time nor the patience. It is Mr. Schmitz, isn't it? Yes, your expression betrays you. If you would allow me to continue, maybe I can refresh your memory." He removed a tattered leather notebook from his breast pocket, referring to its contents. "In April 1945, you deserted your post at an anti-aircraft emplacement and escaped Berlin with a group of children in the care of one Captain Hans Dieter. Captain Dieter brought yourself and the 12 other deserters to this farm." He paused, looking about the farms property before continuing. "In 1946, Captain Dieter immigrated to America, first settling in New York City and later in the Hudson Valley. Since that time, you and your wife, Inga, have been appointed caretakers of the farm." He paused for several seconds as he looked at the Lieutenant then back to Axel. "We at the Vatican believe Captain Dieter secreted some property here on this very farm. The property I speak of belongs to my employers, and we were hoping you would assist us in recovering it. We tend to think Dieter utilized some of the product as an insurance policy to protect himself and his family. Now, assuming the documents stayed hidden, all is well. But with the recent demise of Hans Dieter, we suspect the new owner might try something rash."

Schmitz appeared visibly upset, reaching for the doorframe to balance himself. *How were these people able to gather so much information? What else were they aware of? Could they be out to blackmail Inga or himself? Schmitz started to panic. He had to rid himself of these people before it was too late. He couldn't slip up and betray Mr. Dieter.*

"As I stated earlier, gentlemen, I have no idea what you are talking about, so if you would kindly leave. Or maybe I should call the police to escort you from my property."

Perluci sensed Schmitz was about to break and decided to press on. "Come now, Mr. Schmitz, you wouldn't do that. Do you know why? Of course you do, because such an incident would draw attention to this farm and its Nazi past. How about your wife's past? Now for the sake of not wanting to draw attention to our mission, can we reach an understanding? We just want to search your property. If we find nothing, we will be on our way. You will never hear from us again."

Schmitz realized he was trapped with no easy way out. "Alright, I don't see any harm in just poking around as long as you don't disturb my animals or crops. But I insist on going with you." He grabbed his slicker from just inside the door, stepping out on the porch, positioning himself between the two men.

Perluci looked at the Lieutenant, satisfied he still possessed an adequate interrogation technique after all these years. "Fair enough, Mr. Schmitz. Just think, we can be out of your life forever after this minor inconvenience."

"That is all I require," Schmitz said, "to be left alone and live out my days on this farm. Is that asking too much?" He put on his slicker and corduroy hat, glaring over at Perluci with sullen eyes. He sensed his chance to take a quick verbal jab at his unwanted company. "To tell you the truth, *I never knew you were in my life to begin with."*

Perluci turned to the Lieutenant, then his Vatican guards. "Let's start in the barn and work our way toward the rear of the farm, near the graveyard and the river intersection. Look for anything out of the ordinary, especially recently disturbed earth. If anything were removed, it would have been sometime during the past two days."

"You sound as if you know this area better than myself," Schmitz said, allowing Perluci to walk ahead. "Please, I insist. You lead the way, and I will just follow along in your so-called investigation."

They took almost 30 minutes to scour the property lines located along the east bank of the river tributary for any telltale signs of recent diggings. Satisfied there was none, they approached the rear of the property in the vicinity of the Dieter family graveyard. Located at the south end of the property, a walk that would normally take, on an average day, 10 minutes from the farmhouse. But this was no average day.

Perluci sketched in his notebook as they walked, obviously saving them for later reference. They now approached the 30 by 10 meter wrought iron fenced cemetery. "Exactly how many people are buried in the graveyard, Mr. Schmitz?" said Perluci as he opened the gate, leading them into the well-kept grassy sanctuary, stones of various heights all in orderly rows.

"You seem to know all about the farm and its contents, Mr. Perluci. You tell me," Schmitz spat back in response, trying to extract some satisfaction for his inconvenience.

Perluci smiled at Schmitz's obvious play at sarcasm. "You are right Mr. Schmitz," again referring to his notes. "The Dieter family cemetery had it first internment in 1778. Over a period of some 200 plus years, 20 Dieter family members have chosen to be buried here. The information I am lacking right now is the date of the last internment. Could you possibly fill in that minor detail, Mr. Schmitz?"

Schmitz pondered a response, looking at the burly Vatican Special Team members stationed on either side of him before answering. "I really don't recall," He stammered, "it must have been some time before my employment here. Why do you ask?"

Perluci pointed toward an area in the rear of the cemetery. "Because from that freshly overturned dirt, I would come to the conclusion," adjusting his reading glasses to look at the headstones engraving, "one Peter Goot was just interned. Did he happen to die recently?"

Perluci bent down to examine the writing on the tombstone. "No, I don't think so, because you would have remembered something so recent." He looked accusingly to Schmitz then to the tombstone, writing down the date of Goot's death in his notebook. "Lieutenant, I think we have found our answer. This Peter Goot was obviously an accomplice to Hans Dieter's little job, and Mr. Dieter evidently buried the gold and property with him in the actual grave itself. Am I right, Mr. Schmitz?"

Schmitz looked away.

"I would say this soil was disturbed within the last twelve hours by the looks of its moisture content." He picked up a handful of earth before allowing it to filter through his fingers back onto the ground. "Also, compare the depth of the tire tracks for those entering to the ones leaving. This leads me to the conclusion that they left here laden with our property."

Schmitz searched the faces of the men surrounding him, wondering if they could possibly be cold-blooded killers. "I don't know what you are talking about, Mr. Perluci. The river flooded last week and disturbed this particular grave causing me to reposition the tombstone yesterday."

"Just the tombstone was disturbed, yet you dig up the entire grave? Come, come now. I don't think so, Mr. Schmitz. But it was a good try," Perluci said. He slowly approached Schmitz, leaning in toward him, allowing his face to be only inches from his own. "We will take up no more of your time, Mr. Schmitz. We have our answer. Let us go, Lieutenant. We must report back to The Vatican at once."

**Dulerie Airport, southwest of Paris**
THE DRIVE FROM Weimar to Dulerie was accomplished in a brisk seven hours, primarily on major highways with some small back roads thrown in for good measure. They never knew if they were being followed.

Adhering to Dan's strict timetable, they were able to arrive at the Dulerie Corporate Airport complex, 41 kilometers southwest of Paris, in plenty of time. The small airport was known for its transatlantic corporate jet service between America and France. Mostly it was used primarily by high-profile corporate executives who preferred the quaint atmosphere to the madhouse at the Orly International Airport some 20 kilometers north. Dan imagined the same criteria, selecting an airport with little traffic. They also required the services of a functioning corporate airport due to their accomplice leasing a corporate type jet and the need to blend in.

Motoring past the airports six empty service hangars, they were afforded the view of what appeared to be the only jet occupying the airports concrete tarmac, a Boeing 777. It also happened to be the aircraft leased by Dan's relative.

Jim envisioned a smaller business-type jet where they could still be comfortable but in close quarters. But with a 777 they would undoubtedly have plenty of room to stretch out.

He maneuvered as close as possible to the aircraft.

"This is a beauty, Dan," Jim said, exiting the truck to perform a closer inspection of the aircraft. "I only have one more question to throw your way. How do we clear French customs and get permission for this baby to take off?"

Dan motioned for Jim to follow him over to the aircrafts stairway, stopping short of actually walking up. "Yes, there always has to be one stick-in-the-mud. Up to this point, I have performed a majority of the planning. For the operation to proceed, some of your previous military contacts will now come in handy. I need you to call in a favor from your associate in the French Ministry of Armed Forces. I imagine he's located high enough in the bureaucratic food chain to merely request clearance from one of his equals for our trip to proceed. If he is, he can run blocker for us on the customs issue. Hell, the United States military does it all the time."

Jim stood facing Dan, knowing deep down that he was right. They couldn't possibly depart French airspace without proper clearance. "You want me to just casually call my friend and say that I require a rather large favor of him." Jim picked up an imaginary phone as to speak. *"Yes, Mr. Chief of Staff, could you sign our manifest so we can bypass French customs and take our cargo of Nazi gold out of your country?"*

"Well not as crude as all that. Work with me now, Jim. I envision the discussion a little differently, a little more risqué. The French love that sort of action. Tell him the cargo is a bunch of rich passengers on a little joyride from the United States to visit Paris. Being a close friend you hate to ask for any favors, but one of the passengers on board is a female movie star who doesn't need her identity betrayed by some customs' inspector. Top it off with — *she is going through a very nasty divorce."*

"Do you realize that you spoke those words with a straight face as though it were all true? You can lay some of the best bull I have ever heard, and being in the service for a number of years I've heard some whoppers." He paused for a moment to digest what was being requested of him. "It just might work. I haven't talked to him in over three months, at least since he was appointed to his new position. Hell, what do we have to lose? Okay, I'll go along with your story. He just might buy it. Lead me to a phone my good man."

Dan pointed up the aircrafts steps. "Use the one in the plane while I pop open a bottle of Brut. After all, it is the breakfast hour."

# CHAPTER 34

**French Ministry of Armed Forces – PARIS**

In the two months since assuming his position, Honorable Jacque La Tour was still acclimating himself to the workings of the position. He already aligned himself with the ruling party, settling in comfortably with the *fold*. Regular golf outings and expensive dinners were the norm. Of course, contractors or lobbyists always made sure the bill never found its way to him.

Short in stature with the build of a wrestler, roughly handsome to most, always impeccably attired, Jacque La Tour had been educated at the Special Military School of Saint-Cyr otherwise known as the French Military Academy, the equivalent to the United States West Point. Since graduating many years before, he had assumed a number of increasingly influential posts, mostly diplomatic, culminating with his most recent position upon military retirement.

He adjusted a set of family pictures that lay on his hand-carved oak desk, mentally remarking how blessed he was to have a beautiful wife and four lovely children; all of this accomplished at the relatively young age of 43.

*Yes, he was undoubtedly a rising political star in the French government.*

His brief interlude was interrupted by his secretary walking into his office, pointing to his phone.

"Mr. La Tour, you have a call on your private line. It's from an American named James Dieter, who, if I may so bold, speaks horrible French. Shall I say you are busy, sir?"

Jim always did speak atrocious French thought Jacque, slapping his hand on his desk, laughing aloud. "No, please put him through. He is a dear old friend."

Jacque picked up his ringing phone. "Jimbo, you old, crusty sea dog, how are you doing? I haven't heard a peep from you since you retired from the Navy," Jacque said, reverting to English, one of three languages which he was fluent, Arabic being the other. "I was a little perturbed that you did not invite me to your retirement party."

"I would have enjoyed nothing better, Jacque, but your wife would have killed me, especially since the ruckus we caused last time we were together. Come on, you didn't already forget, did you?"

Jacque paused for a moment reminiscing about the "fishing trip" they had went on -- well, almost went on. *They did happen to cross over a river to visit four separate bars*, finally stumbling home at 3:00 a.m., waking Jacques' wife and the kids in the process. "Yes, I remember. How could I forget? Monica didn't speak to me for three nights after that little episode. Okay, my friend, you are absolved this time. So to what do I owe the privilege of this phone call? Need a place to stay in Paris?"

# THE VATICAN's LAST SECRET

"In that house of yours? Are you kidding? It's already bursting with three children running amuck," Jim said, remembering his last visit.

"Correction," Jacque replied. "Four right now. Monica had the latest addition to our happy clan last month."

Jim felt like a heel for not remembering, making a mental note to send some flowers and a case of wine when he returned to the states. "That's right, four. I apologize. Time flies, Jacque. The last time I had the privilege to talk with you, Monica was eight months' pregnant. Just do me one favor, keep it in your pants so you won't have to worry about number five coming along." He felt sorry for poor Monica. She was stuck with four kids while Jacque flew from country to country representing the French Ministry of Armed Forces.

"Not all of us can be independently wealthy like some people I know," Jacque said.

"You're right. I spoke out of turn. I didn't mean to imply anything. I'm still the same old sailor I always was, just a little more round in the middle, if you get my drift."

"The next time you are on this side of the pond, I am going to fix you up. Yes, that's it. Monica has many pretty friends. You can get married and join the club and stop looking in the window."

Jacque provided Jim with the perfect opening for Dan's fabricated story. He utterly disliked having to lie to a trusted friend such as Jacque, but he had no choice at this juncture. He would make amends at a later time. "As fate would have it, that's one of the reasons I am calling, Jacque. I happen to be outside Paris as we speak. I flew in for a couple of days with some outrageously rich bastards to visit Paris."

"You don't say. You are moving up in the social circles. Now a private jet, eh? Must be nice. Even as a Chief of Staff I am required to fly coach."

"Well, here's the scenario," Jim started, the lie fresh in his head from practicing with Dan. "One of our passengers is traveling incognito. She's a big movie star who is going through a messy divorce, and she doesn't want her whereabouts publicly known. We have to keep everything hush-hush. Do you catch my drift, Jacque?"

Jacques secretary silently slipped in bearing documents for him to sign, depositing them on his desk in order of importance, withdrawing as efficiently as she had made her entrance. Jacque waited until she had departed before continuing. "You're her squeeze, aren't you? Come on, you can trust me. Which big star is it? Come on and tell me, Jimmy. I need to hear some exotic stories," he pleaded. "Just one little tidbit to get me through the day."

Jim pictured Jacque on his knees in some angelic pose. "Calm down you old horn dog. Next time I'll have some juicy details for you beyond your wildest imagination." He paused, weighing the possible repercussions his friend could expect if caught, deciding it best to push on. "But back to more important matters at hand. I would consider it a personal favor if you could get airport clearance for our party to bypass customs so we can vacate the premises as soon as possible."

Jacque was taken aback for a moment, but quickly reconsidered, realizing Jim would not make a request if it weren't important. "No problem, my friend. One of the perks of the job," he replied. "Tell me your airport location, final destination, and the tail number of the aircraft. I will then magically use my newfound power to do my first illegal act and get my friend and his Hollywood starlet back to their love-nest."

*There, it was done.* Jim took a deep breath before proceeding.

"You French are all the same, always with sex on the mind. Then again you haven't changed a bit, Jacque," he said, laughing loudly. "All right, you have your pen ready? We are departing from Paris-Dulerie to Newark International, New Jersey. I will need you to fax the tower at Dulerie with the documents and the U.S. Immigration office in Newark."

# THE VATICAN's LAST SECRET

Jacque scribbled the information on his new letterhead, still admiring his official title. "No problem, Paris-Dulerie to Newark, New Jersey," he mumbled as he wrote down the information. "I will have my secretary draft a letter for my signature and then fax it to the tower and immigration within ten minutes. Jim, next time call me *before you get to Paris* so we can get together. I can't wait to tell Monica about your famous Hollywood starlet. She will be amused, to say the least. Take care, my friend."

Jim hung up the phone feeling ill at having to deceive a friend. Turning to a patiently waiting Dan, him having monitored the whole conversation from across the table. "All right, we are clear for takeoff. Jacque is using his diplomatic leverage to allow us an orderly exit before some customs' official wanders by."

"Excellent news, you've done well, my boy," Dan said. "This calls for a libation. I know we have a bottle of Irish on this plane somewhere. Will you join me when I find it?"

"Find me the pilot you promised first," Jim said, wanting to get underway. "Then I'll join you.

"Who needs another pilot? I'm still qualified to fly," a smile creased his face. "Well I've never flown anything this big or with two engines, but it shouldn't be too hard if you can find me the instructions."

"You can't be serious?" Jim said, not knowing whether to believe him or not.

"Jimmy it's just part bravado and bullshit which equates to an Irish emergency plan, but no worries," pointing over toward the control tower. "Speak of the devil and who shall appear."

Walking towards them was a tall, athletically built gentleman in an awkward-fitting traditional blue blazer, starched blue pants to match, leather World War II Air Force style hat tilted to one side, and wearing a pair of aviator sunglasses. Only a scarf around his neck was missing to complete his ensemble.

Eian Doherty, all of six feet and pushing a solid 220 pounds. His once handsome face attested to the fact that he loved to play a decent game of rugby, and fight. As he approached, a grin was apparent from ear to ear.

"Cousin Daniel Flaherty, you old sod, good to see you, my friend," Eian said, playing up his Irish brogue, heavier than ever as he extended his hand in greeting. "Now stop being a pain in the ass, load your product, and I'll take care of the flying business. This is no little trucking operation driving into Dublin. And another thing, I refuse to fly the plane until I have met all of its passengers."

A thousand pardons," Dan said. "Mr. Eian Doherty meet Mr. James Dieter, the man who is paying our passage and employing you in this most humble yet modest of undertakings."

"A pleasure to meet you, Mr. Dieter," Eian responded sincerely, crushing Jim's hand with his grip. "I don't know how you got yourself mixed up with this man," pointing over toward Dan, slapping him on the back in jest. "But if I were you, I would keep an eye on your wallet. And he's known to cheat at cards."

Dan turned serious for the moment, taking offense to Eian's off-hand comment. "Now, Eian, that's no way to talk to your master. You lost that last poker game fair and square."

Eian displayed a passion for playing cards, badly, with poker being his favorite way to go down in flames. He was known to wager an entire paycheck on a single game. Unfortunately, he sometimes had to borrow money from the local bookies or loan sharks in order to meet his losses. Presently he owed $22,000 dollars to a small-time Philadelphia hustler named Mickey Dolan. Dan knew of Eian's need to score a quick payday thereby avoiding the "bone breakers" Mickey employed to perform his debt collection services.

Eian rubbed his hands over the dirt-encrusted wooden boxes, trying to acquire a sense of what was inside. "Then I want a rematch when we get back to the States with my cut from whatever product you're loading here."

"You're on," Dan replied.

Eian pulled out a clipboard that contained his flight plan and an empty aircraft manifest sheet. "Okay, what lie should I place on the aircrafts manifest under product so we can get this junk into the States without much notice?"

"Just say antiques and religious articles. That should fly for now," Dan said with a quick wink.

"Antiques and religious articles, oh yeah, I got you," Eian replied, annotating the manifest. "Oh, you're a real comedian, Dan. What do you really have in these boxes here: C-4 explosives, grenades? Come on, you can tell me, Danny boy," as he puts his arm around Dan pulling him closer.

"We go back a long way, Danny and I do, Mr. Dieter. Danny, do you remember the time we had the O'Malley twins out on that amusement pier? That was an unforgettable night."

"Alright, Eian, the cockpit awaits your grand entrance, so hop to it, eh," Dan said, realizing this was neither the time nor the place to reminisce.

Amused at Dan's obvious discomfort, his feathers having been ruffled, Jim said, "Eian, you'll have to fill me in on that adventure while Dan's sleeping." He glanced over at Dan, him now busy moving the remaining boxes onto the aircraft.

"It will be a pleasure, Mr. Dieter," Eian said, tipping his hat as he moved off to the cockpit.

Jim walked over to assist Dan with loading the final few boxes. The last thing he needed was Dan to experience a heart attack from his recent exertions. That was if you included the digging, all-night driving, and now the heavy loading. He tapped him on the shoulder, pointing to the aircraft stairway, indicating for him to rest.

Dan appreciated the respite and didn't protest.

"Dan, your cousin is a character from another era or another time. Wouldn't you agree?"

"Don't be fooled by that act he puts on, my friend. That man is as smart as a fox and as dangerous as a rattlesnake. A word of warning: don't get on his wrong side."

"Most of the people I happen to meet with you are from the wrong side of the tracks, and believe me, I wouldn't want to cross any one of them."

"Let me give you a little info on my cousin. During a little trouble in the homeland, Eian was part of my ten-man cell, or unit, as your American military would call it. He was the man responsible for flying in our light weaponry: 45s, M-16s, and the occasional explosive devices from France. It may sound easy to you, but Eian," he looked up to ensure Eian was not within listening distance before continuing, "had a habit of flying his aircraft at 10 to 20 meters above the sea to avoid the British Army radar sites based in England. I can personally vouch for the man, because I was included on one of his little flying adventures from the French coast. We were flying so damn low the plane actually had seawater in the cockpit. Eian had to keep the windscreen wipers on due to the ocean spray obscuring his view. All the time this crazy bastard is singing Irish Folk tunes at the top of his lungs for all to hear. The boy even had the nerve to ask me for his fishing pole as he was flying along, as if he were actually going to drop his line in the water while he was flying. *Crazy bastard!* When we made it to our destination of Tully Meade, they said I was white as a ghost. I did not remember the landing, because I passed out after he turned the aircraft sideways to empty the sea water out of his plane before setting it down.

"Enough," Jim said, shaking his head, wondering if only half of the story were true. "The man's as crazy as you are."

# THE VATICAN's LAST SECRET

# CHAPTER 35

**French Ministry of Armed Forces – Paris**

Mrs. Lafier waited patiently before deciding to approach Jacque in his office.

"Mr. La Tour," she said apprehensively, wondering how he would accept her brashness. "I know you are still new with the position and are still getting acclimated with the workload, but I noticed you haven't reviewed the *Top Secret* message traffic log in a week or so. The former Chief of Staff, Mr. Chavier, read his message traffic every day. It's not my area to suggest such things to a man in your position," she stammered, looking to the floor, averting his piercing gaze, "but it might benefit you to know what is going on, sir."

Jacque was taken aback at first. Allowing a few seconds to pass before realizing that maybe he could learn a thing or two from her. Hell, she was in the employ of the previous Chief of Staff for over two years.

## THE VATICAN's LAST SECRET

"No, no, you are right, Mrs. Lafier," he replied in an all-is-forgotten tone. "Sometimes I get overwhelmed with all the duties assigned to this position and forget the little things. Let's start fresh. From now on I want you to bring me the top-secret message traffic list first thing in the morning. That means I'm at least a week behind, so we better start right away."

"I happen to have them right here, sir," she said, proudly presenting six red folders, each with *Top Secret* emblazoned across their covers.

Utilized by the Ministry of Armed Forces upper level management, the message-traffic system allowed them to keep abreast of domestic situations that could affect national security.

"If I could direct your attention to the top two folders, sir, they came in via special courier almost a week ago," she said, opening them both. "The first is from General Sinclair, and the second is evidently from a Mr. Perluci of the Vatican Security Force, which is unusual, because we normally receive all of our messages of this nature through our security service. Apparently it was rushed through other channels about a week ago."

He casually glanced at the General Sinclair message detailing the escape and manhunt for an Algerian terrorist who has promised a bombing campaign as revenge for his time spent in captivity. "Don't worry, Mrs. Lafier. I'm sure they weren't too important to our little office," he said, quickly picking up the next folder, one that detailed an extensive Vatican, British, and Interpol manhunt for an Irishmen named Daniel Flaherty and one American named James Dieter; both wanted for questioning concerning an IRA incident that had occurred many years before.

Jacque face turned a ghostly white.

"My God, this can't be my friend, Jimmy," he said aloud, brushing aside the rest of the files including everything else that happened to be present on his desk. "Mrs. Lafier, get me the tower at Duliere immediately."

**DUE TO A SERIES** of wide-sweeping government cutbacks, Renee Dupree was the sole air traffic controller on duty at Duliere Airport.

The last thing she needed now was any form of trouble from a government 'big-wig.' She already made mistake number one by picking up the towers phone and not letting it go to voicemail.

*She hadn't even had her first cup of coffee yet.*

"This is the Ministry of Armed Forces Chief of Staff Jacque La Tour calling from Paris. I am trying to locate a particular aircraft that may be at your facility. Can you tell me if any planes have taken off in the past half hour or so?"

Renee picked up her binoculars to monitor the only aircraft she had on site, now assuming take-off position at the end of runway 26. "No sir, it's been pretty slow today. I do have a corporate Boeing 777 ready to roll."

La Tour exhaled a sigh of relief. "I need you to stop that aircraft in the name of French National Security," he ordered. "Do not allow that plane to take off. Do you hear me? Do not give them clearance. Tell them to return to the terminal and await further instructions. Just make up some excuse. Any excuse. Tell them the air space is closed for military aircraft maneuvers or something along those lines."

Jacque let a sigh of relief escape.

Renee's hand started to twitch for the first time since she had first worked the tower at de Gaulle airport, Paris's main airport, many years before. "But, sir, I have received a direct order from the Office of the Aviation Director himself, Mr. Trottier. I cannot countermand his order," pausing, "it would be my job."

# THE VATICAN's LAST SECRET

La Tour sensed the nervousness of the controller. But this was now a potential national security issue and he was not taking the fall. "Yes, I understand. I am the person who asked Mr. Trottier to allow the aircraft to proceed. Now, I need you to stop the aircraft. There are possibly two criminals on board who need to be interrogated by the police. I am giving you a direct order that undoubtedly overrides your boss. Please tell them to stop. You can do that, can't you?"

Renee was mentally reviewing her management's chain of command and wondering whether or not La Tour had the authority to override her boss's order.

"*Why me?*" she thought, her right hand now twitching uncontrollably. She removed an airline-sized bottle of Johnny Walker Red whiskey from her desk drawer, fumbling with the bottles small cap before mixing the contents into her black coffee. She raised the ceramic mug to her mouth, and in one swift motion downed the strong mix.

"If I get into trouble for this… "

La Tour was quick to cut her off. "You won't. And I'm the one who will have full accountability for this action. You have my word." He realized that if any news of him allowing two possible criminals to flee the country hits the press, he would be forced to resign his position.

The controller seemed satisfied with his reply, either that or the Johnny Walker had provided the necessary calming effect. "I will radio them now, sir. Please hold."

"November five zero seven zero nine, please stop your forward progress and return to terminal. Repeat. Abort your takeoff and return to the terminal."


**EIAN GRACEFULLY MANEUVERED** his aircraft directly in the middle of the runway on top of the large, white, luminescent runway numbers. He scanned the aircrafts instrument panel one last time for any warning indications. Satisfied, he positioned the engines throttles to full power.

The aircrafts radio sprang to life just as the aircraft passed the 500-meter mark on the 3,500-meter runway.

"Abort your takeoff. Say again, abort your takeoff," the tower controller ordered, desperation apparent in her voice.

The aircraft now passed the halfway mark on the runway. Eian started the ground emergency process of retarding the engines throttles to abort takeoff when he felt Dan's heavy hand land on top of his, pushing the throttles forward again.

"What the hell are you doing, Dan? The tower said abort," his voice cracking, not wanting to relinquish control of the throttles.

Dan pointed his finger down the runway with his free hand. "We are going full power whether or not you like it, Eian. We are not returning to the terminal. Do you understand me?"

Dan radioed the tower, the plane still proceeding down the runway at full power. "Tower, please say again. We are experiencing radio difficulties."

Renee shook her head. "November five zero seven zero nine, this is Dulerie Tower. You are instructed to abort your takeoff and return to terminal at once."

Dan smiled at Eian. "Dulerie Tower, say again. Our radio is evidently not receiving all of your transmission. We will switch to the emergency frequency for a retry."

The plane gently lifted off into the afternoon sky, banking slightly right as Eian steered the aircraft toward the Atlantic coast.

Renee followed the aircrafts progress until it cleared the airport control area, watching it on radar until it was 10 kilometers out. Realizing she still had the phone line open, she slowly picked up the receiver, wondering if her job was suddenly in jeopardy. The controller stood transfixed, staring at the phone for a few seconds.

# THE VATICAN's LAST SECRET

"Sir, I could not stop them," she said into the receiver. "They are evidently having radio problems and cannot receive our transmissions. There is nothing we can do at this time to make them turn around."

"You're joking!" La Tour said. "They are playing possum, hearing every word you say. Where is the nearest military air base to your facility?"

"That would be Cherbourg Air base, sir, 130 kilometers due west of my location. Come to think of it," the controller said, picking up a pile of recent faxes, sorting through them individually until finding the one she needed, "we received an unclassified message early this morning from Cherbourg stating the base would be conducting military warfare exercises starting today. That's why I originally vectored this aircraft just south of the restricted area."

La Tour focused on his wall-mounted, floor-to-ceiling map of Europe, trying to anticipate the route they would be flying. "Can you tell me how long before that aircraft reaches international air space? Just a guess will do."

Renee plugged several numbers into her calculator. "Judging by the aircraft speed and altitude, they should reach the coast in close to 16 minutes and be out of our airspace totally in about twenty, sir."

"Excellent. I thank you for your assistance," La Tour replied, ending the conversation. Jacque sat at his desk for a minute pondering the plight of his friend. He had to reverse the aircrafts course while it was still in French airspace. Some minor assistance for a friend could turn into his downfall. *How was I supposed to know they were suspected terrorists?* He picked up the phone once more, dialing his secretary.

"Mrs. Lafier, connect me with the Cherbourg Air Base Commander."

### Aboard Boeing 777, west coast of France

DAN ROSE FROM the cramped co-pilots seat, easing his slender frame past the instrument panels center console. He positioned himself behind Eian who still occupied the pilot seat. Dan suddenly reached over, wrapping his arm around his neck, depriving him of oxygen for a few seconds.

The plane took a momentary dip as if hitting an air pocket.

"I want to get something straight, Eian," Dan whispered into his ear. "You are in our employ for this trip. Don't you ever doubt me again. Do you understand me?" He then released his grip from around Eian's neck.

Jim was taken back by Dan's action. He had just come out of the toilet to see Dan release his grip. "Would you just let him fly the plane," he said in the calmest voice he could manage.

Dan rapped Eian on the head with his knuckles. "If I say jump, or anything else for that matter, you don't doubt me. You just do it. Do you understand?"

Eian nodded, trying to regain his breath, coughing several times. He rubbed his neck, moving it around several times to check to see if he still had full rotation of his head. "I'm sorry, Dan. I should have known better. I reacted as trained." Eian tried his best to control his temper, concentrating on the planes instruments, making sure the plane did not veer off its intended course.

Dan leaned over to Eian, his hand extended. "No hard feelings. We go back a long ways, Cousin. You should have known better. I am the boss, and you are the worker bee. Understood?"

"Won't happen again," Eian said before shaking Dan's hand, knowing what would happen if he tried a move like that again, cousin or no cousin. He had heard that Dan sliced off a man's fingers during an interrogation session, and the man happened to be their distant cousin. He could only imagine what would happen if it involved something of real value.

# THE VATICAN's LAST SECRET

Dan seemed satisfied with his response and changed the subject, returning to the co-pilots seat. "Eian, how long do you think until we reach the coast?" He acted as if nothing had ever transpired.

Eian tapped the clock located on the instrument panel in front of him, peering at his wristwatch and comparing the two. "If you look out the window off your right-hand side, you will see what looks to be a bluish cut between two rather large brown spots. That's the English Channel. So according to my trusty clock here, I would say we clear the French airspace in about seven minutes."

Dan turned to Jim who now sat in the jump seat behind Eian. "In seven minutes, we are in international airspace with the next stop in the good old US of A," he said, clapping his hands in approval.

Eian pondered if the conditions were right to inquire about the type of cargo they had brought onboard. After all, it was customary that he receive a percentage of its value. Then again, he realized that dealing with Dan was anything but ordinary. He decided to press ahead anyway.

"I have to ask a question, gentlemen. You're not displaying all of this enthusiasm for a load of guns or missiles, because I know you, Danny. Oh, yes, I do. We had too many run-ins of that sort in the old days. Would your product be so hot and valuable that the law would quite possibly be on our tail? Could that be the reason why the authorities tried to stop us and return to the terminal? Speak up, Danny. You only mentioned something about hauling the usual weaponry."

Dan took Eian's comments in stride, adjusting the positioning of his seat before looking over at him. "I guess you can say a little of both, Eian."

Eian removed his hat, slamming it against the control wheel. "I don't believe this. You can't trust anybody anymore. Stupid me, I should have driven a harder bargain for my services when you first contacted me. We are definitely playing some poker when we land this tub. Do you hear me? I deserve the right to make some extra cash for my beautiful work, wouldn't you say?"

"Eian, when you land us safely in the United States, I'm going to provide you with a special bonus that will keep you set for the next couple of years or so," Dan said, pausing for the full effect, "and a free week's vacation on my yacht in the Keys."

Eian adjusted his cap to one side, the same angle an arrogant WWII flying ace would have after a successful mission over the skies of Europe. "Little Danny Flaherty now has a yacht in the Florida Keys. Maybe I could win that yacht off you in a game of chance, eh, Danny? One simple hand of hi-low, winner takes all?"

"Or maybe I could just win back the money I'm paying you for this job," Dan said, satisfied that the choking incident was truly in the past with no hard feelings. One amusing thing about Eian, promise him money and everything was considered in the past.

Jim leaned back in the jump seat taking in the childish banter that these two were spouting aloud. It was as though they were still 15 years old and battling over who was going to win the heart of the virginal girl next door.

"Gentlemen, how about we call a good old fashion truce? I'll even fortify us with some coffee from the galley. That is, unless you boys had your heart set on a fight?" Jim struck a pose straight out of Boxing Digest circa 1900. "Marquis of Queensbury rules."

Eian nodded. "Good idea, Mr. Dieter, coffee might keep me awake for the next eight hours while I fly this rig."

Dan scanned the various cockpit instruments, all familiar to him, but on a much smaller scale with his experience confined to single-engine aircraft. "Doesn't this expensive tub come with an autopilot, Eian? I can't locate the damn thing with all of the fancy gadgetry we have in here," pretending to turn knobs.

Eian used one of his rolled-up charts to knock his hands away in jest.

"What do you think we have been flying on for the past five minutes since we left French air space?" Eian replied. "I had to wait until I reached our assigned cruising altitude to clear a French aerial war game off the coast." Satisfied no additional questions would be forthcoming, he returned his attention to an in-flight map of the western European airports and radio frequencies, dialing in control numbers for Shannon Air Traffic Control: his next vector point.

"Let's get a jump on things here," he said. "Shannon Air Traffic Control, this is Extended Flight 777 requesting clearance on a western path to Long Island Control, United States."

**ON THE ISOLATED** and rugged western coast of Ireland, in a drab concrete structure, lay Shannon Control. The structure housed 22 air traffic controllers vectoring transatlantic air traffic safely between Europe and the Americas. Each controller had a particular area of responsibility assigned to them, monitoring traffic via "moving white blips" on a sweeping radar screen updated every 10 seconds with flight critical data such as speed, altitude, and type of aircraft.

Occupying one of the controllers' seats for westbound flights was one Michael Shanely. Tall and lanky, the makings of a goatee merging on his chin, tattoos decorated both arms. He had entered the aircraft controllers training program directly out of Dublin University, graduating third in his class. With the prospect of another quiet day emerging, he decided to track Eian's aircraft after its takeoff outside of Paris. He awaited the call that would eventually come when it cleared French airspace.

"Extended Flight 777, this is Shannon Control. Provide me an indent on your position," Michael said.

Eian pushed a small red button on the aircrafts transponder, the aircraft sending a signal that illuminated their position on Michael's radar, identifying him from six other aircraft in the same area but at various altitudes.

"Roger Extended Flight 777. You are clear to stay on present transatlantic course of 245 and ascend to 35,000, light traffic ahead at 25 kilometers. Contact Long Island Air Traffic Control when you are 400 kilometers out. Have a nice day. Shannon Control out."

Michael glanced to the radar screen still monitoring the jets progress.

"**WE ARE SET BOYS**, another hurdle cleared," Eian shouted as if he were a preacher in a church service, yelling from the pulpit. "I say yes! I say it's time for all brethren to grab some coffee and discuss our vacation plans on Dan's little boat in the Florida Keys." He took the cup of coffee that Jim provided.

Jim handed the other cup to Dan. "Sounds like it's time for a toast, gentlemen. We are close enough to international airspace with our little treasure. Raise your cups, gentlemen…"

"Don't celebrate too early boys. We have company," Dan said, showing no anxiety in his voice. "We have a French Mirage fighter jet off our starboard wing."

**NAVY COMMANDER** Phillipe of the Second Maritime Squadron was leading his squadron in an attack of a wooden silhouette that had been set up in the English Channel for target/scoring during the 33rd annual French Air Force/Navy fly-offs.

A highly competitive affair, it allowed one of the services to claim bragging rights until the following years competition. This would be his third run of the day in what was turning out to be an extremely tight affair with the score tied.

As Commander Phillipe approached the stationary target in a steep dive when an urgent radio message ordered him to immediately break from the exercise. He received orders to force a Boeing 777 back into French airspace.

*Shooting was authorized.*

**EIAN MAINTAINED HIS** composure as he set the radio to the general aviation emergency frequency, hoping the fighter would have done the same.

"Hold the toast, Mr. Dieter. Let's see what this guy wants."

"French Mirage, please identify yourself and your intentions."

**COMMANDER PHILIPPE WAS** in no mood to chase after a civilian aircraft, especially when bragging rights with the Air Force were on the line. He pulled ahead of the airliner, and then applied his aircrafts speed brake, allowing him to shift back to no more than five meters off the aircrafts wing tip, hoping to gain the attention of the pilot in the cockpit.

"Boeing 777, this is Commander Recard Phillipe of the French Navy," he said in a steady monotone voice. "I am operating out of Cherbourg Air Base. You are being directed to return to French air space immediately. Repeat: *Immediately.*"

**DAN LOOKED TO EIAN** for some sort of explanation. "What the hell do we do now?" he said.

"If we can just stall him for another 10 minutes until we reach Irish Airspace," Eian replied. "He would not dare go into another nation's airspace if he knows what's good for him. If we were in French airspace, he would have already taken the shot by now."

"And they would say we stumbled into their little air exercise by accident and were shot down by an errant missile," Jim said. "From what I've heard, it's been done before."

Eian pondered his options for a few seconds before responding, trying to maintain his professionalism. "French Mirage, this is air piracy. What is the justification for our course deviation? We are Irish and American nationals flying on board an American registered aircraft in international airspace. What are the charges?"

**COMMANDER PHILIPPE WAS** not aware of any charges nor did he care. He followed orders from his superiors. The civilians controlled the military and he in turn performed as ordered, no questions asked. With a simple flick of a toggle switch on his joystick, he armed his 20-millimeter guns.

"Your aircraft has been identified as being involved in a possible crime. You are requested to return to French Airspace," he replied.

**EIAN AND DAN TURNED** to face Jim, busy strapping himself in the jump seat, no doubt bracing himself for what was about to become a turbulent ride.

"Jimmy boy, it sounds like your buddy sold us out," Dan said, looking over his shoulder at Jim, still struggling with his seat belt. "What the hell did you say to piss him off?"

"Honest, I didn't say anything bad about him or his country," Jim said. "I just said we needed a favor to bypass customs. Hell, he even thought I had some major starlet on board."

"Well, I still have something up my sleeve, boys," Eian said, pushing the engines' throttles forward, increasing the speed an additional 50 kilometers per hour. He waited a few seconds until the fighter jet took notice of the new speed to resume contact.

"Mirage aircraft please provide me with a new course to turn to and a new approach control. I will await your confirmation."

# THE VATICAN's LAST SECRET

**THE COMMANDER DIALED** his radio controls in order to contact his superior at the Cherbourg Air Base.

"Roger Boeing 777, I will have your reply in 30 seconds," he said.

**EIAN EYED HIS WATCH**, hoping the pilot of the Mirage would experience some difficulty in contacting his superiors. "This guy must be a buffoon," he said. "Most of your experienced fighter pilots would have ordered us to perform a 180-degree turn and *then* assign us a new course, that is, if you don't want a 20-millimeter shell crashing through your windshield. His mistake in providing us an additional half a minute. Believe me, we are going to need every second. The longer we can stall him, the closer we approach Irish airspace and freedom."

Jim looked first at his watch and then at the ominous aircraft still on the starboard wing. "How long till Irish airspace?"

Eian provided them with a wide grin. "Its three minutes and counting, time to put my emergency plan into operation."

**THE COMMANDER ANNOTATED** the numbers he had just received from Air Traffic Control at Cherbourg Air Base, carefully maintaining a five-meter separation from the 777's wingtip. "Boeing Extended 777, this is French Mirage," he said. "You will immediately turn to course 134, drop your altitude to 14,000, lower airspeed to 275 knots and establish contact with Cherbourg Tower on Frequency 3472. Acknowledge, please."

**EIAN REALIZED IT WAS NOW** or never if his plan had a decent chance of success. He had to take advantage of the one element all pilots in an oxygen-rich environment were deathly frightened of: *fire*.

"French Mirage this is Boeing Extended 777, we cannot presently comply with your request. We have a fire indication on engine number one and are declaring an in-flight emergency as of now."

He was hoping the ruse would gain them the additional time they required.

**"BOEING 777, THIS IS** French Mirage. I will try to position my aircraft to see if you indeed have a fire in engine one. Please stand by. The Mirage aircraft slowly drifted back into a position 100 meters directly behind and above the 777, seeking a vantage point to scan for any telltale signs of a fire.

**"KEEP STALLING, EIAN**, your ruse is working," Jim said. "We only have one minute till we reach Irish airspace," he said.

All three eyed their watches as if awaiting midnight in Times Square.

**THERE WAS NO FIRE**. Commander Philippe could see he was being played as the fool. They were merely attempting to stall their return to French airspace, seeing no choice but to once again activate his 20mm guns, resuming a position 50 meters directly behind the aircraft.

"Boeing 777, I see no fire, nor do I see an engine shutdown procedure that would have normally followed such an action. Nice try. Now immediately turn to course 134 and drop your altitude 14,000 feet, or I will be forced to open fire," he said calmly. "Repeat. I will open fire."

# THE VATICAN's LAST SECRET

"**FRENCH MIRAGE, MY** number one indicator has a red fire warning light illuminated," Eian said, maintaining his cool. "We are making sure it's not an electrical problem before we start engine shutdown procedures. We are checking the circuit breakers now," lighting a cigarette with a cupped hand, revealing the burning ash to Jim. "I'm not lying, look at the bloody ciggy. It's on fire, right?" extracting a laugh from Dan and Jim, breaking the tension that, up to now, existed in the cockpit.

"**BOEING EXTENDED 777**, you will start your turn immediately, or I will open fire on your aircraft," replied Commander Philippe, angling his aircraft above the 777. Once in position, he squeezed off a warning burst of 20mm machine gun fire, its orange tracers racing by the 777's cockpit window.

"**DAMN YOU," EIAN SAID**, viewing the tracers shoot by threateningly in front of the aircraft. "This bloody bastard is serious. He's firing live ammo at us."

**AT SHANNON CONTROL** Michael Shanely continued to monitor the situation involving the Boeing Extended 777. Having already detected Eian's Irish accent on the radio, he would not allow a French military aircraft to enter Irish airspace nor harm one of its citizens.

Michael decided to lend a hand.

"French military aircraft, this is Shannon Air Traffic Control," he said in a firm tone. "You are ordered to return to international airspace and abandon your proximity to Boeing 777. I say again, you have now entered Irish airspace and you will be forcibly removed if required."

"**SHANNON AIR TRAFFIC CONTROL**, this is a French military aircraft pursuing a Boeing 777 with suspected criminals on board. I am under orders to turn them around. Please advise the Boeing 777 aircraft in your airspace to turn around and return to international airspace."

**MICHAEL SHANELY REPLIED,** "French Mirage, your aircraft is now in violation of the sovereign territory of Ireland," he replied sternly. "We request that you immediately return to international air space or face immediate action. Acknowledge, please."

**COMMANDER PHILIP** realized he was beaten. "Affirmative; French Mirage now returning to international airspace."

**EIAN WAVED AS** the Mirage peeled off from his threatening position on the port side of the aircraft. "Look at that bugger run, boys."

"Can you believe it? Eian said. "We were actually saved by our old Irish government.

Eian called his saviors at Shannon. "Shannon Control, this is Boeing 777. We thank you for your humble Irish welcome," he said. "We would like to request maintaining our present course until reaching Long Island ATC."

Boeing 777, this is Shannon Control. You are cleared for course request. Maintain altitude of 35,000 feet. Good day to you *and Godspeed*."

Dan triumphantly pumped his fist in the air. "You did it, Eian, you beautiful bastard," he said. "You just had your share of the pot doubled, boyo." Realizing his mistake with him caught up in the euphoria of the moment, Dan turned sheepishly to Jim. "That is if you agree, Jim."

"Damn straight, you deserve a medal for the way you handled that French pilot," Jim said. "You are definitely someone to have around in a pinch. When we hit the Florida Keys, we are going to throw the best damn party those fine folks have seen in a long time. Maybe we can even hook up with Jimmy Buffet for a private concert."

Dan and Eian looked at each other before replying in unison, "Who the hell is Jimmy Buffet?"

If it's a party to be, then we need some Clancy Brothers' music," Eian said. "Let's try that toast one more time. The last time that damn fighter pilot ruined it. Raise your cups, gentlemen. Mr. Dieter, you have the floor, or cockpit. Take your choice."

Jim stood up from his seat, raising his cup. "Gentlemen, if it weren't for my father having a set of balls the size of Texas back during the war, none of this would have come to light. So raise your cups to my departed father. May he rest in peace beside my beautiful mother. God rest their souls. Cheers, my friends."

"All right, gentlemen," Eian said, "let's settle in for a long flight to America and on to my next set of devilish plans."

Jim turned to face Eian before replying. "The Americans don't know what they are in for do they?"

"Not in the least, Mr. Dieter. *Not in the least.*"

# CHAPTER 36

**French Ministry of Armed Forces – Paris**

Jacque La Tour sat dejectedly behind his desk, pen in hand, wondering if his "pet" projects would survive the next round of defense budget cuts. Rumors were circulating around the Paris water cooler that they would undoubtedly fall to the axe. *What a way to be initiated into politics.*

A soft knock by his assistant interrupted his train of thought. "Sir, sorry to interrupt you, but the Commander of Cherbourg Air Base is on line two," she said, pointing at his phone. "He said it was urgent."

"Admiral Roche, how are our little captives? Have they landed yet?" said La Tour.

"Sir, that's why I am calling," Admiral Roche replied. "We sent one of our best pilots to convince the aircraft to turn around, but they slipped into Irish air space before we could nab them."

"Admiral, are you informing me that they are not in Cherbourg?" La Tour replied angrily.

"Yes sir, you are correct," Admiral Roche said, standing in his well-appointed office overlooking Cherbourg's harbor, loosening his uniforms tie and collar. "They are not at Cherbourg or anywhere else in France for that matter. Our intelligence sources have informed us that the aircraft continued on a direct course for the United States."

"Admiral, this must be a pretty embarrassing episode for the Navy when a supersonic Mirage aircraft cannot catch and return a fleeing subsonic Boeing 777," Jacque said. He enjoyed having the upper hand with someone who two months earlier was his boss while he was on active duty. *The tables were truly reversed.*

"Sir, we had no problem overtaking the aircraft," the Admiral began. "It was our inability to convince them to deviate from their intended course. That was the issue. But I do have another idea. We could make arrangements for their capture upon landing in the United States by simply notifying their Department of Homeland Security."

Jacque wanted no part involving another government agency, an American one at that. The paperwork alone would burden him for days on end. No, he wanted to drop the political hot potato as soon as possible.

"Admiral, let the Americans worry about this affair. It's out of our hands now. We tried our best, thank you and good day," he said, hanging up before the Admiral could respond.

Jacque slowly rose from his desk, walking over to where he proudly displayed various mementos and pictures from his days as an officer in the French Navy, focusing on one picture in particular.

Removing an aged bottle of Calvados from his bar, he poured a single shot into a baccarat crystal glass, lifting it in mock salute to a picture of Jim Dieter and himself taken only two years before.

# THE VATICAN's LAST SECRET

*"Good luck my friend. Until we meet again under better circumstances."*

# CHAPTER 37

**MI-6 HQ – LONDON**

The early morning fog showed signs it was beginning to burn off as scattered streaks of sunlight made a welcome appearance. A lovely day was surely on tap for those souls lucky enough to enjoy it.

General Parker's military helicopter burst through the scattered fog as it banked over the Thames in route to the MI-6 VIP helicopter-pad. He bore news that could potentially provide his team a second chance to redeem themselves.

Sir Robert was made aware of General Parker's arrival by the helipad control officer. *God only knows what Parker has in mind*, he thought, clearing any trace of his morning breakfast of Earl Grey Tea and hot Irish scones with extra butter, an early morning habit he picked up years before from his dear departed mother.

"Good morning, Sir Robert," General Parker said breathlessly, bursting into the office as if it were his own, his uniform immaculate, an overflowing briefcase and assorted maps in tow. "Thank you for meeting with me on such short notice, sir, but I think we have a chance at redemption concerning the French fiasco."

General Parker hands a recent message for Sir Robert to view. As Sir Robert silently read the message, General Parker unfurled a detailed map of the Eastern United States on Sir Robert's conference table.

Sir Robert glared at General Parker as if he had just crossed an unspoken barrier. "First of all, General Parker, it's not *we* who have to redeem ourselves. It's you and your SAS boys," Sir Robert spat out angrily, tossing the message to one side with obvious contempt. "Secondly, who said I would entrust another operation of this magnitude to you. I am already on the receiving end of a load of buckshot in my ass from the Prime Minister because I asked for your help."

The General ignored him for the moment, scouting the area for something to hold down the edges of the map before it rolled up on him once again, finally settling on a stapler and a hole punch for each corner.

Curiosity caught the best of him, walking over to view the general's map.

"Sir, allow me one last chance. I will personally lead the team. No screw-ups. You have my word as an officer and a gentleman on the issue."

"*You*, General?" Sir Robert spat out, looking at him with obvious disdain. Wondering as to what depths he would succumb in order to save himself. "You've got to be kidding. You haven't seen action since Iraq. Don't you think *the rust is on your sword* so to speak?"

General Parker allowed the snide comment to pass, pressing on with his pitch. "Sir Robert, we don't have much time," he began. "Our listening posts outside of Cheltenham have intercepted communications between a French fighter off our southern coast and a privately leased Boeing 777." He pointed to the map and the last known position of the French fighter. "The reason they tried to turn the aircraft around was due to a suspected Irish and American criminal on board: our

Daniel Flaherty and James Dieter. The message I handed you was intercepted less than 15 minutes ago. Based upon that message, I overstepped my authority and authorized one of our *ready alert* aircraft to launch and follow the aircraft. Our aircraft is faster and should have overtaken the 777 by now. My plan is simplistic in nature. I take the same team that was in operation in France over to the U.S."

Sir Robert started to protest.

General Parker held up his hands to cut off Sir Robert, continuing. "They can eliminate our friend Flaherty. I have our SAS men stationed on another jet at Gatwick ready to be airborne as soon as you give the word. If we launch in the next 30 minutes, we can catch them off the eastern seaboard of the United States and simply trail them in."

"And what if you screw up again, General?" He started looking at the maps the general had spread out. "Are you going to shoot any old ladies as they cross the street? Or will I be forced to lie to my American counterparts as I have to the French? Or even worse, will I have to meet with the Prime Minister with more grievous news? Because if I do General, I will have you eliminated," his fingers cutting across his neck in one swift motion.

"Your point is well taken, Sir Robert," the General said, patting his 9mm sidearm. "I will personally guarantee success."

"All right mister, you sold me," Sir Robert said. "Your personal guarantee on this? I like that. All right. But don't screw it up boy, or I will personally have you hung from Parliament Tower."

"No need, Sir Robert. If this operation turns to mission failure — *I will already be dead.*"

# THE VATICAN's LAST SECRET

# CHAPTER 38

**BOEING 777 – OVER ATLANTIC OCEAN**

Jim's steady hand operated the aircraft controls, gliding the aircraft through the brilliant blue sky. "I can't believe an aircraft of this size is so easy to control," he said to Eian, still seated beside him. "When I was in the Navy, I would always stand mystified behind the pilots as they flew the aircraft. It always looked so hard, or at least they gave the impression that it was."

Eian laughed aloud at Jim's flying analogy, still monitoring the instruments as Jim was having his fun, having begged to take over the controls since leaving Irish airspace.

"To tell you the truth, Mr. Dieter, its pretty easy to fly the plane. Due to basic aerodynamics, the plane actually wants to stay aloft. The trick is on landing and take-off. Then it can get a bit sticky, especially with the harsh elements thrown in like snow or heavy rain. Other than that, a monkey could fly it."

"Oh, I'm sure there's more to it. You're just being modest. I saw how you handled the situation with that French fighter. You were actually going to shut down that engine to simulate an emergency, weren't you?" Jim said, looking over at Eian, searching the man's expression for the half-truth.

Eian enjoyed the captive audience of one, reminding him of his flight instructor days of past. "Your hair would stand on end if I told you what I intended on doing with our fine aircraft here. I have performed many a stunt that most aircraft engineers would deem not possible."

"Please, don't tell me until we get down on the deck. I don't want to lose that fine breakfast you cooked us earlier." Jim's hands tightened on the aircrafts controls as he shot a nervous glance over toward Eian for support. "Any idea on how long we have left? I'm starting to tire from holding the controls."

"No problem," Eian said, eyeing his watch. "Looks like one hour and fifteen minutes to our destination. As a matter of fact, I think now would be an excellent time to contact Long Island Air Traffic Control. We have to keep up our ruse. That and to check our conditions over the target area."

Eian leaned over the center console, casually disengaging the autopilot system that had been flying the aircraft the whole time Jim was in the seat totally unaware.

Jim shook his head in frustration. "You mean to tell me that I wasn't flying the plane at all? The damn computer was doing all of the work? I feel like a total fool."

Eian laughed aloud before turning around to view a red-faced Jim. "Mr. Dieter, do you actually think I would let you fly this aircraft over the ocean, possibly taking us off course? I don't think so. I just humored you all along. After all, you are the boss."

Jim joined in on the laughter at his own expense. "Wait until I have a chance to get even, little man. Your time will come."

Dan slowly made his way forward, rising from a two-hour nap in the rear of the aircraft, arriving in the cockpit as the laughter was subsiding. "Don't tell me, Eian, you pulled the old autopilot joke on young Dieter here?" He handed Jim a cup of coffee. "Don't worry, Jim. He pulls that crap on everyone. He did the same thing to me over 20 years ago." He turned to Eian. "Do we have an estimated time of arrival?"

"Sure do, Dan," Eian shot back confidently, "as long as the autopilot stays off," looking back at Dan and Jim, a smirk still resident upon his face. "We have a little over one hour till we get this baby on the deck and start unloading your mysterious cargo."

Dan removed his Nokia satellite phone from his pocket, keying up two prerecorded phone numbers. "One hour you say? This would make it an excellent time to call our ground transport personnel and make sure they are in position at Millville."

### British Nimrod Aircraft, trailing B777

NIMROD AIRCRAFT WERE utilized extensively by the British Navy for anti-submarine warfare missions in the 80s and early 90s. Since the demise of the Cold War, most were retired from service but several were donated for VIP transport or electronic eavesdropping for the British Foreign Services.

The Nimrod following the Boeing 777 happened to be an extended series model four with the latest in avionic eavesdropping equipment. The crew consisted of eight flight officers whose primary mission was to detect and decode electronic signals. In this particular case, they were trying to detect signals emanating from the Boeing aircraft, hoping to eavesdrop on both sides of any conversation.

The boring eight-hour flight was suddenly interrupted when a signal, the first in as many hours, was detected.

The lead intercept officer was busy scribbling something on a piece of paper before turning to his mates. "Flight Lt. Hawkins, please radio General Parker in the trailing aircraft, and inform him that we just intercepted an air-phone conversation originating from our suspects. Inform him that the Boeing 777 pilot will fake an in-flight emergency and land at an airport called Millville in the state of New Jersey."

## **General Parker's Aircraft**
IN THE COCKPIT, the pilot, copilot, and navigator kept up the vigilance, trailing the lead Nimrod by only eight kilometers. The cockpit crew could clearly view the red and white anti-collision lights of the forward aircraft, close enough to almost reach out and replace the bulbs.

The navigator suddenly hunched over his radio, busily scribing a message, before turning to the general. "Pardon me, sir, but we have a message from our forward aircraft. They've intercepted a cell phone transmission from our suspects."

General Parker quickly read the message before handing it to the SAS team leader, him stretching in the chair beside the general. "What do you make of this?"

The Captain read the message before returning it to the general. "I never heard of this Millville, sir."

"That makes two of us. If our Irish lad deviates from landing at Newark International, how are we to declare the same emergency in order to land behind him at Millville?"

The Captain shook his head. "No sir, we would lose the element of surprise, wouldn't we?" The Captain turned his attention to a map of New Jersey that now lay before them, tracing its coastline in an attempt to locate Millville. "I have a radical plan of attack for our two friends, that is, if you are willing to think outside of the box, sir."

"Captain, I am willing to listen to just about anything," General Parker said. He turned in time to see his navigator had finally located Millville.

"We took the liberty of bringing on board all of our gear because we had no idea what type of operation was going down," replied the Captain. "Translation: we also have our parachutes. So if you will indulge me," he said, pointing to the Millville location, "We can land via parachute over the airport runways here," pointing to two intersecting black lines indicating the main runways at Millville. "We can jump from our aircraft at around 1,500 meters and glide down virtually on top of the suspect's aircraft. With it being dusk, they won't see us coming. If you read the maps legend in the corner here, it speaks of the particulars for this spot. This airport has everything going for it. Its secluded. It has a regular jump area adjacent to it used by the U.S. Military as a nighttime jump spot. In my discussions with our pilot, this aircraft is about six minutes behind the suspect's aircraft, so we should be able to ambush the bastards on the ground and in a location where they would never expect it. In doing so, this allows our aircraft to continue on its route to Newark airport as scheduled, uninterrupted. No one will know the difference. When our ground mission is complete, we can steal transport from around Millville and proceed to the Newark airport in a matter of a few hours." He searched the general's face for any sign of concurrence.

The general poured over the map in deep thought, allowing his finger to trace the route the Nimrod aircraft would have to traverse. "Let me get this straight. You are going to para-jump onto a United States civilian airport and overtake these hoodlums on the ground?"

The Captain casually glanced from side-to-side, wondering what he was getting himself into, especially after the debacle in France. "Sir, I know it sounds a little unorthodox, but this would be a chance to redeem ourselves."

"How do you think the Americans will react to us parachuting over an active civilian airport?" General Parker said.

The Captain looked him straight in the eyes before responding. "Obviously, we don't want the Americans to know, sir," looking at his watch and referring to the digital clock on the aircrafts bulkhead. "Right now, figuring the time difference between our aircraft and American Daylight

# THE VATICAN's LAST SECRET

Savings Time, the operation will commence at or around dusk. No one will see our aircraft nor hopefully will they observe our people parachuting into the airport. For peak efficiency, we will be utilizing our black camouflage outfits with matching parachutes."

The General nodded. "I still don't like the idea of operating in such a brazen, untried fashion in an allied country. That little operation in France was nothing compared to this. The Americans will not just sweep it under the carpet, especially if anyone from their press corps gets wind of this."

"If their press gets wind of this, it's because we're all dead and on CNN."

## **Aboard B777 aircraft**

EIAN OCCUPIED THE pilot's seat, Jim in the copilot's seat, and Dan in the jump seat, each feeling the effects of the long transatlantic flight. Eian was on his sixth cup of coffee in as many hours, wishing he had brought along another pilot to relieve him at the controls for a spell. At least Jim and Dan had been able to take naps in the rear of the aircraft.

"Okay, ladies," Eian said, "according to my trusty cockpit instruments, which would never lie to me, I would put us at about 90 miles east of the Millville airport. So in about five minutes, we are going to put my little aircraft deviation plan into action. Jim, I want you to proceed down into the cargo hold and start preparing our cargo by loosening the straps for when we hit the deck. Now, as soon as you feel the landing gear hit the runway, you will start maneuvering the cargo toward the side-entry door. We will taxi over to an isolated portion of the airport where a truck will be waiting to off-load the cargo. At that time, two of my friends will board the aircraft and take your place. Remember, the manifest states three passengers, and you gentlemen will be exiting stage left. At the same time, we will take aboard a dummy load of cargo, some old furniture that is labeled antique and such. We will only have a few minutes before this aircraft will have to take off and continue on our flight path to Newark. The vehicle you have for your escape is all yours. Think of it as an early Christmas gift. At that time, gentlemen, we will be parting company, at least for the time being."

Eian finished the remainder of his coffee. He then dialed the frequency to Newark's setting. "Dan, when we hit the deck, I will need you to watch the airport tower and ramp for any movement directed toward us." He reached behind his seat for a green flight bag, extracting a 9mm pistol with accompanying silencer. "Only use this if you feel threatened. We don't need a mass of dead bodies strewn about. As for myself, no worries. I still have my trusty Uzi," patting under the pilots seat. "Last but not least, my friends, I will be requiring some good old American hard cash up front for my little flying gig, first to pay for the services of the two gentlemen who will be coming aboard, and secondly there is the matter of the truck and the aircraft lease. Now, will that be cash or credit, Danny?"

"Eian, as always, it has been a pleasure doing business with a man of your qualities and scruples.

"Enough with the build-up for my ego, Danny," Eian said. "Cash is the acceptable form of payment."

"All right, Eian, I must agree," Dan said. "Without your first-rate services we would have been two ducks stuck in a puddle of mud. If you could take the time to look under the blanket located directly behind you, you'll find a small flight bag. In it, you'll find $50,000 in cash and $250,000 in gold to buy yourself something nice. Now remember, that money is also for your two cohorts, plane rental, plus payment for the truck. I also threw in some extra cash for pocket change. However, remember, Eian, sit on the friggin gold for a few weeks and use Nick in New York for the resale. He will give you a good price with no questions asked. Did you hear me? Sit on the damn gold."

"Understood, Danny," Eian said, turning to eye the bag. "You don't want the gold floating around too early after the take. Eian reached back to pick up one of the gold bars.

Dan nodded to him. "Now, let's get down to more serious matters. As planned, we will meet in the Florida Keys on my new boat." Dan handed Eian a piece of paper with an address and telephone number for a boating marina. "I don't have the boat picked out yet, but this will be its berth number when I do. If you have an emergency and find it necessary to telephone, you will ask for a Mr. Pepper. That will be the name I have arranged to get you through. If everything goes smoothly, you are to meet with us on the 30th of next month. But remember, that beautiful stuff you have in your bag cannot be peddled around for a few weeks, so lay low."

Eian slipped the paper safely into his shirt pocket, wondering what the hell type of cargo he was flying for them to be so generous.

It was Jim's turn to speak. "Eian, we may also have some additional flying work for you. Can you provide Dan a phone number where we can contact you in case we require your services earlier than the thirtieth?"

Dan shot Jim a puzzled glance. "What's the deal with the additional flying work? You want to share the details with me, Jim? I thought it was agreed that I would be doing the planning for this operation."

Jim nodded. "Just wait until we arrive in the Keys. I will provide you with the rest of the details.

"So the apprentice takes over from the master, eh?"

"Something along those lines," Jim replied, enjoying the lead for a change.

"Cousin Dan knows exactly where to find me, Mr. Dieter. Believe me, with the salary you gentlemen pay, it will be a pleasure to work for you again. Now, if I may be so bold gentlemen. It's time to assume our positions."

### General Parker's Aircraft

"GENERAL, OUR SURVEILLANCE has tracked them to within 20 kilometers of the Millville airport," the Captain said. "It looks as though their intentions are still the same, to declare an emergency of some type, enabling them to land at the Millville airport in lieu of Newark International."

The General shot him a quick glance. "Captain, are you positive we can catch them before they off-load their cargo?"

"General, I am willing to stake my life on it," he replied, expertly fingering his Uzi machine pistol.

The General nodded. "Captain, you are well versed in the embarrassment we suffered in France."

"We will not let you down, sir," the Captain replied. "The men are all familiar with the repercussions. Confidence is high."

"Right you are, Captain. Proceed to your jump stations."

### Aboard B777 aircraft

"NEWARK TOWER, THIS is Boeing N7364," Eian said calmly. "I have a problem with my left landing gear indicator. I am requesting a touch-and-go at Millville airport for a down-verification prior to our landing at Newark."

"N7364, are you declaring an in-flight emergency?" The Newark tower operator responded, knowing full well that Newark had some of the best capabilities for handling any possible aircraft emergencies.

Eian had to maintain the simple appearance of a faulty landing gear indicator. The last thing they needed was the Newark Tower operator ordering him to change his plans. Eian had his own agenda. No matter what happened, he was landing at Millville.

"Negative, Newark. We are requesting to deviate from our original flight plan for a touch-and-go at Millville for a landing-gear-down confirmation. We think a good jolt on the runways surface will provide a green indication for us to proceed on to Newark."

"Roger that, N7364. Steer to 197, maintain altitude and contact Millville Tower on frequency 2786. Good luck, and contact us on channel 1482 prior to your reentering the pattern."

"Thank you, Newark." Eian said. He leaned over quickly dialing in frequency 2786 before calling the next location.

"Millville Tower, this is Boeing 777 flight N7364 originally in route to Newark International, requesting a touch-and-go for faulty gear-light indicator."

**THE MILLVILLE TOWER** normally lay quiet at this time of day with most of the earlier traffic in the area having been small single-engine aircraft whose owners were out trying to hone their flying skills. None were usually present in the pattern after 4:00 p.m., creating a void until the dinner crowd started flying in from Philly around 7:00 or 8:00 p.m. The "crowd" usually consisted of a few planes flown by middle-aged men trying to impress their girlfriends or wives by flying them to dinner at a local restaurant.

Morris Thompson sat in the Millville tower trying to enjoy his own dinner, a microwave meal his wife packed for him before he left home. *How many times can I eat Salisbury steak?* He pushed it away from in front of him, gravitating toward the vending machine. He was searching his spare change when the call from Eian's aircraft came in requesting an emergency touch and go.

*Finally, a little excitement around here. Don't receive too many heavies in this place.* He placed his change back into his pocket. His snack would have to wait.

"Roger that, N7364. Would you like emergency services standing by?"

"Negative, Millville Tower. Should be a nice and easy touch and go."

"Roger that, N7364, you are the only traffic in the pattern. You are clear on runway 11 for a straight-in approach," Morris said. He decided to be cautious and place a call to the Millville Volunteer Fire Company as a precaution. Located only a half-mile from the perimeter of the airport, they could be on the main runway in a matter of minutes if needed.

Eian provided a thumbs-up to Jim and Dan before replying to the tower operator. "Roger that, Millville Tower, I have a visual on the airport runway lights."

Eian paused for a few seconds before the next phase of his plan, contacting Millville Tower once more. "Millville Tower, this is N7364. I would like to request a deviation from my earlier request for a touch and go. I require a full stop for five minutes to perform a quick visual-gear check. Our left gear-down light just illuminated indicating a full-extended condition. I want to visually check the gear-down switch on deck."

"That's affirmative, N7364. You are requesting a full stop for a gear check," Morris said. "The airports wide open at this time. You may perform your check on the ramp to the west side of runway 11."

"Thank you, Millville. N7364 over and out."

### **General Parker's Aircraft**

THE PILOT SLOWED the lumbering aircraft to 140 knots, *dangerously near the stall speed for the type of aircraft,* in order to facilitate the parachutists who would be attempting to jump from the rear of the aircraft. Any speed above 140 knots would possibly push the jumpers off course. Once the pilot was satisfied with his speed and altitude, he radioed back from the cockpit to General Parker in the rear of the aircraft. They were ready.

# THE VATICAN's LAST SECRET

Four men dressed in black Ninja-like uniforms rose in unison from their canvas-webbed seats in the galley area. They walked through a narrow door in the tail section that led down to the rear exit hatch.

"All right, gentlemen, this is for the big money. Good luck," General Parker said to the men as they stepped willingly into the night's darkness at 1,500 meters.

The four men free fell to 500 meters before activating their Sentry-modified parachutes. The chutes allowed the user to essentially steer the chute, allowing a person, depending on the crosswinds at a certain location, to land within several feet of their objective. From 500 meters, it turned out to be a quick ten-second tight corkscrew maneuver with a near perfect landing 100 meters to the rear of the now-parked 777 aircraft.

Upon landing, they expertly gathered up any evidence of their illicit landing on American soil.

*A first for British combat troops since 1814.*

"Welcome to America," the Captain said aloud to no one in particular.

# CHAPTER 39

**BOEING 777 – MILLVILLE AIRPORT**

"All right, people, no time for chatter. Let's slide this container into the truck," Eian yelled, looking at his watch. "We have three minutes before Newark starts asking questions about our location."

Eian had to yell over the loud whooshing sound of the aircrafts auxiliary power unit (APU), a small jet engine used exclusively for ground power. He helped the men maneuver the three-by-four-foot pallet into the Ford pickup truck for Jim. The truck had a modified lift consisting of four hydraulic auto jacks installed in its rear to handle the pallet, allowing it to be gracefully lowered into its bed.

Eian now turned his attention to Sean and Colin, his new crewmembers. Distant friends from youth, fresh out of prison for armed robbery, they needed the quick cash this job would provide.

From his experience of traveling the US/European route, the U.S. customs' inspectors casually waved through any planes bound from the European continent. Just a cursory check was the usual status quo. They were more keenly focused on the South American routes due to the notorious drug traffic trade, that and the fact that they were spread thin due to a hiring freeze.

"I need you two boys up in the cockpit for take-off," Eian said before turning back to Jim and Dan. "And I will see you gentlemen in a few weeks when we divide the big cash. Until then, my friends."

"Good job, Eian. Until then, my friend," Dan said, shaking Eian's extended hand, shaking it vigorously, patting him on the back with the other. "We are going to have one hell of a poker game. I might even let you win a hand or two. Now get the hell out of here," he shouted above the whine of the APU.

Dan's reflexes were still in prime condition considering the events that had transpired over the previous 48 hours. *Of course, a gallon of coffee didn't hurt.* But something about the situation didn't feel right. His grandmother called it "Irish beforehand."

Dan tapped his pocket out of reflex. His weapon was still safely in its place. Glancing to the rear of the aircraft, he noticed something moving on the tarmac. His "Irish beforehand" was clearly working. The hairs on his neck rose. His heart raced. Its confirmation came quickly with several black-clad figures appearing out of the darkness brandishing weapons.

"Damn it, gentlemen, we have company, four figures with weapons toward the rear of the aircraft."

"Jim, go up front and start the truck. We have to get the hell out of here," Dan said, extracting his Beretta 9mm in response, quickly checking its ammunition status.

"Eian, close this aircraft door and get the hell out of here. We'll see you in a few weeks."

Eian saluted Dan in the aircrafts doorframe before turning to yell up to the cockpit. "Sean and Colin get back down here. We have trouble brewing."

**CAPTAIN ROBINSON LED HIS** three fellow SAS troops in their race towards the B777 aircraft, stopping a mere 50 meters from its rear to reassess the situation.

"Sergeant Major, when we are in range, concentrate your weapon fire on the truck just in case our birds of prey are trying to off-load and flee."

Turning to face his other two commandos, he said. "We will split into two groups. Jennings and Astor, I want you gentlemen to assault the aircraft from the port side over the wing entrance. The Sergeant Major and I will move to the starboard side of the truck.

Remember, we cannot screw this one up, gentlemen. Safeties off and I'll see you after the mission. Cheers."

**DAN FIRED SINGLE SHOTS** at the fast approaching figures forcing them to take cover on the tarmac for the moment. "Let's get this truck the hell out of here, my friend," he said to Jim. "We have company and its not the local police. They would have identified themselves by now, cutting off any possible escape route with a hundred cars surrounding us."

Jim struggled to locate the keys to the truck, finally locating them overhead, stuck in the drivers visor. "Who the hell are they?" he said, bullets now impacting the side of the truck with soft, dull thuds as they struck. He hastily stuck one key after another into the ignition before finding one that brought the truck to life with the roar of its eight cylinders.

Dan ducked behind the safety afforded by the wooden containers, they offering some protection from the SAS bullets that seemed close to finding their mark. "FBI or SWAT would also have also identified themselves. No doubt thieves got wind of this little operation. Get this rig the hell out of here before we are dead on arrival."

The van suddenly swerved from side to side as Jim tried to get control of the rapidly moving vehicle.

Dan held onto the truck with one hand, with the other firing at the dark clad figures.

"Who in the hell are they?" Jim yelled back once more.

Now empty, Dan quickly reloaded his weapon. He viewed only two figures versus the original four, they still firing blindly at the truck from an ever-increasing distance.

Jim slowed the truck to negotiate the curve that announced the airports exit, now searching for the main road. *"That was close,"* he said to himself in the empty cabin of the truck.

Dan managed to squeeze his way into the truck's cab through cabs small window, now sitting in the passenger seat. "We are heading for a gas station about two miles up this particular road," he said, looking in the trucks mirror for anything suspicious that might be following them.

"I just hope Eian and his friends are okay," Jim said. "There were a lot of fireworks going on back there."

"Eian's a big boy," Dan replied, "he can handle himself."

## **Millville Airport**
THICK DROPLETS of blood marked Eian's course on the aircraft floor as he weaved his way forward, rushing to close the forward service hatch, the last door before he could ready the aircraft for take-off. Checking the area outside the door, he couldn't believe his luck when he found two SAS men kneeling on the ramp no more than 25 meters away, firing at Dan and Jim. Eian positioned his weapon against the

doorframe, his Uzi coughing out a short burst, immediately killing both Captain Robinson and the Sergeant Major.

Eian next turned to Sean and Colin, both having made their way down to the cargo hold when they heard the first shots being fired. "Sorry boys, but you missed the action," he said, a smile creeping onto his face as he fought the obvious pain in his wounded arm. "Sean, go back upstairs and make sure nobody entered the aircraft from the topside. These gentlemen," pointing to the now lifeless bodies on the ramp, "most likely have friends. Colin, I want you to close this access door and secure it for flight. We are getting the hell out of here."

**PRIVATE JENNINGS AND CORPORAL** Astor took advantage of the confusion on the opposite side of the aircraft, scaling up and onto the aircrafts port wing, entering the aircraft through its emergency over-wing door.

Positioning themselves on opposite sides of the aisle, they moved forward toward the cockpit area.

**SEAN SCALED THE** aluminum steps from the cargo hold, reaching the top of the steps as Private Jennings and Corporal Astor were moving toward his position. *Damn it!* Sean cried aloud as he caught a short burst in the upper torso from Corporal Astor, killing him instantly.

In the cargo area, Eian turned in time to notice Sean's feet protruding from the top of the steps, him obviously dead. *The topside of the aircraft was compromised.*

He realized he was dealing with professionals. Eian decided to make his way back to where Colin still struggled to close the aircrafts door. Eian caught Colin's attention with a slight tap to the shoulder, yelling above the still whining APU. "I think it's time to retreat out of here and allow these buggers to meet their fate." He brandished two grenades. "I want you to go over on the side of the tarmac. Once you're safely in place you can provide me with covering fire. I'm going to give these buggers a real surprise by dropping these grenades by the planes center fuel tanks."

Colin fingered his own weapon, wondering what the hell he had gotten himself into. "You didn't warn me about the possibilities of a firefight, Eian. You told me to simply drive the truck here, load some goods, and hop on the plane for a 20-minute ride to Newark. A total of four or five hours work and I would get five grand, real easy. This is going to cost you extra, boy."

Both nervously eyed the steps leading to the topside of the aircraft.

"It's like Vietnam around here," Colin yelled back.

"Relax, you will still get your fiver with a bonus, but let's get the hell out of here first. Dead men can't be paid. Now take up a position 50 meters from here."

A quick shove from Eian sufficed as Colin dropped out of the aircraft, limping slightly from his fall as he quickly moved toward cover.

**PRIVATE JENNINGS AND CORPORAL** Astor finished their topside sweep of the aircraft, cautiously starting down the stairway leading to the darkened cargo hold. From their vantage point, they could see the hold contained three individual compartments for separating various types of cargo. A narrow passageway on each side allowed access to the rear of the aircraft.

Corporal Astor detected movement in the rear of the aircraft. "We have someone in the third hold," he said, moving carefully to the bottom of the steps. "A flash grenade should stun them. I'll break to the right and you take the left side. On my command, ready…"

**EIAN COULD SEE THE COMMANDO'S** dark image at the bottom of the steps. The timing couldn't be more perfect, rolling his grenade toward the center of the aircraft as he jumped out of the aircrafts door, running like a fox from the hounds and toward where Colin lay in wait.

**"GO," CORPORAL ASTOR SAID**, tossing the stun grenade into the aft cargo hold, closing his eyes, covering his ears, and opening his mouth to minimize the effects of the impact. The stun grenade exploded three seconds after he had pulled the pin, a blinding luminous flash followed by a thunderous bang intending to momentarily blind and stun the intended victims.

They moved rapidly into position, breaking to the left and right respectively, quickly slipping past the first empty cargo hold.

In his last moments alive, Corporal Astor viewed Eian's grenade.

Shrapnel laden explosions soon punctured the aircrafts interior, consuming the entire aircraft in a fireball that rose up a hundred feet in announcement.

Eian's grenades had evidently blown over the center fuel tank, *as intended*.

**COLIN HELPED EIAN UP FROM** the concrete ramp, the force of the explosion having tossed him as if he were a rag doll.

"Eian, what the hell did you do?" he said. "I thought you were just dropping a couple of grenades to knock off the boy's topside, not destroying the whole friggin plane." Colin looked about the immediate area in case additional attackers still lurked.

"Well now, the whole damn plane is history, isn't it? Eian said. "Let's get the hell out of here before we attract any more unwanted attention." He glanced over toward the airport tower.

# THE VATICAN's LAST SECRET

"Don't look now, but here comes the emergency response team. Let's move our position. How much money do you have?" he said, moving toward the same fence line that Jim and Dan had escaped through minutes before.

"I have five bucks," Colin replied, trying to keep pace with his sprained ankle, a gift from Eian when he was pushed from the aircraft.

"And I have ten, so we have a lousy 15 lousy bucks between us," Eian lied, holding tightly onto his flight bag that contained his real cash and gold. "Maybe we can hitch a ride to Philly?"

"Just a minute there, Eian," Colin said. "What about my five grand you owe me? I was promised five grand upon completion. Let's have it so we can split up and make a run for it."

Colin looked menacingly at Eian, advancing towards him. "You probably have it in that bag, don't you?"

"You're being a real pain in the ass, Colin, you know that? You can't wait, can you? We have a burning plane right behind you, and I just killed four people in a span of five minutes. Don't you think this might be a bad time to inquire about your money? You are a real jerk, you know that? No, you know what? Here, take your damn money." Eian extracted a bundle of cash from his flight bag, tossing it at Colin's feet.

The aircraft in flames behind them created a surreal scene as Colin stood looking down at the cash. Eian extracted the Beretta from his jacket pocket, pointing it at Colin. "And I owe you this too, you…" he said. "Pick up your money so I can say I paid you with a clear conscious before I administer some Irish justice."

"Eian, come on, man, I was just kidding. I knew you were going to pay me. Don't do it, man," Colin pleaded, now on his knees.

"Goodbye, Colin," Eian said, placing two well placed bullets to Colin's head. "You couldn't wait till we got to Philly?"

Eian quickly gathered the money from Colin's lifeless body before disappearing into the airport tree line and freedom.

# CHAPTER 40

**ROUTE 55 – SOUTHERN NEW JERSEY**

"That was too damn close for me," Jim said. "Who the hell were those cast of characters? They dropped out of nowhere and started shooting like it was the Wild West. Any friggin ideas?"

"It wasn't the U.S. Special Forces or police, I can assure you of that," Dan said. "Not their tactics. They would have taken us out with snipers, and then assaulted the remaining forces in the plane with precision. I would place my money on the Brits. Their SAS troops utilize techniques similar to the one you just had the privilege to experience. That's their top-notch people. They drop out of the night like owls onto their prey. They never let those boys out of their cage unless they really have a bad-ass character on their hands."

"Do you think they got wind of what we were doing? I don't think there could be any other excuse for it. Somebody dropped the dime."

"Now calm down," Dan said. "We are free and clear of that place. Nobody can find us, I assure you. What I'm worried about is Eian and his friends. If any of them get pinched and drop the ball on us, we may have some trouble."

"Do you think Eian's alive?" Jim said, looking to Dan rather than the road in front of him.

Dan shook his head. "I have my sincere doubts about it. If they were SAS, nobody would get free of those boys. They would have had that place buttoned up tighter than a virgin's sweater."

"I can't believe the Brits would have the nerve to pull something like this in our country. Our government wouldn't allow them to operate over here."

"I can only think that I'm to blame for this one, Jimmy. They finally pinned that bombing on me. It's the only rationale for them coming here. They wouldn't give a damn about the gold, or you for that matter. But first things first," pointing to a well-lit area containing a variety of fast-food restaurants. "Pull over at that Denny's up ahead. I want to check our cargo and the truck for any obvious damage. We took a few hits from those bullets back at the airport. I don't think the local police would take too kindly to our driving through the area with bullet holes everywhere. We might attract a little attention. Besides, lad, it's time for my hourly caffeine fix. I need a little java to keep me going."

# THE VATICAN's LAST SECRET

# CHAPTER 41

**NEWARK INTERNATIONAL AIRPORT – NEW JERSEY**

General Parker nervously paced up and down the aircrafts narrow aisle, a mad scowl upon his face. The General's staff had lost communication with the assault team 15 minutes earlier. He stopped beside the lead communication's officer.

"Lieutenant, play it back," the General said in a low voice, not wanting to be overheard.

"Sir?" the communications officer questioned, puzzled by the request.

"Go the hell over your goddamn notes and replay what had previously transpired," he yelled loudly, surprising even himself at his tone. Realizing it wasn't the young officer's fault, he quickly corrected himself. "Accept my apologies, Lieutenant. Circumstances dictate that I have a lot on my mind." He paused, looking about, before smiling. "A word of advice, Lieutenant. In the future when you eventually assume a command position, you will realize that the human brain can only take so much before it either shuts down or snaps." He patted him on the back. "Please read the notes you have on the action report."

The Lieutenant picked up his notepad nervously searching for the appropriate page that the ground operation started. "Yes, sir," he said, his finger traveling down the page to locate the precise moment of the parachutists' exit from the aircraft.

"As you are already aware, at 7:45 p.m. local time, we had confirmation from Captain Robinson that they were on the deck approaching just aft of the target. At 50 meters, they were spotted by the suspects and chose to press on with their attack. At that time, we picked up small arms' fire for three minutes' time until the Captains radio went dead. Sensing a bad connection, I switched over to try to raise the Sergeant Major on the same frequency, finding it was inoperable."

The General allowed the information to replay fresh in his mind in case he had missed something. "Could it be a total radio failure on our part or theirs?" speaking with no hint of anger or sarcasm in his voice.

"I checked and rechecked our controls, sir," the Lieutenant replied, pointing to the built-in test controls for the Rascal communications set, a state-of-the-art unit that was standard issue equipment for SAS troops. "Doubtful on our end, General. I would say the radios are working fine, sir. The failure is due to our people being incapacitated."

If you mean dead, Lieutenant, then say dead," the General snapped back in a fit of rage, taking off his jacket, throwing it against the communications panel located above the Lieutenants head.

The Lieutenant picked up the crumpled leather jacket, brushing off the jacket before carefully handing it back to the general. "They are most likely dead, sir," retreating to his communications console.

The General flopped down in his chair. He picked up a piece of paper and a pen from the metal table in front of him.

He started scribbling some words, speaking softly to himself in the same instant. "Damn, this was a royal screw-up," rolling up the sheet of paper into a ball, throwing it toward the open cockpit door at no one in general.

"General, I am picking up a live feed from CNN concerning Millville Airport," said another flight officer from his seat next to the lieutenant.

The General perked up. "Damn it! Put it on the main screen! Quiet everyone!"

The crew huddled around the 24-inch screen, all jostling for a decent view of the picture. Only the pilot stayed at his post, monitoring communications with the airport control tower.

"CNN has just received updated information on an aircraft explosion from one of our sister stations located out of Philadelphia," the commentator said. "We now go live to WPVI."

The location changed from CNNs Atlanta studio to show a live feed of a middle-aged, yet attractive female reporter standing a half-mile from a fire. The only way to realize it was an aircraft was the tail section protruding through the flames.

"This is Monica Torri of WPVI News reporting live from Millville Airport in Southern New Jersey where a jet aircraft has exploded on the ramp." She now referred to her hastily prepared notes, hoping she could read her own chicken scratch. "Our sources say they heard an aircraft flying low over the area five minutes before the explosion. They also saw four parachutists descend to the aircraft tarmac before the parachutists charged to the aircraft located behind me. Shortly after, an intense gun battle erupted, then within a minute of the gunfight a loud explosion ripped through the aircraft, destroying it in the process. We are only speculating about possible motives, but this could be drug-dealers with an FBI capture gone astray. Again, we are only speculating. We really don't have anything concrete at this time. WPVI will keep you updated as we receive additional information."

## THE VATICAN's LAST SECRET

Upon hearing the news report, General Parker collapsed into his seat, his hands covering his face in disgrace.

In the cockpit, the pilot was busy stalling the Newark Control Tower, time was of the essence until they heard from their SAS ground troops. "Sir," the pilot began, "the Americans would like confirmation of our planned departure or if we are requesting transient ramp space for the night."

General Parker allowed a full 30 seconds to elapse before responding, staring at the floor in disgust. "Inform them of our intention to depart after we refuel, Captain."

The pilot and SAS Captain were friends, having served together in Iraq. He couldn't just abandon his friend. Gathering enough bravado to confront his commanding officer he said. "But sir, what about our troops on the ground? Should we at least give them a few hours to communicate with us? We can't leave them for the wolves, sir."

The General slowly looked up at the pilot, staring intently at him as if he were going to rip his head off, his face changing from peach to the color of a deep crimson. "I said now. Those boys are dead," he barked. "You just saw it for yourself on their television network. If Captain Robinson were alive, he would have communicated with us by now. Captain, you will notify the control tower that we are departing."

The General quickly rose from his chair, marching solemnly off to the planes lavatory. Upon closing the lavatory door, he extracted his service revolver, staring at the aged image in the mirror. *Is this how my career is to end?* He saluted the image as the aircrafts number one engine was starting.

# CHAPTER 42

**SOUTHERN NEW JERSEY**

"Dan, I think our bullet holes are going to get us a little unwanted attention in the daylight hours. So what's your big plan?" Jim asked, fingering one of several well-placed holes in the windshield.

Dan placed the plastic lid back onto his coffee cup, sliding it in the holder he had pulled out from the dashboard. "We can go to a shopping mall just a little north of here and find a new vehicle in the parking lot," he said, pausing to see if Jim was catching on to where the conversation was heading.

Jim grinned in acknowledgement.

Dan continued. "The parking lot will have a few available SUVs. We can drive our new truck behind the mall and exchange plates with this one and reload our product. We then torch the old truck to get rid of the evidence. After that festive bonfire, we head south on Interstate 95 to Florida, home free."

## **MI-6 Headquarters, London**

SIR ROBERT SHUFFLED through the last remnants of the days paperwork when Rufus Sneed interrupted him.

"Sir Robert, I have a secure phone transmission from one of our special mission aircraft. It's concerning your American operation."

"Put it through," Sir Robert said, quickly picking up the receiver on his Marconi scramble phone, a remnant of the cold war days, but still handy for operations such as this. "With whom am I speaking?"

With the message being electronically scrambled from phone to phone, it was still possible to intercept the signal and achieve some partial translation. Due to this, the operators were ordered to speak in a collection of "reference phrases." This would provide anyone who did have the capability to intercept certain words with a jumble that would be impossible to break.

"This is the lead truck driver, sir. I have updated information on our Irish package. We are reporting four of our packages lost, and the postmaster has resigned."

Sir Robert referred to his notes he had fastened under his calendar blotter on his desk for the quick translation. "What happened to the Irish package? Did it get shipped?"

"We suspect that since the vehicle was lost, all packages were also lost."

"Until we get a positive address on our package, we will keep the slot open. And as far as the postmaster is concerned, he experienced a heart attack during a mission and died in the line of duty. Upon your return, we will have a crew meet you to take care of the situation."

"Yes, sir. Over and out."

# CHAPTER 43

### ARCHDIOCESAN HOME FOR ABUSED CHILDREN – NEW YORK CITY

The early morning streets of the North Queens business district were nearly deserted on this, the first Sunday of July, with one notable exception. A group of young children played hopscotch on the trash-laden sidewalk in front of a dilapidated brick building. The building appeared out of place in the center of a city block dominated by merchandisers of dollar store products, cheap liquor, and check-cashing outlets.

The building was referred to as *'the last stand'* by most of the cities social workers. The New York Archdiocesan Home for Abused Children being the only difference between the children and the city's mean streets. Unfortunately for the Archdiocesan Home, its interior matched its aged exterior in the areas of plumbing, air conditioning, and electrical wiring. The building lay on the verge of being condemned by the city's license and inspection bureau, literally taking away shelter for its 24 children in residence. For the poor children to once again face a sense of uncertainty, having already been abandoned and abused once in their young lifetimes, they were now on the verge of abandonment for a second harrowing time.

Thomas Jankowski was the homes group leader or "head dude" as the children would endearingly refer to him, having worked in the home in one capacity or another since graduating from NYU ten years before. At 6'4" and 250 pounds, he could command the children's attention through sheer intimidation, if he so chose. However, to them, he was a gentle giant. A teddy bear always ready to lend a hand or listen to someone's problems.

His college friends shook their heads at his choice of careers. "You could be making the big bucks" was the most frequent comment he would hear from his Wall Street friends.

What they couldn't understand *is that he actually enjoyed his work in the home*. He could see progress and results each and every day. How many of them could say that? Most of his friends already had ulcers, downing containers of anti-acids just to make it through their workdays. The worst scenario he faced was the occasional fight or shoplifting charge. No big deal to him. Just an average day dealing with the constant tug-of-war the streets provided.

He sat finishing his traditional breakfast of four pieces of bran toast and a bowl of Wheaties as he eyed the New York Times box scores for the previous night's Mets game. After seeing the Mets dropped another close one to the Phillies in 10 innings, he tossed the sports page to the floor in disgust. "When are the Mets going to get some decent pitching," he said aloud, only to be interrupted by his older assistant, Mrs. Klein. She held a rather large envelope for him.

"Tom, Federal Express just left this package for," she said.

"Fed Ex delivers on a Sunday morning at 7:30 a.m.?" Tom asked, looking at his watch in amazement. "And I thought we were the only ones with horrible hours. Thank you, Mrs. Klein. You can leave it on the table. I'll get to it as soon as I find out if the New York Times offers any hundred-dollar vacation deals. That's about all I can afford right now."

"You don't have the time, Tom," she said with a mysterious grin. "You also have a phone call in your office. The man says it's important. He would not tell me a thing. Should I inform him you're still sleeping?"

"No, it's okay. I'll get it. But just once I want to be able to sit and eat my breakfast in peace and quiet," he said before directing a smile at Mrs. Klein.

**JIM WAITED PATIENTLY IN** his car across the street from the children's home, cell phone in-hand, watching the children play on the sidewalk, ready to uncover another piece of his father's past.

**"HELLO," TOM SAID**, "And what can I do for you on this lovely morning?" The sarcasm clearly evident in his voice, wondering what one of his kids did this time to piss somebody off.

"Sir, this is going to sound a little crazy to you, but please bear with me," Jim said, taking a deep breath to try and calm his nerves. "You don't know me, and we have never met but I am hoping to fulfill a last request from my recently departed father."

Jim eyed the buildings crumbling façade, a smile now creasing his face before continuing. "Let me provide you with a little background information so you know I'm not pulling your leg. Before my father died, he informed me about the rather large donations he had been providing to your institution. Usually once per year, he would send a check in the amount of $60,000 to cover your expenses. Now as far as I know, only six people are even aware of this information.

Counting the two of us, that sure narrows the list down even further, doesn't it?"

Tom stared at the phone for several seconds before responding, wondering where the man was heading. "I guess that would be a correct assumption."

"Good. If you would kindly open the Federal Express package that was recently delivered to you, I will proceed."

"You're not joking with a man whose job is on the line, are you?" Tom said, having already received his layoff notice due to the homes expected closure. "My life is already in turmoil over what's going to happen to my kids. I can't even sleep at night."

"Tom, this is no joke. Please open the package. I think you will enjoy what you find," Jim said. He looked once more at the children playing across the street, thinking back to his father's ordeal in leading orphaned children from Berlin in its dying days, rescuing them from certain death. Seventy plus years latter his father was once more reaching out to administer aid, only now from his grave. A tear ran down his cheek wishing his father could be standing there beside him.

*Then again, who said he wasn't?*

"All right, all right. I'm opening it now," Tom said, ripping open the red, orange, and blue envelope, extracting a single sheet of paper with a check attached via a paper clip. Tom stood staring at the check and its seven zeros, still wondering if he were on the receiving end of a practical joke. But it couldn't be. Who else knew of the $60,000 donations? Surely none of his friends were aware of the generosity from the anonymous stranger. Gathering his thoughts, he finally responded. "Oh, come on now. Who is this? Tell me the truth because you can't be serious—a certified check for twenty million dollars? You can't," he said, pausing for a moment. "It can't be real. No one can write a check for this amount unless he's Bill Gates, *and you don't sound like Bill Gates*."

"I assure you Tom, it's real," Jim replied, amused at his beneficiary role. "I want you to call the phone number attached to the check. It's the number for the First Bank of New York. You will ask for the manager, a Mr. Pete Simmons, he will confirm its authenticity. I have made special arrangements for him to be at his desk this Sunday morning awaiting your call. This was the last wish of my father. Tom, please allocate these funds to your children who really deserve it. Don't allow the funds to become lost in some internal political shuffle. Until we talk again, please take care."

Tom was performing a little dance with the check in his hand as Mrs. Klein came back into the room. "Mrs. Klein, we are finally going to build a new house for the kids. I want you to personally telephone everyone on our staff," before placing the check onto the table in front of her. "Someone has just saved our kids."

# CHAPTER 44

**MARATHON KEY – FLORIDA**

Many a worldly traveler referred to the Florida Keys as *the American Caribbean Isles* because they happen to feature many of the same amenities as its tropical brethren: plenty of sun, surf, sand and boozed up tourists. However, the Keys possessed a more laid-back feel then their uptight island neighbors, with a 1960s vibe reverberating through the area. San Francisco if it were warm and had access to fabulously sunny beaches.

The Craggy Dog Marina was a suitable fit with its Keys neighbors, as it contained all the fundamentals the new generation of baby-boomer retirees necessitated for their vacation abodes: a freshwater lap pool with a swim-up bar, an on-site health club, tennis courts, private beach, and a 200-foot pier suitable for fishing. At every turn you could view palm trees softly swaying with the continuous warm ocean breeze, each tall and wide enough to provide shade where desired. To top it off, the weather hovered around a constant 85 to 90 degrees.

Life is good.

Eian exited the marinas office dressed in sandals, baggy white shorts, and a Hawaiian print shirt, topped off with a panama hat. His arm hung precariously in a sling.

Having squared off his debt with Mike Dolan in Philly, he was free and clear of everyone *but possibly the FBI, Interpol, or the British SAS.*

He was following directions provided by the head Craggy Dog himself, but he had a strange feeling that the rather large boat at the edge of the marina belonged to Dan.

At the moment, only 17 boats lay moored to the Craggy Dogs piers, a number that could easily reach a peak of 40 when the *snowbirds* from Pennsylvania and New Jersey returned in winter. The boats currently tied up ranged from a "low-end" 23-foot King Fisher sail boat to a "high-end" 57-foot Jefferson Motor Yacht with the name "Irish Rebel" painted conspicuously in emerald green on its stern.

The "Irish Rebel" slept six, with a full galley, three bathrooms or *heads* in nautical speak, teak decking throughout, and a small two-person hot tub on the stern. Rumors circulated about the origins of its owner's wealth, something mysterious involving Nazi gold. But no one knew for sure.

A familiar Jimmy Buffet tune hung in the humid air, tracing its origins back to the *Irish Rebel.*

Evidently the party had already started. He approached within five feet of the boats stern when he heard a loud metallic click from behind, the same unmistakable click a 45-caliber made when sliding a round into its chamber. Eian dropped his bag on the dock, still facing the boat, waiting for the inevitable.

He should have realized it was too good to be true. The cops were on to Dan.

"Damn it," was all Eian could muster in response, looking to the water as an escape route, his lame arm quickly extinguishing that notion. *Just when I had a few dollars in my pocket, the clouds of illusion part to drop a bit of rain.*

The gun now pressed against the base of his skull, only prolonging Eian's agony. "Just friggin shoot me," he said aloud, wondering where the rest of the arresting officers were hidden.

Deciding it was too much for Eian to handle, but still extending his agony by pausing several seconds, Dan replied in a low voice, disguising it as best as possible: "Eian, you old sea dog, give your long-lost cousin a hug."

Eian turned slowly to face Dan, his face now lacking all color.

"You scared the shit out of me. Jesus, what the hell did you do that for?" Eian said, pointing to the gun in Dan's hand.

Dan howled with laughter before extending his hand in welcome. "We're just having some fun at your expense. Let's go on board my new vacation home so I can show you around."

After several hours, all was forgiven. At least it appeared so. Dan and Eian were locked in a high-stakes poker game, its conclusion riding on the next card.

Before them they eyed the eight poker cards that lay on the table, four in front of each, a small stack of fifties separating them.

Eian looked up at Jim, smiling as he triumphantly held up his final card for Jim to view, then looking to Dan, his eyes sparkling. "Beat a full-house, Danny boy," he said. Eian held up a red queen for Dan to appreciate before tossing it down on the table.

Dan stared hard at Eian, shaking his head before replying in an even heavier Irish brogue: "How many times do I have to beat your ass in poker until you finally learn how to play?"

Eian rolled his eyes. "You've got to be kidding me? Are you telling me you can beat my full-house?"

Dan ran his hand through his thick white hair before holding up a black ten, placing it beside the three already showing on the table. "Four tens, my man," he said aloud as he cracked a slight smile, greedily raking in the pile of money.

"I can't believe it, you're the best damn liar I know. You should play in Las Vegas with the professionals."

Dan laughed heartily in reply. "I believe you could be right my friend."

Jim placed a pitcher of Margaritas and several glasses on the table. "Peace offering," he said, pouring each a glass.

Eian shuffled the cards before placing them before Dan. Dan cut the cards before sliding them back over to Eian. "Tell me the truth on this one, Danny," Eian said in a low gravelly voice as he dealt the cards. "On our last little adventure, those English SAS bastards were really after you, right? They didn't care about Jim's father and his little *'deal'* with the Vatican and their Nazi gold. Hell no, they finally caught up with the great Flaherty, Mr. IRA himself."

A smile concealed Dan's silence.

Eian boldly pushed on. "Those Brits must be royally pissed that you screwed them." He observed both men, his eyes betraying him as they darted anxiously between the two of them.

*He was holding something back.*

Dan noticed it first. "Spit it out, Eian," he said. "You're a painfully dreadful liar and you sure as hell can't play cards. Say what's on your mind."

Eian nodded. "Okay. You got me, Cousin Dan," he said as he took a sip of his drink before placing the glass back on the table. "Quick synopsis. We loaded the gold from Jim's father's farm in the hold of our plane. I flew the plane across the Atlantic with the Brits, unbeknownst to us, on our ass. I land us at the Millville airport. My friends Colin and Sean board the aircraft to help us unload. Then we have our little shootout with the Brits. The shootout was soon followed by an explosion that destroyed the aircraft and basically ended my chances of ever leasing another one again. Well, at least under my Christian name."

Dan looked at Jim and then to Eian wondering why the history lesson. "Speed it up my friend, I have a tee time in a couple of hours."

Eian smiled. "Okay, the down and dirty version for the hurried amongst us. Remember gentlemen, the authorities found six dead bodies in the wreckage or in its proximity: *four British SAS troopers and two of my boys, Colin and Sean.* When I was up and about in Philly last week, I just happened to be playing in a high-stakes poker game with a few homicide detectives who knew more than they should have about the case. Of course, they weren't aware of my involvement. Over the course of a few hours, a few drinks, and me losing a couple thousand bucks, they opened up. They let it slip that the autopsy had come back on the criminals who had a shoot-out with the British SAS. Big news considering British troops were on US soil tracking a known IRA terrorist. The detectives went on to say that the bodies on-board the destroyed aircraft were burned beyond recognition, but one of them was thought to be," he paused, looking coyly to Dan before continuing: "One, Daniel Flaherty. If you think about it, you are dead as far as they are concerned. So they won't be coming after you. The great Dan Flaherty is a dead man. They will be in mourning at Whitehall on that one."

Jim turned to Dan, "I guess after 20 years of playing dead, *you really are dead,*" he said.

Dan smiled as he nodded. "As long as those bastards leave me alone, I will leave *them* alone. I'm just sick of constantly being on the run."

Eian saw his opportunity and dove right in. "Dan, you have your ghost status. Come on cousin, it's what you always wanted."

Dan nodded.

Eian pressed on. "And, as you have always told me, business is business."

Dan knew where Eian was leading him but allowed him to proceed.

"That piece of information was considered valuable. Am I right?" Not waiting for Dan to respond, he continued. "Well, I'm under the assumption it is. So, as I see it, I should receive my little bonus that was promised to me. That and a little vacation time on your yacht here." Eian regarded his surroundings on the yacht appreciatively. "She's a beauty, Dan."

Dan poured Eian another frosty margarita, a serious look on his face. "Come on, Eian, you impetuous little bastard. Asking for the money so quickly? That's not being polite. Didn't you just lose $50,000 at the craps table in Atlantic City?"

"You should have seen the lovely lass I had standing beside me. I had a system, Dan. It was working up until...."

"Up until you lost it all," Dan countered, knowing his cousin all too well. "And how about the other $50,000 you paid to the bookies that have since rescinded the contract on your ass? That's it boyo. I'm keeping you on an allowance. I owe it to your sweet mother. *God rest her soul.* That and because we may be willing to cut you in on Jim's next little adventure."

Eian took the frosty glass in hand, wiping the excess salt from around its rim. "What do you mean next little adventure? You almost succeeded in getting me knocked off on your last *little adventure.*"

Eian downed the margarita with one long swallow, placing the empty glass down in front of Dan, indicating he would like a refill.

"You are one of us, Eian, an adrenaline junkie. Now as I see it, we still owe you $250,000 from our last trip, and if we are successful on our next one, you could clear close to $1.2

million. How does that sound? Such a lovely figure, wouldn't you say?"

Eian's eyes went wide. "Are you serious? Who do I have to kill?"

"It's true. And you don't have to kill a soul."

Eian pondered his response for all of two seconds. "If I heard you correctly state the figure of $1.2 million, then it would be a pleasure to do business with gentlemen of your stature."

Jim moved toward the boats main stateroom, gaining Eian and Dan's attention as he did. "All right, gentlemen, enough. Let's get down to the main reason why we are here." Jim knocked on the door of the main stateroom. "Are you awake yet," he said.

An elderly man emerged, swiping a comb through his thinning white hair, a forced smile upon his face. "Good afternoon, gentlemen," said the small, almost gnomish man with a hint of an Italian accent. He had the resigned look of one who knows that at his age, life has stopped giving and only takes away.

He looked at Eian, smiling. "Allow me to introduce myself, Mr. Antonio Perluci, formally of the Vatican Special Action Team, at your service."

# THE END

## THE VATICAN's LAST SECRET

**The Vatican's Deadly Secret (James Dieter Part 2)** is now available.

What 75-year-old secret links a prospective US President to $350 million dollars in Nazi gold bars and Vatican Bank accounts that contain vast sums of money stolen during World War II?

In this fast-paced action-packed thriller, James Dieter (retired Navy SEAL), his wife Nora (investigative journalist), and his best friend, Dan Flaherty (ex-IRA) battle their way across Europe as they attempt to unearth a secret guarded by some of the world's most powerful and shadowy organizations.

They soon realize why it's one of the most closely guarded secrets of all time.

But will they live to tell the tale?

*There's only one way to find out.*

Amazon Best Selling author Francis Joseph Smith has traveled to most of the world during his tenure in the Armed Forces and as an Analyst for an unnamed Government Agency, providing him with numerous fictional plot lines and settings for future use. His experiences provide readers with well-researched, fast-paced action. Smith's novels are the result of years of preparation to become a fiction writer in the genre of Clancy, Griffin, Higgins, and Cussler.

    Smith lives with his family in a small town outside of Philadelphia where he is currently in work on his next novel.

Made in the USA
Las Vegas, NV
21 March 2025